# DESERT FIRE

# DESERT FIRE

*A Novel*

## SHANNON VAN ROEKEL

Kregel
*Publications*

*Desert Fire: A Novel*

© 2009 by Shannon Van Roekel

Published by Kregel Publications, a division of Kregel, Inc., P.O. Box 2607, Grand Rapids, MI 49501.

All Scripture quotations, unless otherwise indicated, are from The Holy Bible, English Standard Version, copyright © 2001 by Crossway Bibles, a division of Good News Publishers. Used by permission. All rights reserved.

Scripture quotations marked KJV are from the King James Version.

Scripture quotations marked NASB are from the NEW AMERICAN STANDARD BIBLE, updated edition. Copyright © 1960, 1962, 1963, 1968, 1971, 1972, 1973, 1975, 1977, 1995 by The Lockman Foundation. Used by permission. (www.Lockman.org)

All Qur'an quotations are from *The Koran Interpreted*, Arthur J. Arberry, trans. (New York: Macmillan, 1955).

The original drawings on pages 66–67 by the children of Darfur are included with the permission of Waging Peace, London, UK. Waging Peace campaigns against genocide and systematic human rights abuses—with a particular focus on Africa, on atrocities overlooked by the international community, and where minorities have been persecuted on racial or religious grounds. Waging Peace works to secure the full implementation and enforcement of international human rights treaties wherever they campaign. Their current priority is Darfur where they are fighting for an immediate end to the atrocities, and a stable and secure peace settlement that will bring about long-term safety and security for Sudan's citizens. Their experienced team produces regular high-level and in-depth research reports that enable them to support the call for urgent, effective, and measurable action from the UK government and the international community. For more information visit www.wagingpeace.info.

ISBN 978-0-8254-3922-3

Printed in the United States of America

09 10 11 12 13 / 5 4 3 2 1

*For the Father,*
*who cares for every*
*widow and orphan.*
*May His Word blaze*
*forth.*

# Acknowledgments

⁓

Inspiration for this book came from the faithful reports of Mel Middleton and Eric Reeves, who were saying what the media wasn't saying, long before it was popular to say it, and are still faithfully saying what many others won't. I owe a debt of gratitude to them and to the children of Darfur who drew pictures of what happened to them. Thank you to Waging Peace for permission to print these drawings, and thank you to the people who brought them to the attention of the world.

I could not write without my husband's and children's love and support. Thank you, Brian, Brandt, Holly, Danielle, Kieran, and Zachary. I love you all *so much!*

A big thanks to my mother, Euna Haynes. What a blessing you have been to my life, not only as my friend, but also as an encouraging editor!

Thank you, also, to Elsi Dodge: I am privileged to have your friendship and the benefit of your edits. You have spent countless hours weeding this manuscript, not to mention driving to Canada in your Moose. I look forward to many more happy visits!

To the editors at Kregel Publications, you have been wonderful to work with!

And finally, thank you, Steve Barclift, for all your work and efforts on behalf of this project.

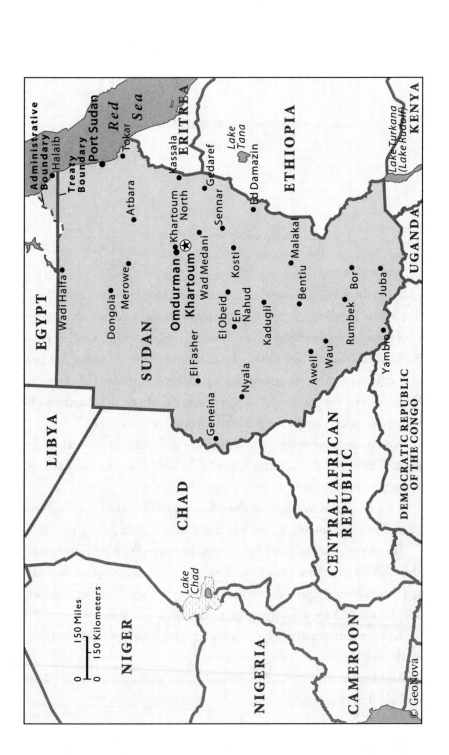

# PROLOGUE

The Son of God suffered unto the death,
not that men might not suffer, but that their
sufferings might be like His.

GEORGE MACDONALD, *UNSPOKEN SERMONS*

OCTOBER 2008

Dust mixed with Peter Kuanen's tears and slid down his cheeks. Years ago when he was a little boy, he'd had time to cry. Now he was old and often wept while going about his daily chores. Life had brought pain: living through drought, watching his wife and three of his seven children die of starvation—his story wasn't so different from other men in his village. Today, however, crying would demand every ounce of his strength. There had never been pain like today's pain.

Peter sat cross-legged on the hard, dry ground, swaying back and forth like the long grass, his wails filling the soulless place that had been Qasar. He had been born and raised in this small village. He had lived here with his family growing potatoes and groundnuts and keeping a few goats and chickens, working hard every day of his life. A way of life forever taken from him now.

Today the Janjaweed had come to Qasar. They had left behind hundreds of corpses: men, women, and children. Peter had pulled three of his sons, his daughter, and two of his grandsons from the gruesome aftermath of the massacre. Laying their bodies side by side under the baobab, he had buried them in a shallow pit he dug. The stink of flesh and blood rose in the heat. Peter wiped the sweat from his eyes, pushing away the flies that gathered.

Other survivors had fled for refuge, urging him to come with them, but Peter couldn't leave. He could not run away. This was his home and his family. This was his life.

"Father!" he shouted, lifting his arms to heaven, his fists clenched. The vast sky stretched overhead, softened now from the merciless heat of the day by the curtain of dusk.

"Do You see? God in heaven, do You weep with me? Oh, God! Oh, God."

Grief touched insanity as Peter's keening went on and on. Eventually, shuddering overtook him . . . the shock would not leave him for many days. Sorrow never would.

"Mercy. God, have mercy. How can I live? How can You let me live after this? God, have mercy. Take me, Father. I have loved You. I have served You. All I had, I gave to You. Let me die now.

"Evil conquered today. Evil men fill our lives with fear. How long will You let our people suffer? God help us . . . deliver us.

"Do not let evil take Your servant's soul. I do not know how to go from here."

Sobs wracked him. Hurt and vulnerable as a baby, he sobbed until nothing was left in him but a strange stillness. It wasn't insanity. It wasn't death. It was peace. Peace from outside that settled over him like a mama chicken setting over an egg. He knew relief from the drowning pain. And he knew whose presence he felt comforting him and washing the evil off like the dirt that washed away when he bathed in the wadi. No words were given to him. No voice spoke out of the African night sky. The baobab leaves rustled; the cicadas sang. But deep in the center of his soul, he knew that God in heaven saw him, felt his pain, and heard his prayer. It was enough.

Night came, drawing a curtain over the day and filling the heavens with multitudes of stars. He gazed at the familiar constellations by which he fixed his compass and measured the seasons. Lowering his aching body to the ground, the old man curled into a fetal position, his hand resting on the mound of earth that covered his family. With a rasping voice, he whispered to the unseen presence, "Into Your hands, I commit their spirits."

Encourage the exhausted, and strengthen the feeble.
Say to those with anxious heart,
"Take courage, fear not.
Behold, your God will come with vengeance;
The recompense of God will come,
But He will save you."
Then the eyes of the blind will be opened
And the ears of the deaf will be unstopped.
Then the lame will leap like a deer,
And the tongue of the mute will shout for joy.
For waters will break forth in the wilderness
And streams in the Arabah.
The scorched land will become a pool
And the thirsty ground springs of water;
In the haunt of jackals, its resting place,
Grass becomes reeds and rushes.
A highway will be there, a roadway,
And it will be called the Highway of Holiness.
The unclean will not travel on it,
But it will be for him who walks that way,
And fools will not wander on it.
No lion will be there,
Nor will any vicious beast go up on it;
These will not be found there.
But the redeemed will walk there,
And the ransomed of the LORD will return
And come with joyful shouting to Zion,
With everlasting joy upon their heads.
They will find gladness and joy,
And sorrow and sighing will flee away.

ISAIAH 35:3–10 NASB

# ONE

THE LITTLE GIRL KNELT IN THE WHITE SAND, energetically scooping it with her green plastic shovel into a matching bucket. Through half-closed eyes, Julia Douglas watched her. Carting the bucket down to the eddying pools by the shore, the child added pints of ocean to her bucket and then ran on chubby legs back to the building site, where she dumped the mixture upside down.

After waiting for a moment, crouched with pink tongue extended past a pinker mouth, the girl impatiently lifted the bucket straight up. Anticipation met reality. Huge eyes filled with tears as her bottom lip quivered. No castle appeared. Only a crumbling mound of sand. Turning away from her failure, she started crying in earnest, stumbling across the sand, only to be picked up by a tall, tanned man who held her tenderly in arms knotted with muscle. Kissing away his daughter's tears, he whispered something into her ear. Like sunshine after rain, her cherub cheeks dimpled with joy as she curled her arms around her daddy's neck.

Julia looked away. She would not watch. It only produced memories she did not want and an unreasonable sense of rage that she could not and would not deal with.

"Piña colada, miss?"

Her hand shading her eyes from the afternoon's glare, Julia turned her sun-drenched body and looked at the young Mexican waiter.

"Yes, thank you." She placed the chilled glass against her cheek, letting it cool her skin as well as her tongue. Avoiding the sight of the child and father now building a castle in the sand together, she turned to her friend.

"This must be the hottest day yet, eh, Caroline?"

Caroline held her own iced beverage, something pink and slushy, and reached down to check her BlackBerry.

"Ninety-seven degrees in Cancun today, with tomorrow and Thursday supposed to be getting even hotter."

"That's what I like to hear." Julia's lids closed as she leaned back into the chair. "Wanna swim some more?"

"Yup. Ready when you are."

The two friends spent a moment securing straps and adjusting their bikinis, then ran toward the turquoise Caribbean. Julia dove first, managing to get under a wave and through it before breaking the surface again. Caroline was already body surfing in the next breaker. Paddling toward her friend, Julia admired the multicolored fish swimming beneath her. This water was so clear, it played havoc with her depth perception. She flipped over on her back, enjoying a calm. *This is the life,* she thought. *Sun, surf, book, and a friend.*

They sunbathed and played in the water all afternoon, losing track of time and, more to the point, responsibilities.

"What do you say?" Caroline asked. "Almost time to go in, I'm thinking."

"Just a few more minutes, Caroline. The sun is so wonderful. I am starting to feel hungry, though."

"Julia, you had tortilla chips and guacamole not more than an hour ago. How can you be hungry again so soon?" Caroline asked, a wistful tone in her voice. "If I ate like you, I'd look like a house."

"Maybe I have worms—we are in Mexico." Julia smiled with fondness at Caroline. They had been best friends since fifth grade, and their shared love for books and writing had led them to take the same degree, with different minors, at the same university. They had landed similar careers working for the same magazine. Julia worked as a staff reporter for *Women Informed*, and Caroline as assistant to the senior editor, Tabi Barnette.

Darn Tabi, anyway.

Tabi, her boss, and sometimes her tormentor. Even on holiday in Mexico. Julia had opened an e-mail from her at breakfast.

"We're in Cancun, how can it hurt to look at just one?" she had muttered to Caroline as she clicked on Tabi's name in the in-box:

> Julia,
>
> Would like you to consider assignment in Sudan. Women are suffering unbelievable atrocities there. The world needs to be aware. We cannot let these crimes against our own sex be ignored. Our power is in the story, and I think you'd tell it well.
>
> Call me after you've had a chance to look at the attached folder.
> —Tabi
> PS How is Cancun?

Julia had smiled when she read it. She had been writing pieces for this national magazine—boasting a readership of more than six million— for the last two years and counted herself lucky to be one of the few in Tabi's stable of regulars. Her editor had not become successful in the competitive world of journalism by being the warm, fuzzy type, yet Julia had a soft spot for Tabi.

But Sudan?

"Pretty harsh," she commented to Caroline.

She shouldn't have looked at the attached file. But she had.

She thought about those pictures now. All shots of Sudanese women and children living in what could only be described as squalor but were called IDP camps. Internationally Displaced Persons. Driven from their villages after first enduring torture, then being forced to witness the violent murders of many of their families and friends, these people had become refugees in their own country at the hands of their government's militia. The militia was made up of Islamic extremists and regular Sudanese boys and men forced to join either at point of death or to escape torture themselves. Equipped with machine guns, helicopters, and bombs; trained to hate their "infidel" countrymen; and bribed with an empty promise of a serial killer's paradise, they became barbarians. Barbarians called Janjaweed.

Julia knew her history. She had read about the Huns, the Vikings, and the Crusaders. She knew the scars of the twentieth century, including Hitler's Holocaust and Hiroshima. The events of 9/11 were forever burned into her mind. She understood the tragedy and injustice of it all. But she believed in progress and the age of information. Sifting the soft, white sand through her fingers, she sighed, thinking that the world's diverse societies were just beginning, after eons of war and tragedy, to accept and understand one another. *Sure*, she thought, *there will always be setbacks, but with modern cooperation and understanding will come friendship and ultimately peace.*

Watching the Mexican and American children nearby building a sand castle together, their voices rising and falling in the universal excitement and energy of childhood, Julia knew it was true: the basis for world peace was not war, but communication. It was up to those who were educated and informed to enlighten those who weren't. *Women Informed* did just that. Exposing social and cultural narrowness to the public was the path to greater understanding and awareness. The women in Sudan were suffering at the hands of religious extremists, men who lusted for control and power. Empowered and educated women around the world needed to be made aware of this, and then change would begin. Women in Canada and the U.S. had lived in similar subservience to men within the last hundred years. Maybe not with as much physical violence, but certainly with terrible emotional abuse.

"Another piña colada, miss?"

"That would be wonderful, yes, please." Julia beamed up at the white-coated waiter as he handed her another drink.

"*No problema.* Can I get you anything else? Something to eat, perhaps?"

Julia shook her damp curls.

"*No, esta bien,*" she replied, impressed with the service at the resort. Being waited on hand and foot was wonderful, and by such handsome men, too. She sighed blissfully, pushing thoughts of Sudan from the forefront of her mind and concentrating on enjoying the last few days of her vacation.

Three weeks and several hours of travel later, Julia tried to figure out what it was she'd forgotten to do. The voice of the British Airways captain broke into her thoughts. "Good morning, ladies and gentlemen, this is your captain speaking. I'd like to draw your attention to the White Nile flowing below us." Julia squeezed her eyes tightly together, trying to remember. Goliath's favorite dog treats? Yes. She'd grabbed them off the top of the fridge and put them into the suitcase that also contained his sleepy blanket, his throw toys, food dish, brushes, and shampoo. She'd handed this to Caroline with some trepidation when she dropped him off on the way to the airport. Not that Caroline wouldn't take good care of him; she would. But Goliath, a 120-pound Leonberger, had a way of taking over. No, for the umpteenth time, it wasn't the dog treats, but it had to be something; it just wouldn't stop niggling her. Shirley, her landlady, was coming in to water the philodendrons—philodendrons because other plants kept dying on her. Julia had finally given up and bought scads of philodendrons so she wouldn't feel guilty when she forgot about them for weeks at a time. The effect of this had been to turn her two-bedroom, attic flat into a sort of green jungle full of oxygenated air. The opposite, in fact, of this jet, not to mention the desert below.

Julia rubbed sleep out of her eyes. Coffee. Pungent aroma from a fresh brew filled the cabin. The flight attendant had begun to make her way down the aisle, pushing the trolley—roll, stop and pour, roll, stop and pour—placing steaming Styrofoam cups into grateful hands. Julia needed coffee. After a red-eye from London plus the ten-hour killer out of Vancouver, she had totaled two whole days of traveling to get to Khartoum. The nice thing about red-eye flights was that she traveled while she slept. The bad thing was that she didn't really sleep.

Reaching forward as far as possible without hitting the seat in front of her, she stretched, rotating her shoulders forward, then backward, turning her head gingerly, left and right. Bones creaked. A definite pinch in the neck. Great, and once installed near the IDP camp, she'd have about as much chance as a snowball in hell of finding a chiropractor.

The dentist appointment tomorrow! That was it. She made a mental note to text Caroline and ask her to notify the dentist's office. They practiced a strict fifty-dollar fine for cancellations without at least twenty-four hours notice—or a death certificate.

With that out of the way, she rested her head back and smiled peacefully. She'd remembered everything. She hoped.

"How did you sleep?" her neighbor inquired of her solicitously. A bit more than middle-aged, he wasn't handsome so much as striking with his Seville Row suit, silk tie, olive skin, and jet black hair. Julia wondered how he managed to look so unrumpled. She swept pretzel crumbs from her lap—remains from the late-night snack—noticing a smudge of chocolate had stained her slacks. She draped her hands over the spot in her best attempt at "calm and cool."

"Quite well, thank you," she lied.

"What brings you to Khartoum?"

Julia smiled politely at the man beside her and shamelessly lied for the second time. "I'm just visiting friends."

Khartoum did not welcome reporters. Julia knew that the government would not hesitate to give her the boot if they discovered she was attempting to wake the world to the annihilation being meted out to its African population. Rwanda's genocide would have nothing on Sudan if Khartoum was not soon stopped.

She could feel the man's eyes linger on her just a little too long, but Julia, hardened to male attention, practiced indifference.

Removing the pillow she had slept so uncomfortably against, she turned away from him, releasing the window blind with a snap and squinting at the glare of the sunny day. Far below, she could make out the hazy blue outline of the river, source of life for many cultures since ancient times. The Nile had always held a sense of mystery for Julia; this may have had something to do with seeing Charlton Heston, while playing a convincing Moses, turn it into blood in *The Ten Commandments*. Seeing the river winding below her, blood long since washed away, she began to listen with interest to the captain's discourse.

"As they enter Khartoum, the Blue Nile and White Nile meet and join together as one to travel northward to Egypt. From the source of the White Nile, it runs some four thousand miles before draining into the Mediterranean, making it the world's longest river.

"We will be approaching Khartoum in about ten minutes. We hope you have enjoyed the flight . . ." Julia tuned out the rest of the airline's commercial.

Clenching her jaw, she steeled herself for what lay ahead. What would life be like at a displaced persons camp? If the horror stories were true, this would not be a picnic. More like a torture chamber, she guessed. Still, her commitment to tell a story the way it was had often led her into difficult situations. She had spent two weeks in a shelter for battered women and a week in a Mexican women's prison. Her latest and most successful report was from the two-month period she had spent undercover in an Amish community.

Gazing again out the window, Julia could see Khartoum. "Offspring of the union of the life-giving Niles," the pilot had called it. The city had certainly grown and matured, stretching out below her for miles in every direction and, not unlike a spoiled child who gets everything he wants, it had grown into a raging, murderous criminal. Gazing down on the neat, white building blocks that made up the residential and industrial sections, she thought Khartoum didn't look like the base of a sinister government so much as an overgrown slum.

Leaning over her shoulder, the man beside her pointed out, with obvious pride in his voice, the white block that made up the Hilton Hotel.

"I have often sat in the restaurant there and enjoyed the view of the two Niles as they merge. It is a truly romantic spot for dinner with the lights of the city reflecting on the water, but so much nicer with someone else. Perhaps you would care to join me sometime?"

Julia pretended not to hear the question and asked one of her own.

"What is that tiny little island just before the confluence?"

"Indeed, its name is Tuti Island. See how it resembles a crescent moon? It is by no mistake that the symbol of Islam sits in so strategic a place, reminding Sudanese Muslims of why we are in this land."

He smiled as he spoke, but Julia didn't feel like smiling back. She choked off the words that could expose her and said nothing. Scrunching herself against the window, she turned her shoulder to the man and hoped he'd get the message. It seemed to work, as he didn't attempt any further conversation while the plane circled and prepared for landing.

The world had turned its back on Sudan's crisis. Her job was to open people's eyes to the truth, give the facts, and let politically powerful and free Western women speak out on behalf of their Sudanese sisters. That was her job and her duty. And she loved both. Working for *Women Informed* was the crowning achievement of her journalistic career.

As a child, she had written in a journal every day. Every entry started with Dear Dad. In her mind, the father she was writing to was someone like Andy Griffith: strong, good, kind, and a pillar of the community. The opposite of what she knew was the truth. Children were great survivors, and she had survived her own tragedy by creating an alternate reality. One she could accept.

In first grade, she had encountered the hard wall of truth in the form of Sandy Ellis, a pretty little girl with long blond braids whom she had desperately wanted for a friend.

"Your daddy is a bad man. My mom said he killed some people, and I'm not allowed to play with you."

Julia had never felt pain like that before. It had shocked and terrified her. It had also set her life in motion, for after her mother had drawn the sobbing confession out of her, things were never the same. Abbotsford, Kamloops, Hope . . . the names of the places they had moved to in the next year blended together in her memory, a blur of new schools, new teachers, old apartments. Mother said they were trying on places, like trying on shoes in a shoe store, to see which one would be the best home for them. Mother also tried on men. Apparently one couldn't be too choosy.

Port Coquitlam was the last stop. The place that finally fit. Mom had liked her job at the hotel, working as a receptionist, and she also liked a new man. This time, Julia liked him too. Heaven had decided to smile on them. Into their lives had entered James Douglas. "Not to be confused with British Columbia's first governor," he always said. But from what Julia learned in school later, the two men shared more similarities than he realized. Both were stocky, lumberjack types who loved the wilderness and had big bushy beards. But she didn't think the James Douglas from her history books had ridden a Harley. It was after James moved in that she had started the diary to her imaginary daddy. For in spite of the genuine affection she and James had for one another, he still wasn't the image of the father she craved.

Image, she had decided, was important. People respected Caroline's father, who was a dentist. He had a nice car and a big house. For some reason, Caroline liked her, Julia, with the ugly apartment, floozy mother, and James's Harley. Caroline was only ten years old when they became friends and would not know what the word *Bohemian* meant for some years, but she fit the description. Her mother, Mrs. Laurant, let her wear whatever she liked, and she liked long skirts, baggy sweatshirts, and sneakers. The two girls were soul mates, sharing all their secrets—of which there were a surprising number. Caroline was one of the few people who knew about Julia's real dad. To her credit, Caroline never divulged that information as far as Julia knew. Probably because Caroline entrusted Julia with equally damaging reports concerning the dentist. Also a bad man, but respected.

Something in Julia's childish mind had clicked with this worldly understanding, and the journaling began. Every entry began with "Dear Dad," her imaginary composite of James Douglas and the dentist— minus the faults: someone who wore nice suits, drove an expensive car, always had answers to her questions, was generous and caring, and, most of all, loved her with all his heart. A smile touched her lips. That was a long time ago: Before graduation had arrived with a healthy journalism scholarship. Before James had died of a stroke. Before she knew how to say thank you to him for loving her.

Her reverie broke as the plane's wheels hit the tarmac, bounced, then connected with terra firma once again. Automatically, she reached for her laptop bag. She had arrived.

# Two

There is a God-shaped vacuum in the heart
of every person and it can never be filled by any
created thing. It can only be filled by God, made
known through Jesus Christ.

BLAISE PASCAL, *PENSÉES*

Dear Julia,

I want to die better than I've lived. So I ask you, please read this letter to the end.

It's the only one I'll send.

Cold, fluorescent light shone down on the metal desk where Fred Keegan sat. His hair was closely shaven along a massive neck between a pair of muscle-bound shoulders. He hunched over white notepaper, his right hand engulfing the pen.

A sigh escaped him, a moment passed, and then the pen scratched its way across the paper again:

If you receive this, it will mean I am gone from this world—so you can relax, I won't come and disturb your life.

There are some things, however, that I'd like you to know about me.

One is that I've always loved you. I guess your mama didn't spend much time talking about the father you probably had no trouble forgetting. I don't blame either of you for having nothing to do with me. I was a real jerk. I was guilty, as charged, for the crimes I committed. That life, I am ashamed of, and I paid a high price. Thirty years in the slammer. And counting. I won't bore you with the sorry-old-me stuff. Mostly, I want to tell you about the last eight years. Something important happened, and you should know not just who I was, but who I got to be and the Treasure I found. This is why I write to you.

I've got a picture of a cute kid taped to my wall. You're missing your front teeth and have two of those pony things. You're a cute gal and no mistake. Pretty, like your mama. The picture came in the last letter with the divorce papers.

Fred stopped, head bowed, eyes squeezed shut. The memories of that day still filled him with remorse. The rage he'd felt and his inability to control it. Two guards had taken the brunt, both of whom still carried scars marking the event. Two weeks in solitary was his punishment. Regrettably, not long enough to cure him of his anger-management problem.

Picking up his pen again, he gazed at the photo. The tape had yellowed with age. The girl never aged. She smiled back with sweetness and youth.

I guess you were seven in that photo. That means you'd be thirty-three now. I wonder if I'd know you if I saw you today. Can a man walk past his own kin and not feel the bond of blood that connects them? Recognize the spirit in the other who shares his same history, ancestors, and perhaps God? Maybe that's why we get goose bumps. Maybe I'm a crazy old fool who's had too much time to think about the inner workings of this thing we call life.

"Keegan, you got a visitor."

Fred looked up as the guard unlocked the steel door and stepped aside, allowing a tall man access into his cell. His frown at being interrupted from his writing smoothed immediately into a grin when he recognized his guest.

"Mr. Lawyer, good to see ya."

"Good to be seen, Keegan. How are you feeling today?" Joel Maartens returned Fred's grin with one of his own.

"Feeling? I guess I'm fine. I've got things to do, and that helps keep my mind off the pain." Fred tried to ignore the pity in Joel's eyes.

"Let me guess, you've got new books?"

Fred followed Joel's gaze as he glanced at the bookshelf on the opposite wall. His cell was compact: bed, desk, chair, toilet, sink. But the bookshelf reaching from floor to ceiling was the focal point.

"Nah! Not books this time. I've got a letter to write, and it's not an easy thing to do, Mr. Lawyer." Fred folded his large frame into a sitting position on the edge of his bed so Joel could take the chair. "That's why I asked to see you. I need some help with its delivery."

"You need a letter mailed?" Joel asked.

"Not mailed, delivered," Fred explained.

"Got an address, Keegan?"

"Well, no. No, I don't. But it's to my daughter."

Fred watched Joel, wondering how his lawyer would respond to his proposal. They had known each other for the last five years, and during that time, he had learned to value the man's opinion. Joel seemed less like his lawyer and more like a nephew.

Joel leaned forward, his elbows resting on his knees and his fingers laced together as he spoke.

"I wouldn't think it should be too difficult. There'll be a marriage certificate if your ex remarried—would she be the type to remarry?" As Fred nodded and grimaced, Joel continued. "And of course, school registration forms. Maybe with some help from the Web, I could find an address or addresses where you can send the letter—"

"No," Fred interjected. "I don't want to mail it. It's taken me a long time, Joel, but now that I have something of value to offer her, I want to know that it'll get put into her hands. I don't know who else to ask. I thought this thing through till my head feels like I've got two tumors, not one, and I keep coming back to you. I need you to do this.

"My daughter, Julia, will be my only heir, and you will be the executor—if you agree to it, that is. This search shouldn't be complicated, but if it is, you can take any funds you require for it from the inheritance provision that you will write up with my signature and a third-party witness. I'm not a rich man, but I'm not a poor one, either, thanks to some of the investments you've helped me with." He stopped. His outburst had winded him.

Fred prepared himself for disappointment as he watched Joel struggle with the ramifications of his request. Things that should be simple and straightforward were sometimes the opposite. For a lawyer to take on the unknown with no guarantee was a leap, and Fred knew it.

Joel hesitated for a moment, then gave a quick nod.

"I'll do it, Keegan," he told him.

As they shook hands over the agreement, Fred sighed with relief. He knew Joel would see it through. It was enough.

Four weeks later, Joel stood by a mound of freshly dug earth and pulled his gray, woolen collar up around his ears against the fingers of a cold autumn trying to creep past it. The prison chaplain and a few people Joel had never seen before were the only ones at the burial service for Fred Keegan.

"The Lord is my shepherd, I shall not want . . ."

The skin on Joel's neck grew itchy as the Bible reading went on and on. He disliked sappy words and sentiment. As a lawyer, he was hardened by the hypocrisy of even the nicest people, and it had left him repulsed by religion. He looked at the ugly blue coffin that would sink into the cold dirt and freeze there all winter. Fred Keegan was one of the few people he knew whom he also trusted. But Fred, a convicted murderer, had had nothing to hide. Real, like no one Joel had ever known, and now he was gone. It was sad. Not just that he was gone, but that quality human beings were so often ignored, while the rich, famous, and beautiful were looked up to and lauded regardless of their crimes against their fellow humans. The face of the woman he had divorced four years ago on grounds of infidelity came to mind. Crossing his arms over his chest, Joel tried to protect himself from a sudden cold gust.

"Even though I walk through the valley of the shadow of death, I will fear no evil . . ." Joel hunched deeper into his coat, his thoughts full of unrest. He felt like turning his back and leaving, but respect for Fred held him frozen in place. It was also why he had taken on the task of delivering the letter to Fred's daughter. Fred Keegan had been a friend.

"Surely goodness and mercy shall follow me all the days of my life, and I shall dwell in the house of the Lord forever." The chaplain finished with an amen. Joel wondered who believed words like that these days, even as they continued to echo through his head as he walked away from the grave, his feet crunching the fallen maple leaves underfoot.

# THREE

❧

He makes the clouds his chariot;
he rides on the wings of the wind; he makes . . .
his ministers a flaming fire.

JULIA WOKE WITH THE RISING SUN. Slipping her clothes on, she grabbed her laptop and stepped outside to survey her home for the next several weeks. Plastic shelters stretched over sticks and patched with woven grass mats extended as far as the eye could see. A civic engineer's worst nightmare. The tendency seemed to be for people to set up tents in concentric areas with others, presumably from the same families or villages.

Hassa Hissa was the name of her new residence. It covered several square miles of land, Jonathan, the camp's director, had informed her upon her arrival two days ago. In her jet-lagged state Julia had not taken in everything he'd said, but she remembered being shocked at the idea that hundreds of new arrivals came to this IDP camp each day, extending the parameters and adding to the confusion. The relief workers' stations and camp areas were separated from the rest of the dishevelment by walls and a gate. The area included warehouses for storing

28

relief supplies, a school, vehicles, and a medical clinic. Laid out in neat right angles, American style, it stood in contrast to the rest of the camp.

Those needing assistance entered through the gates to register their names at the office and to be entered on the list of those who would receive aid. There was a long line. People would often end up camping along that line, Jonathan had said, sometimes for days, before they could get official camp status and be eligible for the daily allotment of food and the plastic sheeting that would protect their lean-to shelters from the rains. The line of those waiting for medical attention had grown so long that it had become an unofficial open-air clinic, where treatment was given on a strictly emergency basis. The needs and demands were constant.

Julia sat cross-legged in a patch of shade she'd claimed as her own. With her laptop on her knees, she described the scene in front of her, her fingers slowing only slightly as she occasionally looked up to smile at the herd of very black children huddled four or five deep and watching her. Most people here spoke at least some basic English, so when she said, "Hello," the children responded shyly. A tiny boy who looked like he was two or three years old flashed a set of yellow teeth with a gap on the top row. He was missing his right arm. It wasn't the first child she'd seen severely maimed here. Delimbing, she had been told during her orientation, was a common form of torture practiced by the Janjaweed. Children were not exempt. *Janjaweed*. It sounded so benign—like an herb or a wild flower. Instead, it was militant Islam. Men with machine guns and hate.

Two little girls, each wearing a bright colorful *taub,* the loose cotton shift and head covering Darfurian women wore, gazed at Julia with glassy stares, no returning smile on their faces. After the first couple days in this camp, Julia had begun to realize a sad truth. Some children did not know how to smile. Both girls were holding babies almost as large as themselves.

Julia's fingers started flying across the keyboard, her heart full of emotion. From experience, she knew this could produce some of her best writing—or possibly some of her worst:

> Living here are the world's poorest, most abused, and mistreated. Where, one must ask, are the voices shouting in defense of women and children and each person's rights (not to mention the whales, owls, or trees)? Their absence is particularly odd, given that most of the people in this refugee camp are victims of the worst injustice known to humankind. Genocide.
>
> "The farmer and the cowboy should be friends" are the words to a song in Rodgers and Hammerstein's "Oklahoma." In Sudan, one would sing "the farmer and the nomad." Years of fighting between these two groups has escalated into a tragedy of epic proportions. The small Sudanese farming villages dotted across the region of Darfur are almost gone: not because of the drought or harsh circumstances of a difficult existence, but rather because of Janjaweed, the militant, Islamic, Arabian nomads supported by the government in Khartoum.

A box flashed on her screen: Low Battery. She'd have to recharge it soon. To send her report and the photos, she would have to wait until she was back in Malha, where there was exactly one building with Internet access: the butcher shop.

Julia's stomach growled. She would go down to the mess tent and eat breakfast. But she knew that each of the children surrounding her was hungry, too. Relief aid provided them just two meals per day—standard, tasteless, and beige. A little girl, maybe five years old, was holding a bowl of the porridge-like meal and sharing it with a smaller child, probably a little sister, who was hunched on the ground beside her. One would think it was chocolate, the way their eyes lit up at each bite.

Julia frowned, troubled with the reality of this great injustice. She could go and get a regular meal whenever she wanted, but these children waited for what wouldn't be enough even when they got it. This was the aid the world was offering. To be sure, it was on a grand scale; more than 2.5 million people were in the IDP camps scattered across Darfur, an area that was almost desert, hostile to fertility at its best, and now lying mostly in ashes thanks to the Janjaweed. The resources of the nations, Julia knew, were adequate, even abundant. Didn't people throw away perfectly good food at home all the time? It made her feel guilty just thinking about the meals she had left on her plate. Here, the reality of hunger, hunger and children, was irreconcilable.

Storing her computer in her pack, she hefted it onto her shoulder— a light load at five and a half pounds—and stepped into the sunlight. Hot even in the shade, in the sun it felt like an oven.

Children, black as coal, came from everywhere as she walked, chattering constantly: "Where you go, miss?" "Do you have sweetie for me?" "Will you be my mother? My mother dead . . ." Their voices had a singsong cadence. These children were a mixture of the three main non-Arabic tribes of people who made up most of Darfur: the Zaghawa, the Fur, and the Massaleit. They now blended into one common denominator, *refugee*, united as victims of violence. Julia didn't watch the children who ran alongside her but gazed at the ones sitting or lying outside their tents. Blank faces turned toward her with empty eyes. These children were the dying. She knew some camps reported up to two hundred deaths in a single day.

She had realized a significant fact the first time she walked through the camp. Her life would never be the same again. She would return one day to beautiful British Columbia and rejoin the queues at Starbucks and Costco. But Darfur would never leave her. Her heart would always carry the scar.

In the mess tent, she went through the food line, her stomach revolting at the thought of eating while the images of the children outside filled her mind.

"Sit yourself down, girl." A young man sitting with a very pretty woman invited Julia, pulling a chair away from the long trestle table, scratching lines in the dirt floor as he did so.

Balancing her plate of chili and a clear plastic cup of water, Julia joined Kelly and Dave Butler, a volunteer couple also from the West Coast—Portland, Oregon—and both of them nurses, if she remembered correctly from the brief orientation and introductions on her first day.

"Hi, guys." She contemplated lunch: the meaty aroma wafting upward, her fork poised in her hand, stomach growling. Time to eat. Instead, she laid the fork back down and sipped her water, noticing as she did that Kelly's and Dave's heads were bowed silently over their food. Good grief, she hadn't seen that for a long time. Somehow, the thought of praying—even just at a meal—seemed incongruous in a place like Sudan. If there was anywhere that God was not, it was here. Dave looked up first, caught Julia's stare, and grinned. He didn't even seem embarrassed.

"Not hungry, huh?" He shoveled a forkful into his mouth; his eyes steady as they met hers.

She shifted uncomfortably in her chair and agreed, shaking her head. "How do you eat here with . . . everything outside?"

Kelly finished her religious ritual, then looked straight at her, eyes wide with understanding.

"It's terrible, isn't it? I couldn't eat at first, either," she said.

"She lost ten pounds in the first three weeks," Dave shook his head in disbelief at his little wife. Kelly smiled back at him.

"But you quickly realize how useless you are to make a difference"—Kelly shifted the chili on her plate with the fork, making rivulets of juicy tomato sauce bleed into the paper plate—"if you're not healthy."

Taking her first bite, she chewed with purpose, as if to emphasize her words. "I'm a midwife and need to be awake and alert because—for some reason God will have to explain to me one day—birth seems to happen only in the middle of the night."

"A lot of workers get sick here," Dave added. "Sometimes it's so bad they have to go back home."

"Have either of you been sick?" Julia asked, scooping a forkful into her mouth. It was good. Her stepfather James had always said that hunger was the best sauce. He was right.

Dave and Kelly shared a little smile. "We were just talking about that this morning—Julia, isn't it?" Julia affirmed her name with a nod, and Kelly continued. "We've been here for six months and haven't been sick yet."

"Wow. You must take good vitamins."

"Just the regular, but we believe God is honoring our prayers and the prayers of our folks back home." Dave peered at her intently, waiting for a response. He made her feel like a bug under a microscope. But she liked him. If she was a bug, then he was a kind—but mad—scientist.

"Hmmm," was the only response she could manage as she nodded with her mouth full, inviting them to tell her more.

*I definitely like this couple*, Julia thought. And although she didn't agree with them or believe in God, much less a God who could keep people from sickness and disease, compared to her roommate at university who had spent hours meditating in front of a small statue of a very fat man, they were almost rational. She'd watched Dave and Kelly and other volunteers working in camp. They could not do what they did if they weren't strong people. Where that strength came from was a question she had never asked herself, until now.

"You're here with the press, aren't you?" Kelly's clear blue eyes brimmed with interest. "A career in journalism . . ." She sighed enviously and shook her head. "How does Sudan measure up to other places you've been?"

"In truth, I haven't done anything quite like this. The big earth-quake in India was the closest in damage proportion, but it was a lot cleaner emotionally. Here I see not just grief and loss, but the effect of cruelty written on faces—especially children's faces." She paused, her mouth working. Dave and Kelly nodded.

"Do all the kids here speak English? They seem to understand most of what I say to them, but I'm not sure."

"A lot of the people here have a bit of English," Dave explained. "Remember, the British ruled Sudan for over fifty years. Some Suda-nese speak English fluently, especially if they've lived near a town with a school or clinic. Once in a while, you come across people who don't speak any, but that doesn't happen too much.

"You know"—Dave paused, as if assessing her—"we're heading to Qasar today. A report came in last night that they've found a few sur-vivors after last week's Janja raid. Would you like to come with us?"

Dave's invitation was not easy to accept. Julia knew from other reporters and from people at the camp what she might expect to see. Her heart didn't want to go, but she was a journalist, and the world needed to be informed. In addition, while Dave and Kelly might not know it, they were under her microscope now. How did they stay so strong emotionally—if they really were—after six months in a place like this? After today, she might find out.

"Yes, I'll come, but quite honestly, I can think of lots of places I'd rather go."

# Four

"But ask the beasts, and they will teach you; the birds
of the heavens, and they will tell you; or the bushes
of the earth, and they will teach you; and the fish of
the sea will declare to you. Who among all these does
not know that the hand of the LORD has done this?
In his hand is the life of every living thing and the
breath of all mankind."

JOB 12:7–10

"How does it feel, sir?"

"Oh, yeah . . ." Joel felt the tension in his shoulders dissipate into the vibrating leather chair. A hundred thousand square feet of home improvement inventions left him with sore feet and information overload. Whoever was marketing these chairs in a place like this at the end of the first floor was a genius.

"Our product is truly superior to anything the competition offers: imported Italian leather, state-of-the-art technology enhancing your ability to customize the therapeutic aspect—we believe we've thought of everything." The salesman hit another button on the chair's remote.

Immediately, warmth flooded the entire six-feet, two-inch length of Joel's body, adding to the massage effect. He relaxed fully and closed his eyes. The world's hectic pace seemed to recede.

"Oh, hon, it's amazing!" From the chair beside him, Celeste's voice broke into his pleasure. A nerve pinched in his neck. He swung his legs over the side of the La-Z-Boy, smiled curtly at the salesman, and took Celeste's hand.

"Time to move on."

"I could stay here forever," she moaned ecstatically.

"Yeah, we've still got half the floor to see, and our dinner reservations are in two hours." His reminder acted more effectively than any mere request he made of her ever could. She jumped up, generous sections of artificially tanned midriff exposed as she yawned and stretched, shaking her long, burgundy brown hair as she did.

The look in the salesman's eyes was obvious, and he made no attempt to hide it.

"Come back any time; I'll be here for the next two days in case you're interested. Remember, it's imported from Italy, made to bring you maximum pleasure." He leered at Celeste.

Joel looked away in disgust as his girlfriend smiled knowingly at the slime, even while holding Joel's hand. He knew the days of this relationship were numbered, and he had lost patience with the game. It always happened like this, and he had grown cynical and jaded from the experience. Somehow, to protect his own personal standards—admittedly not as high as they probably should be—he had to go through the motions of treating this female with respect until he could dump her gracefully. He wondered why he had started dating her at all. She was boring. She sucked in attention like a vacuum cleaner. One man couldn't give her enough. She needed her own male fan club. In return for what? More fancy dinners, clubbing, and gifts? The cost of this relationship was beginning to outweigh the benefits, and he would never get back interest. A total loss, his head told him. What he couldn't, and wouldn't, calculate was the toll each broken relationship cost his heart and integrity.

Morning sunlight shone through the UV-protected windows, one screened panel letting in the crisp autumn air. Left eye first, then the right. Joel didn't like to face the day all at once. He stretched, feeling refreshed, and wondered what was different. Yesterday: the office, then the home show—he'd really like one of those massage chairs—dinner, and . . . His mind focused, and he knew. Celeste was over. That awkward conversation in which he had tried to convince her she'd be better off without him and, when that hadn't worked, how he needed his independence. "It's over," he had finally said. She had not liked hearing them, but at least his words had managed to silence the woman.

No Celeste, and it was Saturday. He flung aside the duvet, padded barefoot across the hardwood floors, flipped the switch on the automatic coffeemaker in the sterile, stainless steel kitchen, and headed for the shower, whistling as he went.

Afterward, taking his coffee and his cell phone outside onto his twelfth-story balcony overlooking the city center of Vancouver, he breathed in the fresh morning air. Looking west, he could see whitecaps out on the ocean. A cruise ship was making its way proudly out into the Strait of Georgia, like a resplendent, chubby bride. The breeze was up, bringing with it the smell of saltwater and the cries of the gulls. Looking north and east, he could see whitecaps of a different kind. The mountain peaks were powdered with fresh snow. Next weekend, he'd head up for some early season skiing if the weather held. Today, he needed to catch up on office work.

Inhaling the fresh morning breeze blowing in off the ocean, he palmed his cell phone and punched in the numbers, bringing up his messages. One from his secretary, Elaine: an appointment needing to be rescheduled with a client; one message from Celeste, she loved him so much, she whimpered, "Couldn't they work it out?"—no way, baby!—and one from the prison warden: "This is George Westraa from the penitentiary. I have a box of effects from Fred Keegan, one of our deceased inmates, with your name on it. Please pick it up as soon as it is convenient for you. Thanks."

A box of Fred Keegan's effects?

"To delete this message, press seven," instructed the prerecorded voice. "To save it, press nine." He pressed seven.

Blowing softly through his pursed lips, he shrugged away the sense of guilt for having put off the dying man's request—to place his letter into his daughter's hands—longer than he should have. He had had good reason. Finding Fred's daughter had turned out to be more than a little complicated. Maybe the box of Fred's stuff would disclose some contacts: names of relations, old friends, anything that would give him a lead . . .

One last message: Celeste again. How long would it take her to get it? It was over. One discarded girlfriend had dogged him obsessively for six months. His lip curled in annoyance at the memory as he pressed the seven button once more. Hard.

He closed his eyes, wrapped his hands around the oversized mug full of black coffee, and cleared his mind. He had no mantra; he just knew it helped to come to a complete stop sometimes.

The cacophony of sounds from the city below drifted up to him, sounds of people moving busily about their lives. It always had an energizing effect on him. Taking the last sip of coffee, he knew what he would do today. The drive out to the prison took about forty-five minutes. If he left right away, he could get back by lunchtime and start checking out Fred's box for any clues to Julia's whereabouts. If all went well, he might be able to hand her the manila envelope containing her father's letter by evening. It would feel good to get this one off his mind.

He took the elevator down to the basement car park. As soon as the steel door began to slide open, he was already walking and pressing the unlock button on his key fob.

The sound of a basketball halted him in his tracks.

Dominic loved that ball. Or hated his apartment. Joel's money was on the latter. He headed around one of the concrete walls to where the empty car lots were and slid his keys inside his pocket. They could wait.

"Hey, Dominic, try and get it past me."

The kid's face lit up with pleasure at the sight of Joel, and he started a fake. Dribbling pretty well for an eleven-year-old, he kept tight control, siding toward Joel and guarding the ball with his body. Joel worked him a bit, encouraging him as he did.

"Atta boy, try and block me. Good crossover! Trying to fake me out, huh?"

And so it went.

Twenty minutes more and Joel started to slow it down.

"How's your mom doing?"

Dominic shrugged.

"Been to your dad's lately?"

"I was supposed to go this morning. He said he'd take me to the BC Lions game tonight and buy me a T-shirt."

"Cool."

"'Cept he phoned and told my mom we'd have to do it another time cause he's got a bunch of office work again. Then there was another long fight, so I came down here."

"Sorry, kid." Joel tousled the back of his head. "I bet your dad is so bummed he's missing that sweet game with you. He's gotta hate that office!"

Dominic paused, considering this angle of his circumstance. The light in the kid's eyes was ever so slight, but Joel saw it flicker, then catch.

"Yeah, I bet he's yelling at that bimbo secretary right now."

"Darn right."

"Darn right!"

Joel passed the ball back and pulled out his keys, turning toward his car.

"See ya."

"Yeah, see you later, kid." Joel started to walk away, then stopped. "Hey, Dominic, you want to hang out with me tonight?"

"Sure I do! Can we play your Wii?"

"Actually, I've got tickets to the Lions, too. If you want to come, that is. It's not the same as going with your dad, and if you don't want to, I understand."

The grin on Dominic's face did not need words.

Nor did the grin on Joel's.

Books. The box of Fred's belongings Joel brought back from the penitentiary was full of well-used books. Joel took them out one at a time, reading the titles and flipping through the pages, checking to see if any letters or memorabilia were stored there. Ten lay neatly in a stack on the pine table alongside his fast-food chicken sandwich. Curiosity had won over hunger, but as he looked at another twenty or thirty books still to be checked, he decided eating food while it was still hot was good practice.

Grabbing his lunch and the newspaper he'd picked up from the lobby, he sank into the leather couch and threw his feet onto the coffee table. As he bit into the sandwich, his eyes scanned the front page.

*Domestic violence leaves 3 dead*
*Computer company sued*
*Over 2,500,000 displaced people in Darfur*
*Can the B.C. Lions freeze the Eskimos?*

He flipped to the sports section and became fully absorbed for twenty minutes as he pored over scores, plays, and stats. Crumpling the empty food wrapper into a ball, he shot it into the waste bin twelve feet away. Swish. As he made the move, the news section slid away from the folds of paper.

His eyes fell on the back page as he bent to pick it up and were held for a moment by a picture of a mother's thin, dark hand covering the body of her baby, who was barely more than a skeleton. The child's dark eyes seemed too large, the skin on his face stretched. Sudan.

Experience told him someone, somewhere wanted to use the picture to motivate him to give them his money. Overexposure to the world's suffering had left him indifferent, but in spite of that, the picture continued to capture his attention.

He read the caption: "A mother holds her child in the Hassa Hissa refugee camp in the Darfur region of Sudan, Friday, October 3, 2008. Refugees in their own country, an estimated 2,500,000 people have been forced to flee their homes due to violence from militant Islamic factions."

Joel belched, folded the offending picture back into the newspaper pile, and stretched out full length on the plush sofa, sleep coming almost as soon as his eyes were closed.

He was searching for Julia Keegan. He called her name over and over, but no one answered. Someone was walking toward him. He started running, but when he got close enough, he saw it wasn't Julia. It was Keegan. Fred gazed at him with sad, soulful eyes, his hand held out toward Joel, reaching for him. Wondering what he should do, Joel extended his hand to Fred in response and suddenly felt that huge, familiar hand grip his own warmly.

He woke up, Fred's hand still holding his. Coming fully awake, Joel pulled his hand from under the warmth of the cushion that he'd been resting on. *Huh.* Clearing his head with a shake or two, he stood up.

It was time to pick up Dominic.

⁂

The Lions won that night. So did Joel. He hadn't enjoyed an evening that much since before he met Celeste. After dropping a sleepy Dominic off at his front door, he went back to his apartment.

Tossing his keys on the counter, he spotted the box waiting on the table. How the man had loved his books. Handling them, Joel felt more moved than he had at the funeral. It was like he was visiting a part of Fred. He placed a hand on the table and stroked the smooth, satiny wood. Fred's hands had held these books; Fred's hands had made this table . . .

Joel had walked into Fred Keegan's cell for the first time five years ago, after Keegan found him in the yellow pages. Joel's first impression: *that's a lot of tattoos.* His second: *huge biceps.* So when Fred spoke, his soft, quiet voice had surprised Joel. Almost as much as his question.

"I'm wondering if you can manage my money. You know . . . set up some investments or something. I don't really care what. There's not much I can do with it in here."

"You've been earning an income in here?" Prison had never seemed a likely place for business opportunities.

"I've been making some furniture. I didn't think anyone would like it. I just made it to please myself, you know. But one day, the instructor asked me if he could take a few pieces to some kind of show, and I told him, 'Why not?' Well, to make a long story short, it caught on pretty good, and now it's created a bit of a dilemma. It's brought in a tidy profit, and I mean to protect it. Do you think you can help me?"

"I'd be pleased to, Mr. Keegan. I'm certain I could find some investments that would do the job for you."

"Don't call me *mister*. Just Keegan will do fine."

With that, they had begun a professional relationship that had eventually turned into a more personal one. Joel couldn't remember when it had changed or how, but he knew it had. One day, he had gone for a regular business appointment and ended up staying for three hours, walking the prison grounds with Fred and just enjoying his company. They were an unlikely pair: young successful lawyer and tough old prison inmate.

It had been early spring, warm with promise. Crocuses had been in bloom, and the ornamental cherry trees had blushed in pink blossom. Gladly leaving the bleak cell in exchange for the yard outside on that beautiful afternoon, they had found a bench to sit on where they had a commanding view of rolling prison grounds and inmates strolling or sitting with wives or girlfriends. Some were playing Frisbee or catch with children. It could be a scene from any nice park in the city. Joel was always amazed at how nice prisons could seem. Good, tax-paying citizens keeping criminals in comfort. Right then, he didn't mind.

"How's the furniture coming, Keegan?" he'd asked after a moment's pause in their conversation.

"You wanna see it?"

"I sure do. I meant to ask you to show me last time and then completely forgot during that heated discussion on politics."

"It weren't heated. I was telling you what you didn't want to admit was the truth."

"Uh huh, same as our religious 'debates,' right?"

"I'm glad you're finally seeing the light."

"Keegan, the day I see the same light you see, shoot me dead."

"Son, the day you see the Light, you'll already be dead. To yourself, that is. Dead to yourself and alive to Jesus. It's the only way to live." Fred's tone was sincere and gentle, but his eyes were intense and dark. Joel had enough experience to gauge the impending conversation by the eyes. But he was also experienced in decoy.

"You are a sneaky devil! You just about got me sidetracked, too, but we're not going to hash out that one on such a nice day, Keegan. Take me to the woodshop!" Joel grinned at his friend, a twinkle in his eye.

Anyone looking at the man's record for violent outbursts during his stay in this place would assume Keegan was a fighter. Funny thing, Joel had never felt afraid of him. Respect, yes. Afraid, no. Maybe age had mellowed the man, or maybe the fact that Joel was a fighter, himself—and as a karate black-belt, he wasn't easily intimidated—he didn't know. But somehow, Fred's violation records that Joel had viewed seemed to belong to a different person, certainly not to this gentle giant.

They entered the woodshop, located in a building detached from the main prison. It was large and spacious inside, with that good smell of wood shavings and varnish. A few guys were working at benches; someone was using an electric drill. At the back corner, Fred and Joel stopped. A dining-room suite made of pine filled the space. Keegan proudly rested his hand on the back of a chair.

"This is my stuff," he said simply.

Joel was impressed. Once slender branches now filled a new function as the slats of the chairs, but they still kept their natural shape. The inside of the chair backs had been molded and sanded down to provide maximum comfort. The chair legs were young saplings, the bark peeled coarsely to leave a dark contrast against the exposed sunny color of the heartwood of the chair slats, the wood seats, and the tabletop.

Joel's eyes rested with pleasure on the table itself. It was a masterpiece. Fred had chosen knotty two-by-six slabs and sanded and polished them to a golden hue. The four legs were small tree trunks, supporting the weight of the tabletop and adding to the solid, rustic appeal of the entire set.

Joel felt a sense of warmth and nostalgia that took him by surprise. Images of farm kitchens, log cabins, and homemade pancakes with melted butter and maple syrup filled his mind. He ran his hand over the tabletop, admiring the silky smooth finish.

"Keegan, it's beautiful."

"You really like it? You're not just being nice?"

"I more than like it, Keegan. How much are you asking for it?"

"I'm embarrassed to tell you what they sell for. I couldn't believe it at first, but then they told me I had to start asking more. Now I think it's silly. So much money for a table and chairs." Fred shook his head in disbelieving wonder at the purchasing power of the younger generation. "But this isn't for sale."

"It's not?" Disappointment filled Joel's voice.

"Nah. This was a custom job."

"Oh." Joel considered for a moment. "Would you do one for me, Keegan?"

Keegan had hesitated, looking at him intently. Maybe Joel hadn't been the only one who'd had to reevaluate his first impression. Fred probably wouldn't slot him as the rustic furniture type but—sophisticated lawyer image aside—he felt strangely drawn to it. Finally the answer came.

"It would be an honor."

Three days later, that same dining-room suite had been delivered to the penthouse Joel called home, lending a warmth and character that had never been there before. A card came with the suite. It read: *Happy Birthday, Joel. —Keegan*

It wasn't his birthday till February, but when Joel had pointed this fact out to Keegan, trying to persuade him to take payment, it had had no effect.

"Sorry it's late," was all Fred had said, looking smug.

Joel's hand ran over the table now, remembering his friend. A slight frown creased his brow at the thought of Fred's daughter. Where was she?

# FIVE

The LORD your God is in your midst, a mighty one
who will save; he will rejoice over you with gladness;
he will quiet you by his love; he will exult over you
with loud singing.

ZEPHANIAH 3:17

IT WAS THE ROAD TO HELL, BUT IT WASN'T smooth and broad. Julia held
onto the seat in front of her. Her hands were wet with sweat, but not
just from the heat. The Land Cruiser jolted and jerked and bucked like
a wild thing. Her backside would never be the same. She thought she
had known how ineffective Khartoum's public road system was, but
this was way off the charts as a "need for improvement" road.

"How you doing?" Dave yelled.

She nodded, her mouth shut tightly, knowing that if she opened it to
speak, the chances of biting her tongue hard were very good.

Beside her, Kelly had also grown quiet and serious about clinging to
the seat in front of her for balance. Once in a while a little "Yikes!" emitted from her petite form, a religious form of swearing, Julia decided.

Their guide, Hassan, sat in the front seat beside Dave. The worried frown on his face and the beads of sweat on his forehead did not comfort Julia.

"How much longer?" She braved the question during a relatively smooth section.

Dave and Hassan said something she couldn't quite hear; the Land Cruiser revved and whined a bit louder with each new abuse it suffered.

"I could really use a bathroom," she shouted.

Dave took his eyes off the "road" momentarily. "We'll be at Qasar in ten minutes. Can you hold it that long?"

That was Dave: Mr. Thoughtful of Others.

"Yeah, I'll make it." What choice did she have? Open spaces of what had once been African veld, now barren and dry from the drought, spread out in all directions. Sudan, she remembered, looking out on endless horizon, was the largest of all Africa's countries.

When they finally pulled off the main bumpy road and headed down what was basically a ditch with some high spots, she spied small huts in the distance. If she hadn't been looking for it, she would never have noticed what had once been the village of Qasar.

Nearing the area, they were struck by the smell. Kelly wordlessly passed out facemasks. Julia's stomach heaved. Bumpy road plus a stench she didn't want to know about or face . . .

A roughly circular formation of smoldering ruins lay where the village once had stood. Dave stopped the Land Cruiser under a large cypress tree smothered in purple bougainvillea. Bold beauty in the midst of smoke and ashes.

Julia and Kelly crawled out of the back of the Land Cruiser and went looking for respective huts to hide behind while they answered Mother Nature's call.

Chickens clucked somewhere. Closing her eyes, Julia tried to pretend she was in a decent facility instead of behind a hut in a forsaken place. A goat cried for its ma, making Julia jump. Bad timing. *Journalism in all its glory,* she thought, *minus toilet paper.* She made a mental note: *while in Africa, don't leave home without it.*

"So what do we do now?" she asked, back at the Land Cruiser. "It doesn't look like anyone's here."

"The people, they are very scared," Hassan told her, the whites of his eyes seeming unusually large above his facemask. "If they are here, they don't know who we are. Maybe we be more Janja, they think."

Kelly had joined them, and Dave tucked her protectively under his arm. "I think it's a good idea if we walk around. Julia, are you OK going with Hassan? If we split up, we can cover the village faster."

Julia and Hassan picked their way across a debris-strewn path, moving away from Kelly and Dave, dust puffing up with each step. A dirty, torn bra lay on one side of the path, creating images in Julia's imagination that she didn't want.

Directly in front of them stood four burned-out huts, still smoking. Julia and Hassan skirted away from these, keeping their distance in order to avoid the stench that rose up and choked them.

They passed chickens, a few goats, and some skinny acacia trees, but they didn't see a soul.

"If there were survivors, where would they go?" she asked Hassan.

He shrugged, tilting his head to one side as if to hear the answer from the sky. "Maybe they walk away somewhere. If they have family in city, they try to go there. If they have no one, they probably try to get to camp. It is hard choice, leaving everything behind to go to live at camp. But harder to stay in village where bad things happened."

Nodding, she realized the truth of this.

"Did you—" She started to ask and then changed her mind. Maybe it was too personal.

He didn't reply for so long, she thought maybe he hadn't heard her.

"I have wife and baby," he spoke very quietly. "Seven months ago, Janjaweed came in helicopters, with machine guns to our village. After that soldiers on camels, with rifles. Many people died. Many people suffered. We ran from our village to Hassa Hissa camp. We ran from fear. But we could not run far enough. Fear is everywhere."

"Aren't you safe now? Janjaweed don't attack the people in the camps, do they?"

"No, not so much. But we must still gather firewood. Many men are shot by Janja outside the camps as they search for firewood. Our women go for us now. It is hard work for them. They walk many miles to find wood for just one day's cooking. The Janja do not kill women. They rape them. Every day my wife goes for wood, I pray God to keep her safe. So far, she is not harmed, but there are many women in camp who carry babies from Janja."

Julia stopped, her hands covering her eyes. Somewhere from some place in her memory's archives the words *see no evil, hear no evil* flitted past. Well, here she was. Now she had seen. Now she had heard. And oh, how she would speak out against what was happening.

"I'm sorry." He was apologizing, she knew, for the pain of the knowledge.

"It's all right. It's why I came." She looked up at him, surprised by the genuine worry she saw in his eyes. "I'll be okay, Hassan."

Glancing ahead, she saw a large tree standing alone, a distance from the village. Someone sat below it, sheltered in the shade.

"Look, there's someone still here." Surprised at the emotion that rushed over her, Julia pointed toward the tree.

"You go. Get Dave." Hassan patted her shoulder and then gave her a very gentle push toward the village as she hesitated. "Dave has medicine for this man."

Understanding dawned and gave movement to her feet. She ran back along the path, calling as she went.

No one was at the Land Cruiser.

"Dave! Kelly! We found someone!" No answer. She started off at a trot, heading the way she knew they had gone. More burnt huts, pots scattered and broken on the ground. A blouse, or what had once been a blouse but was now a filthy rag, drifted along in the breeze.

She stopped, catching her breath. She could feel pressure on her chest. She inhaled deeply. Was she winded? No. She was used to running three kilometers every day. The pressure, she realized, was sorrow. It clutched her heart and squeezed.

Normal people had lived—and died—here. A few mornings before, people had set out pots to cook in, gathered eggs, and hung clothes to dry. Looking around, she could see evidence everywhere of difficult, impoverished lives made suddenly a thousand times worse.

How could this be happening in the same world that she knew to be reality, the world of her Jetta, spa membership, and gourmet dining? How could that world, soaked in an age of information, be ignorant of this? Or indifferent?

"Julia, is everything all right?"

Turning to meet Kelly, Julia's jaw slackened momentarily in surprise.

On Kelly's shoulder, his head turned toward her, rested a beautiful black baby wrapped in a soiled blanket. Dave, walking just behind, had in his arms a little girl who looked to be four or five years old. But Julia had learned from her short stay at the camp that these children were so stunted in their growth from starvation and malnutrition that they were often three or four years older than they looked. The girl's hair was tinged with rust, a sign of malnutrition, Julia knew, but her eyes were wide and bright.

"Oh," she gasped, "they're adorable."

"Dirty and adorable," Dave corrected her.

Kelly's mask was pulled down, hanging under her chin, and her smile was bigger than Christmas.

"Parents?"

"We don't know. We found this little one huddled with the baby in one of the huts. She was humming to him, letting him suck on her finger to pacify him. She doesn't talk. Just hums and moans." Dave spoke matter-of-factly, but his eyes held tears.

"We saw someone under the tree over there," Julia said. "Hassan told me to come and get you."

"Are you okay waiting with the kids here, hon?"

Kelly nodded, and Dave helped her get the children in the Land Cruiser. The baby lay on Kelly's lap, and the little girl snuggled up against her side as Kelly sang a song Julia did not recognize but the children seemed to enjoy, gazing up with wide, brown eyes at the first white woman they had probably ever seen.

*A natural mother*, Julia thought with just a hint of envy. It was kind of infectious, the maternal feeling. She grabbed her camera and walked away from the domestic scene, hurrying to catch up with Dave.

Neither of them spoke as they made their way back to Hassan and the villager.

Julia fought her feelings. *I'm a journalist on assignment*, she reminded herself. *I cannot afford to let the sorrow of this place get to me. Focus. Emotions can undo a person here if you don't control them. I cannot let that happen.*

The man was old and gnarled and very black. He had dirt on his face and clothes, even in his hair. He sat, arms wrapped around his legs, his face resting across the top of his knees. Tears coursed down his cheeks in muddy rivulets.

Hassan glanced up at them, the hurt showing in his eyes as they arrived with the first-aid bag and a water bottle.

"He's in shock." Dave opened the water bottle, knelt down beside the man in the dust, and spoke softly to him. No response.

"There is a new grave not far away," Hassan whispered. "I think this man has buried his family there."

"Oh, Father in heaven, please bring peace to the heart of this man.

Help him to know You weep with those who weep. Father, comfort Your son."

*He's praying*, Julia realized in surprise. Praying in a way she had never heard before, as if he really thought God was listening. The full irony of praying to a God who had let all this tragedy occur was not lost on her. Regardless of whom Dave thought he was calling on, she knew no one was home.

Dave continued, his head bowed, his hand resting on the man's shoulder. "In the name of Jesus, and for His sake, do not let evil have victory here."

Slowly, the man's black, twisted hand reached out to rest on Dave's thatch of blond hair.

The old man worked his mouth for a moment, then spoke, his voice hoarse yet deep, like a drum, the sound of it bringing tears to Julia's eyes.

"My name is Peter Kuanen. God has brought you to me."

# Six

❧

The night is far gone; the day is at hand.
So then let us cast off the works of darkness and
put on the armor of light.

ROMANS 13:12

*WHAT'S SO AMAZING ABOUT GRACE? Good title,* Joel thought, as he shelved
Keegan's books. Maybe he could recommend it in his next litigation
case. Except for a few westerns and spy novels, the only books already
in residence on his expensive, built-in shelves were his tomes from law
school: juicy titles like *Criminal Law and Institutions, Methods of the
Law,* and *Black's Law Dictionary.*

There was a lot he hadn't known about Fred Keegan. With a curled
lip, he shoved *Mere Christianity* and *The Jesus I Never Knew—and was
not ever likely to,* he thought—toward the back where they wouldn't be
visible to a casual observer.

What was up with Keegan? Joel knew he was religious, but he had
seemed like a normal guy—for a prisoner—not a fanatic. No, Joel
admitted to himself, he was better than a normal guy.

Five more spiritual titles got shoved to the back. A set of Reader's

Digest Condensed Books got a front place. He pulled the last book out of the box. It was a largish hardback, dark green with gold trim. He glanced at the spine. There was no title. He opened the front cover. Again no title. Opening it wide, flipping through it, he saw Keegan's distinctive script, a cross between printing and cursive, running over the pages. Keegan had kept a journal.

> I need to write some of the things I'm thinking. It feels like re- cently a light's been turned on and I can see things I couldn't before. A lot of it's jumbled up, though, and I think writing it down will help.

Joel clapped the book shut. Reading Keegan's personal diary felt like trespassing or something. Yes, the man was dead, but it still felt weird. He placed the journal beside the other books on the shelf, picked up the empty box, turned off the light in his den, and shut the door behind him.

Saturday night and no Celeste—in a word, freedom. He luxuriated in the thought: not having to please a female, he could do what he wanted, when he wanted, and where.

An hour later, a sigh of satisfaction escaped him, simultaneous with a large belch. Sitting on his sofa, remote in one hand, pizza and, alter- nately, beer in the other, he watched sports highlights on his fifty- five-inch plasma screen home theater. Life didn't get better than this. And in that moment, womanless for less than twenty-four hours, he believed it.

Three hours, one *CSI* show, and a movie later, he turned off the TV, plastic-wrapped the pizza he hadn't eaten, and stored it in the refrigera- tor. Picking up and depositing the four empty beer cans and the pizza box into the recycling while humming a Nissan commercial, Joel made his way to the bathroom. He liked to kick back as much as the next guy, but who could go to bed without brushing their teeth?

Sleep came quickly, ensconced between a down duvet and a Dux mattress. *Yes, life's sweet,* was his last thought.

⁂

Wide awake at 3:30 AM with beer and pizza repeating on him, Joel tried to fall back to sleep. Nothing happening.

*Shoot.* He knew what he had to do. He turned onto his belly and covered his head with his arms, groaning. Fred's journal was calling him.

Why couldn't he just ignore it? He tossed and turned for fifteen more minutes. No go.

Finally giving in, he went and retrieved the journal from the den. Taking it back to bed with him, he flipped on an overhead light and read:

> I went back today. I didn't plan to; it was like my feet almost took me on their own accord.

*I know what you mean . . .*

> And once I was there, it was fine. I like these people. I really do. They're not hiding anything, they're just—different. If they weren't all cons themselves, I'd feel out of place. Like I shouldn't be there. Like maybe this is too good for me or something. But they're just guys like me. Harry talked about forgiveness and joy tonight. I felt like a man who's been offered a cup of water after crossing a desert. But I just look. I want it so bad, but I know I can't get it. I'd give an awful lot to have it, but even if I did, it would just get dirty and muddy the minute I put my mitts on it. Like everything else.
>
> Somehow, tonight made me think of Sunday school and Aunt Rose. She sure was some lady.

*Aunt Rose?* Joel read a bit further, but no other reference to Aunt Rose was made. Just a lot of spiritual seeking stuff . . . yada, yada, yada . . .

But Aunt Rose? Maybe, just maybe . . .

Old Vancouver, which meant young compared to almost any other city in the world, had streets lined with Japanese cherry trees. In the spring, these trees were one of the earliest to bring hope with their delicate pink blossoms. In the autumn, the leaves turned all shades of red and orange, glorious in their dying. Joel drove his car slowly down roads richly carpeted with the vivid hues.

This was a section of town unfamiliar to him, old houses stuccoed in pink, blue, and white huddled together as if against time. Some showed definite signs of age, and others, like well-kept women, still looked good. All of them blended their pastel shades together into a soft glow under the afternoon sun, bringing to mind a page from *Dick and Jane.*

A little white picket gate stood in front of the house with the address from the phone book that Joel had scribbled in his day planner. It was tucked under an arbor heavy with twining vines and green leaves. He lifted the latch, the gate creaking as he swung it open, to step inside the stamp-sized yard. Actually, garden.

Flowers blossomed everywhere. Orange ones, all shades of pink, burgundy so dark as to be almost black, red ones with white stripes. It looked like an old-fashioned candy shop. The flowers massed together in chaotic color, some of them almost as tall as he was, so that Joel didn't see the woman working on the other side right away.

"'Ello?" It was a question. "Do I know you?" Her voice was low and throaty; a bit of an accent—Joel guessed Irish—lilted there. Her white hair was streaked with gray and pulled back tightly into a bun. Wisps of it curled around her forehead and neck. Kneeling on a gardener's bench, she held a knife in one gloved hand and what looked like a shriveled potato in the other. She looked at him with intense, dark eyes. *Raisins in the face of a snow lady,* he thought.

"No, ma'am, you don't know me." Joel thought if he had had a hat, he'd take it off to speak to her. "I'm looking for Rose Keegan."

"Well, then," Aunt Rose said, tilting her head to him, "you found her."

Putting the old potato and the knife down, she clapped her hands together, shedding little clumps of dirt. Carefully, she peeled off the gloves, revealing long slender hands spotted with age. Gripping the handles of her bench, she pushed herself from kneeling to bent.

"Thank you, I'm fine." She rejected his offer of assistance, shaking her head vigorously. "I take a minute to straighten out these days, and even then, it's not what you'd call straight." She assessed him, with hands on hips. "And now that you know who I am, what might your name be?"

"Joel Maartens, ma'am, attorney-at-law. Your nephew hired me . . ." Joel caught himself at a loss for words momentarily.

"Which one?"

At the blank look on his face, she repeated, "Which one hired you, Tom or Hank?"

"Oh, I see. No . . ." He looked around, wishing he were anywhere else than inside this lady's flower garden, about to tell her that her nephew had died. "No, ma'am, it was Fred."

"Fred." Her face shadowed. An image of a Norman Rockwell painting of a mother waiting for her son to return from war flickered through Joel's mind.

Turning away, Aunt Rose beckoned Joel with her hand. "Let's sit, shall we?"

She led him to a couple of deeply worn wicker chairs. Rose bushes, clipped back and covered with black plastic in preparation for frost, formed a sort of hedge behind them.

Joel told her about Fred. He explained his search for Julia, the woodworking business, and the letter. Aunt Rose listened without making comment, head down, apparently entranced by the juncos and chickadees hopping about, all oblivious, searching for seeds and bugs.

There was a moment of silence, except for the soft, melodious *tickkadeedeedee* coming from the birds and the sighing of the weeping birch leaves. Joel felt a chill that hadn't been there earlier.

"Why?" She didn't look up. "Why would he write Julia a letter? Why now? He wasn't the sentimental type. Definitely not the dramatic type. Why?" Aunt Rose's lined face furrowed more deeply in puzzlement.

"I got the impression it was pretty important to him. He insisted it be hand delivered." Joel tried to remember everything Keegan had said. "Something of value to offer, I think, is how he put it."

"Something of value?" Aunt Rose dwelt on each word as if quoting a beloved poet. Looking up at last, she studied Joel thoughtfully.

"Mr. Maartens, I used to visit Fred. Back in the days before I had the stroke. That was eight years ago. Afterward, it was difficult for me to get out there, but I still sent Christmas and birthday cards. And I've never stopped praying for him. Maybe the sheaves are finally coming in, eh?"

Joel had no idea what wheat had to do with it, but nodded and smiled politely. Sometimes old people got confused.

As if to confirm this thought, Aunt Rose smiled, got up, and led him back over to the flowers.

"Pick up this root, young man," she ordered.

Deciding that she meant the old potato, as no roots were in sight, he accommodated her.

"Do you know what that is, Mr. Maartens?" she asked.

"A potato, isn't it?" he answered.

"No. It is not a potato. That ugly, dirty root is a flower." She said this earnestly, smiling and making little nods at him. He figured it was time to go, and smiled and nodded, too.

"Yes, I see," he lied.

She pulled a large box toward him that was open and filled with sawdust. Reaching her hand inside she pulled another "flower" out.

"This one is called"—flipping a little tag that was wrapped around the root with thin wire—"'Elsie Huston.'"

Aunt Rose gave him 'Elsie' to hold. She was fairly brown and ugly. Definitely an old potato. He was ready to leave. He cleared his throat.

"Yes, she's a very pretty flower, but I think I must leave—"

"No, dearie, it's an ugly root, and make no mistake, but guess which one is her." Aunt Rose pointed to the riotous mass of flowers he had walked past earlier. Joel played along.

"The purple one?"

"Nope." Aunt Rose grinned at his mistake. "That's 'Dorothy May.' This one's 'Dorothy.'" Fishing through the sawdust she grasped another old potato and held it up, obviously pleased with herself.

"Aah." A scene from *Silence of the Lambs* flashed through his mind. Aunt Rose made a very unlikely Hannibal Lecter.

"Guess again."

He pointed to a brilliant red flower, standing about five feet tall.

"Wrong, but you're getting close. That one is 'Holly Huston.'"

"Sister of 'Elsie'?"

Aunt Rose raised her brows at him, reminding him that she had once been Keegan's Sunday school teacher.

"Guess," she ordered.

"The pink one?" He wasn't enjoying this.

"Well done, Mr. Maartens! That's 'Elsie.' Isn't she stunning?"

He couldn't help but agree. The rosy pink bloom spanned at least nine inches. Not a gardener himself, he figured he knew a rose from a daisy. But 'Elsie' was no daisy, and he'd never seen such huge, colorful flowers before.

"Dahlias have an ugly root, to be sure, Mr. Maartens, but some of the prettiest flowers God ever made. No scent, though. I always thought He chose not to give them any perfume so He would still have a reason to make the rose."

Aunt Rose knelt down on her gardener's stool again, picked up her gloves, and proceeded to put them on. Softly, almost to herself, she said, "I think Fred might have been a dahlia." Tears had filled her eyes, and to Joel's horror, one slid down her wrinkly cheek.

She fumbled for her hand shovel. The name game was obviously over. It was definitely time to go.

"Pardon me, ma'am. If you could just tell me Julia Keegan's whereabouts, I'll be on my way."

"Julia Douglas, you mean. She took her stepfather's name several years back. But it doesn't matter; Julia's not here. She's a journalist, you know." Loud sniff.

He didn't know.

"She left two weeks ago for Sudan. There's some kind of war going on, and they're killing the black people. Isn't it horrible?" Aunt Rose shook her dirty spade at him. Joel watched the dirt fall in tiny clumps; an image of a Sudanese mother clutching an infant to her breast flashed through his mind.

"Did you say Julia's a journalist?"

"She rushes into the most terrible places," the old lady continued. "I guess journalists have to, but I don't like it. That one needs praying for, and no mistake." She sighed at this, shaking her head sorrowfully.

Joel thanked Aunt Rose for talking with him. She nodded, barely looking up, busy, it seemed, with her dahlia roots. He swung open the little gate and stepped out into a far less charming world than the one he was leaving. At the sound of the gate's click, Aunt Rose called out, "Please come back again sometime, Mr. Maartens." Joel turned to see her waving at him, the old lady canopied by a natural cacophony of color. He smiled and waved back but couldn't imagine ever having a reason, in the world that was his, to return to a place like this.

# SEVEN

⌇

"Blessed are those who mourn,
for they shall be comforted."

MATTHEW 5:4

JULIA WOKE WITHOUT OPENING HER EYES. She could see a little dot of light behind her lids and played her old game of trying to follow its zinging pattern. She lay still, knowing that the scorching heat of day would be even more unbearable as soon as she began to move. Somewhere in the distance, women were singing. Their songs permeated everything they did: cooking, working, playing. The melodies and beats echoed the rhythm of their hips, three-dimensional, undulating with power and passion. She had never heard anything like this raw African music before.

With the tragedy of Qasar still fresh on her mind—as well as the suffering of the old man, Peter Kuanen, who had lost all his family—she wondered how these people could sing at all. She could hardly bear knowing the pain and horror of such desperate lives.

Her lids opened. She let the day in. But her heart was reluctant.

Then the morning progressed in its on-assignment-in-Sudan routine:

editing the notes she'd jotted down yesterday; adding a few new ones; reviewing the pictures she wanted from her camera card and deleting the ones she wouldn't use; a hurried, tasteless breakfast; and then a walk through the camp, shooting more pictures and looking for stories to tell.

She found Kelly in the large tent that served as a clinic, arms wrapped around the now washed and clean baby from Qasar.

"How's he doing this morning?" Julia asked.

"He's wonderful," Kelly answered her, "and his name is Samuel, according to Peter Kuanen. The little girl is his sister, and her name is Mary. But Julia, you won't believe it; according to Peter, the baby is more than a year old, and Mary is at least seven!" Shaking her head in disbelief, Kelly tightened her hold on the little one in her arms. Motherhood definitely suited her, Julia decided again.

Glancing around the clinic was painful. Three rows of beds joined head to head stretched out in long rows and, except for a few adults, the patients were mostly children. Several had severely shortened limbs wrapped in fresh bandages. Many had bandages around their eyes. Julia's jaw slacked as comprehension set in.

"The Janja did this?"

"And more. Most of the wounds they leave are impossible to bandage, and you can't see them. But believe me, they bleed."

"Oh, Kelly . . ."

Julia walked down one narrow aisle and back up the other, taking time to smile and visit with each patient who wasn't asleep or too ill to care. The ones who were well enough looked at her not with childish curiosity, but with eyes dimmed by pain and memories. Many just turned their heads away.

"Come on, Julia."

Kelly guided her gently away from the scene. "I want to show you something else." They left the clinic, hot desert air smacking them in the face as they stepped into the sunlight.

Entering a smaller tent a short distance away, Julia was immediately impressed with the change in the atmosphere from the last one. Here there were children also, but these kids were all busy. Sitting at small tables or on mats, they worked with paper and crayons and markers. A few of them were chattering animatedly together, apparently trying to settle an argument of some kind about something they were drawing. At the back of the room, little Mary sat by herself, humming softly, focused entirely on her coloring.

"An art class?" Julia asked. Searching Kelly's face, she saw only the same expression of resigned grief.

Moving toward the first table, Julia bent down, mingling her head with five Darfurian boys who huddled over the table, markers clenched tightly in their fists.

"Hey, boys, what're you drawing?"

The first picture had a group of thatched circular huts. "Was this your village?" she asked the little boy beside her. He nodded, barely looking up at her.

Black men in the picture were shooting bows and arrows with a few women watching nearby. *A typical African scene*, Julia thought. No, some of the villagers were lying on the ground. Lighter-skinned men in uniforms were holding guns. Like a macabre children's connect-the-dot picture, little dots from the tip of the gun barrels connected to the women on the ground and to some of the men. Julia had loved doing connect-the-dots as a child. But these dots her mind resisted. She did not want to connect them to the bullets that they were. Red patches marked people lying on the ground; red patches were on people still standing or running. On their chests, and on their heads, and on their arms.

Julia had no words.

Staring at the figures drawn on the paper, the bright colors emboldening a scene that should never in a sane world be depicted by a child, Julia saw and comprehended.

Walking slowly around and then past the first table, she worked her way through the room, studying each picture. Drawn by different hands, in different styles, and with different colors, the artwork revealed Darfur: Janjaweed bombing and burning villages from helicopters, pictures of beheadings and amputations, blood spilled from men and women and even children, females rounded up and chained together being led away, dead babies.

The children continued to draw and color earnestly as Julia finally reached little Mary.

"Hi, Mary. Can I see what you're drawing?" Julia spoke quietly, keeping her tone gentle, not knowing how well, if at all, Mary understood her words. Her only response was to look up at Julia briefly, her eyes lost in a soulless place, before glancing down again. Julia looked down, too, bracing herself for what she might see.

In slightly modified stick figures, the picture showed a Janja on a camel shooting one of two babies held in a girl's arms while she stood in front of a burning hut. Two other Janja were killing men nearby, one with a knife and the other with what looked like a club or a gun. A helicopter overhead dropped two red bombs, shaped like pears. Three more Janja with machine guns firing at people stood in the forefront. Beside each dead person on the ground, Mary had drawn a cross.

Tears rolled down Julia's face, blinding her so that she couldn't see the horror in crayon markings any longer. Resting her arm, ever so gently, across the young girl's frail shoulders was the only inadequate comfort she had to offer. When Mary's little body shifted closer to her own, Julia swallowed hard. This was hurt greater than any she had ever experienced. Every fiber in her being cried out to protect this child from ever being hurt again, to do everything in her power to make the world a safe place for her.

Her thoughts were interrupted by a young American woman, whom Julia hadn't noticed before.

"Hi, I'm Hannah. Kelly left but said she'll come back for you after the story time." She smiled with warmth, patted Julia's arm in understanding, then leaned down toward Mary.

"Mary, would you like to hear a story?"

"Yes." A whisper.

"Good. It is one of my favorites. I hope you will like it, too." Turning to the room, she announced, "It's story time, children. Please put the crayons and markers down now." Hannah paused while a teenage Darfurian girl standing nearby interpreted for her.

Julia was surprised at the prompt obedience of the kids. There was no acting up or attitude here as she would expect to see in a group like this at home. It kind of made sense, though; they had had enough chaos in their lives. Order and structure would be welcome after what they had lived through.

She watched Mary's tiny black hands place crayons deftly back in the box, then froze as the child calmly climbed onto her lap, molding herself to Julia's body as she did. Of course, Julia realized. Storytelling was a huge part of village life. This child must have learned to take advantage of those times of bonding with adults who probably were too busy the rest of the time for much physical affection. Mary was doing the natural thing. And so were two other little girls who had snuggled up on either side of Julia. Feelings of panic rolled over her, even while her arms instinctively encircled them all. She knew she was inadequate to truly bring comfort to these children. She could produce a good, logical report about injustice and cruelty, but to hug and cuddle someone was not her strong point. Overwhelmed would be an understatement to describe her feelings at this moment. Scared. It was scary to feel this much.

She couldn't leave, even if she wanted to. Which she did, as soon as Hannah started telling a Bible story.

"Who remembers what happened to baby Moses in the last story?" Hannah asked, the interpreter repeating every word in a common dialect. Several hands went up. She pointed to a little boy wearing an old rag for a shirt.

"He got put in a basket."

"Yes, he got put in a basket. Why did his mother put her baby in a basket in the Nile River?"

Julia felt a surge of anger. What kind of false religious Band-Aid did Hannah think she was offering? How could the woman be so simplistic in the face of the complexity of what these children had lived through?

An older girl answered. After a short pause, the Darfurian girl interpreted, "Because the Egyptian soldiers were to kill all the boy babies just like Janja want to kill all blacks."

"Yes, Fatima, that is correct. The Egyptian king, called the pharaoh, had ordered his soldiers to go and kill all the Hebrew babies. Do you remember why he did this terrible thing?"

"He was scared for the Hebrews to become more than the Egyptians and maybe decide to fight them." The boy who answered looked about eleven or twelve, Julia guessed. "That is what our president says is his reason to make war against Darfur, because we try to fight him. But he lies. He wants only to kill us all because he hates blacks." Several children were nodding. The feeling in the room was charged. Julia wondered if Hannah had waded in deeper than she meant to. This wasn't exactly a Sunday school class, and those certainly weren't Sunday school papers that the children had colored.

"The Bible says, 'You shall not murder.' It is wrong what the Janja do. It was wrong what Pharaoh did. But God had a plan then, and I know He has a plan today. The Bible says that God has plans of good for us. Remember that Miriam, Moses' sister, had talked to the princess after she found him?"

Children's heads nodded, all eyes were fixed on Hannah.

"Miriam had told the princess that she knew a Hebrew woman who could nurse the baby. And of course, that was Moses' own mother. I can just imagine his real mother telling him stories when he was little about how the Hebrew people were waiting for God to save them from the Egyptians—"

"Like Darfur is waiting to be saved from the Janja," loudly interrupted the same boy.

Hannah nodded imperceptibly, then calmly continued.

"The princess who found him floating in the basket took him and raised him as her own son in Pharaoh's household. When Moses grew up, he knew that he was really a Hebrew, even though he was raised as a prince in Pharoah's court. The Bible tells us that when he was a man, Moses went out and saw an Egyptian beating a Hebrew slave. He was angry, so he killed the Egyptian and buried him in the sand.

"Do you think that was what God had planned for Moses to do?"

There was a mixed reaction. Some of the children shouted yes, but others shook their heads no. A few just looked concerned and confused. Little Mary, still cocooned on Julia's lap, had covered her eyes with both hands and was alternately nodding, then shaking her head. Julia felt the same.

"Well, as it turns out, that was not God's plan. The next day, Moses went out again and saw two Hebrew men fighting one another. He tried to make them get along, but one of the men said, 'Who made you ruler and judge over us? Are you thinking of killing me as you killed the Egyptian?' Then Moses was afraid and ran away into the wilderness because he was afraid everyone knew he had murdered the Egyptian.

"God had a much bigger rescue operation planned for His people than Moses could dream of, but first Moses had to learn about the ways of God and how to follow Him.

"How many of you children have watched over sheep or goats out in the grass?"

A few children raised hands.

"How hard is it to keep all the animals safe and together?"

After a moment, the interpreter spoke for one of the boys who was answering.

"It is hard work. The sheep and goats are always wandering away, and you have to watch them. They are not smart like a horse or a camel that can find its way home again. They just wander around until they are taken by hyenas or die from lack of water."

"Yes, it is hard work," Hannah answered, her brown eyes warming to the story, "and it was hard for Moses because after living in a palace for most of his life, God made him become a shepherd. Moses ran away into the wilderness, and the Bible says he married a shepherd girl and then became a shepherd to her father's flocks for a very long time. But God didn't want Moses to be just a shepherd to sheep and goats. He wanted him to be a shepherd to His people, the Hebrews.

"So one day, God talked to Moses out of a burning bush. At first, Moses was very afraid and hid his face. But God said, 'I have indeed seen the misery of My people in Egypt. I have heard them crying out because of their slave drivers, and I am concerned about their suffering. So I have come down to rescue them from the hand of the Egyptians and to bring them up out of that land into a good and spacious land, a land flowing with milk and honey.'

"God told Moses to go and talk to Pharaoh and tell him to let the Hebrew people go free. He told him exactly what to say to Pharaoh and what to do. He even sent Moses' brother, Aaron, along to help him. God did many miracles and signs through Moses to show Pharaoh His power so that the Egyptian king would set the people free. But it wasn't easy, and it took a long time before Pharaoh finally made up his mind to do it. But he finally did. And do you know why?"

Silence. Every face was turned to Hannah, waiting for an answer. They had not heard this story before.

"The pharaoh of Egypt changed his mind because he found out he could not fight against God.

"So Moses took the people into the wilderness and became a shepherd again. A shepherd of people, not animals. It was his job to lead them all the way home to the new land God had promised them. It took a long time, and there are many stories about what happened along the way, but finally they got to a new land where they were safe from the Egyptians and free to serve and worship God."

Several hands were up.

Hannah pointed to a girl wearing an orange and green striped dress.

"When will God rescue us?" she asked.

The sadness and desperate hope written on the upturned face of every child in the stillness of that moment made Julia's heart ache. She felt angry that Hannah was planting false hope in these kids. Angry that she was portraying God as some magician who would come and sweep all wrongs away. These kids didn't need more disappointment in their lives. Surely, if they believed this story and this God that Hannah was sharing, they would be disappointed. So she was surprised at Hannah's answer.

"I don't know, Jamila. Sometimes I wonder if God has His hand on one of you children to be His 'Moses' to the Darfuri people. I wonder about a lot of things. But one thing I do know: God hears the cries of His people."

Hannah led them in prayer, and several of the children prayed fervently as well. Julia was relieved when it was finally over.

Afterward, walking back with Kelly to find the men as Mary held tightly onto Julia's hand, she tried to explain her confused emotions about what Hannah had done.

"But don't you think it's good for them to be able to acknowledge the reality of their lives in the context of others who have lived through something similar?" Kelly asked.

"Yes, I guess so, but all the God-is-going-to-rescue-you propaganda seemed a bit much."

"Well, the UN isn't going to, nor the States. The International Criminal Court has accused President Omar al-Bashir of war crimes, but nothing seems to change. Khartoum talks peace to the world and agrees to let the African Union peacekeeping force come in, then plays games of delaying tactics and logistical problems and does nothing at all, while continuing its genocidal war in Darfur all the while." She shook her head in frustration.

"I'd say that if anyone is going to be able to rescue Darfur, it will have to be God. There doesn't seem to be any other power on earth that is able or willing."

"But Kelly, be serious. Do you really think God cares?"

"Oh, I know He cares. I'm here because He told me to come, Julia. Dave and I could be living more than comfortably. We both had good jobs when God called us to Darfur. At first, I didn't want to. But as I asked God to share His heart for Darfur with me, something changed. It's like in *The Grinch Who Stole Christmas* when the Grinch's heart grew and grew and grew. Suddenly, I had this love for these people that had never been there before. I am constantly overwhelmed at how much God cares because He lets me feel just a bit of what He feels for them."

"Well"—Julia lowered her voice, reached down, and covered Mary's ears—"from what I've seen so far, I'd have to say the opposite. If there's anywhere on this earth that God has forsaken, I'd say it's Darfur, and the sooner people realize that He's not here, the better."

Dave held baby Samuel in his arms while he and Peter Kuanen sat together at a picnic table surrounded by a group of children, all talking animatedly. Mary climbed up on Peter's lap, huddling into his ragged shirt.

"Are we interrupting?" Kelly squeezed in beside her husband with a sure grin that did not expect rejection.

"Not at all. Peter was just telling me how he met the Lord."

Julia waited, wondering what fantastic tale she was about to hear next.

"I love hearing how God draws His people to Himself," Kelly encouraged. "I've wondered how you are Christian, Peter, in the midst of a mostly Muslim area. It's unusual, isn't it, to meet many Christians in Darfur?"

"It is true," Peter confirmed. "It is very unusual. You see, a Christian family came to live in Qasar many years ago. They had fled the civil war in southern Sudan. Over time, as we watched them live and work and pray to this other God, we began to ask questions. You see, they were different from us. They were not afraid of the spirits or of making Allah angry. They had a joy that we did not know; they loved each other, and they loved us. It bothered us a great deal, so we watched them and asked questions.

"They told us that there was only one true God, and that it was not Allah. They said that Allah was a god of jihad, that he only brings hate, but the true God brings love. That was why they were different: they had love, and they had peace. I wanted what they had.

"It was hard for me at first, so sure I had been that the Muslim way was the only truth. But God was calling me. After a time, this family started a school. You could come to the school to find out more about God. I started to go sometimes and learned that God had a Son, Jesus Christ. I learned that Jesus came and lived a life without any sin and died, even though He was God. He shed His blood. Allah had never done anything like that, I thought. Jesus died, so that I could live, then rose from the dead. Jesus took away the power of death. By trusting that He paid the price for my sins on the cross, I could be forgiven and set free from sin.

"Best of all, He filled me with His Holy Spirit when I believed. He

wrote His law on my heart"—Peter placed his hand over his chest—
"and His Spirit lives right inside me, teaching me and guiding me. I am
blessed above all men because through His Spirit I walk with and talk
with the God of heaven and earth."

Julia was quiet for a moment, struggling to pick out the lies from
what Peter was saying. Except Peter wouldn't lie. Somewhere inside
her, she knew this man would not deceive. But maybe he had been
deceived.

"What happened to the missionary family?" Kelly asked.

"They died some years ago. But it is their daughter Margaret who is
the mother of these two precious little ones." Peter gestured with his
chin toward Mary and Sam.

"And who we think might still be alive." Dave filled them in. "Unfortunately, as you can probably guess, she was taken by the Janjaweed."

Julia assimilated the information as she struggled to hold three
kids on her lap simultaneously. Mostly speaking their dialect to one
another, she noted that these experienced refugees knew a few English
words, too.

"Sweeties, miss? Sweeties, please?"

"Kids are the same everywhere," Julia laughed, but she had been
warned beforehand. Handing out candy directly was strictly forbidden
due to the riots and chaos it caused in the camp life. "You know the
camp rule," she said. With groans, the children corporately accepted
this appeal to their ultimate authority. It meant once a week, at a specific time, they would have a treat. Everyone would receive the same
amount. For kids who until recently had never had anything made
with processed sugar, their desire for "sweeties" was astonishing.

"You kids be nice to Miss Julia." Hassan then spoke sternly to them
in their own dialect. Instantly, the children slipped off Julia's lap and
ran into the maze of camp tents.

"I don't mind, Hassan," Julia said a little sheepishly, but before she could finish, three other children had clambered onto her lap, filling the brief vacancy.

Hassan nodded. "Yes, I know you like children, but they are greedy for love. They do not like to share you, but each one needs to know love."

Julia's arms instinctively tightened around her groupies. She looked up into the stricken face of Kelly, sitting across the table with Samuel now nestled again in her arms. She could only guess at the emotions that might be going through her. Making a mental note to herself to hug as many children as possible each day she was in camp, she only partly heard Hassan's conversation with Dave.

". . . It is common. I think your word is *bounty*. He is a very strong leader of Janjaweed. Qasar is like a medal. It is an honor to this man." At that, Julia turned her full attention to what Hassan was saying. "It is said he has wives and children. They will come, too."

"But he is Janja." Dave was incredulous. "Does he have no feeling of guilt or remorse for the evil done there or for the part he played in it?"

Hassan's calm demeanor as he spoke was betrayed only by his jaw line as it worked back and forth. "It is common."

"Would this Janja person know where Samuel and Mary's mother has been taken?" Julia asked.

Hassan leveled his dark eyes on her.

"Yes, this man knows," he answered.

"Well then, why don't we ask him?"

No one answered her, which did nothing to quell Julia's racing thoughts. Peter Kuanen placed his hand tenderly over hers. His lined face looked very tired, but he said nothing. Finally, Dave tried to explain.

"Julia, this Janjaweed is a terrible evil. These men do not regard human life as anything to value. They behave like monsters. If Margaret is alive—"

"Please, God," Peter sighed.

"If she is alive . . ." Dave tried to continue, but then he left the thought unsaid.

Julia's thoughts, however, would not stop.

Once the idea was planted in her mind, she worked it over until every angle had been covered, every contingency met and managed.

And she decided that the idea was good.

But also worth guarding.

It wasn't until dusk and after the cooking fires had almost all been extinguished that she made her way to Kelly and Dave's tent. Julia had discovered that moving about the camp during the evening mealtime, when the heat of the day joined force with the heat of the supper fires, left one's eyes streaming with tears from acrid smoke.

As a reporter, Julia knew she had a fair amount of courage and a large amount of daring, but she wasn't an idiot. She would need a companion if this was going to be successful.

Knocking on tents was not only impossible, but also not necessary. Mostly screen and only minimal flap was arguably the best way to survive the heat and insects. Kelly already had an LED lamp glowing on a small crate. Julia could see her sitting, back toward the opening, cross-legged on her bed mat. She was rocking back and forth, singing a haunting melody that caught Julia off guard with the beauty and longing of it:

> "The Lord bless you and keep you,
> The Lord make his face shine upon you
> And bring you peace
> And bring you peace
> And bring you peace, forever . . ."

Julia realized then that Kelly was rocking baby Samuel. She could make out another small form curled on the mat beside Kelly—Mary, obviously. Julia hadn't known that Kelly and Dave had taken the children into their tent, but she knew it was the most sensible thing they could have done. To burden the other impoverished families in the camp with two more mouths to feed and care for would have been unthinkable, but to let these two little ones join the homeless children of the camp wasn't an option. So Mary and Samuel lived here. All these thoughts flitted through her mind while Kelly continued her lullaby:

"The Lord be gracious to you,
The Lord turn His face toward you
And give you peace, and give you peace,
And give you peace, forever."

A hand on her shoulder startled Julia from the sanctity of the moment. Glancing up quickly, she saw Dave's eyes, pearly in the moonlight, watching his wife and shining with a love that hurt to witness. One finger over his lips and a squeeze to her shoulder signified that he also was not willing to interrupt Kelly's bedtime vigil.

But the words to Kelly's song had come to an end. Softly humming, she turned her head, saw the two of them through the screen, acknowledged their presence with a slight nod, then gracefully, smoothly, careful to make no sudden moves, she placed the slumbering baby onto the bed beside his sister, covered them both up with a light sheet, then came and joined them outside.

"Hi, guys," she whispered, standing on tiptoe to peck her husband's cheek. "Enjoy the opera?"

Julia's arms reached out in a warm hug, surprising Kelly and Dave as much as herself. Somehow a hug was the only way she could think of to convey the appreciation she felt for Kelly at that moment.

"How are the kids?" Julia asked, feeling uncharacteristically tongue-tied.

"Oh, fine. Asleep, thankfully. Sometimes it takes ages before they finally give in to it. The singing helps them relax. What brings you our way tonight, Julia?"

"Well, I have something I'd like to talk about with you. But—no offense, Dave . . ."

"None taken," he responded quickly.

"Could we chat together alone for a few minutes?" Looking directly at Kelly, she saw surprise register at the unusual request, followed almost simultaneously with a questioning look she shot her husband to obtain, Julia decided with a flicker of impatience, what could only be permission. Dave gave his wife a quick smile and nod, and the women walked toward the bench several feet away. Julia had a moment of doubt as she wrestled with Kelly's seeming doormat mentality toward Dave. They obviously loved each other, and Julia respected that, but the deference Kelly showed to her husband was a little over the top. Julia had always assumed independent thinking and decision making were basic building blocks to mature relationships.

Well, it probably wouldn't cause a problem, Julia decided—it might even help their cover as Islamic women, if her plan succeeded. After all, Islamic women appeared to be nothing if not submissive and docile to their husbands.

The two women sat down together, surveying a sea of rough camping shelters spread about them in the shadows. *Like a huge Woodstock,* Julia thought, *but without the rock 'n' roll and drugs.*

"What I wouldn't give for a green tea frappé right now." Kelly sighed.

"Ditto!"

For a moment, neither woman spoke as they contemplated another place in another world.

"But I have never lived like I've lived here," Kelly spoke thoughtfully, "or felt like I've felt here. It's like everything else was just pretend, but this is real." She spoke softly, almost whispering in the quiet stillness.

"Yeah, I know. I guess that's partly why I wanted to speak with you. I've been thinking a lot about what Hassan said . . . about today . . . about the Janja general or whatever who's gone to live at Qasar. I just can't let it go. It feels like there's more we have to do to try to help Margaret. How can we just forget about her when we know she's probably alive and enduring incredible torture right now?"

"I know," Kelly whispered. "It's wrong."

"Exactly. It's wrong. So I started thinking that maybe, just maybe, if I were to go into Qasar as a journalist looking to write a story about a real, live Janjaweed general, appealing to his ego, of course—"

"Oh, Julia!" Kelly exclaimed. "It's brilliant." Then, more slowly, "But how would you ask where Margaret is? You can't just say, 'So I was wondering where you put the women that you torture,' can you?"

"Don't worry, Kelly. It's amazing what people will blabber about if they're trying to sound important to the press. Especially men."

Kelly smiled, a small frown on her brow as she nodded.

"But what about you, Julia? You're an infidel woman, a prostitute or less to his way of thinking. I don't think waving a camera around and taking pictures will make him respect you."

"I know, I thought of that. That's where you come in."

"Oh, oh . . ."

"Don't worry. I don't think we'll run into any trouble. What we need is a couple of burqas and a man—maybe Hassan?"

"Hassan would be perfect."

It would take some doing. It would take a bit of luck. But after going over and over it with Kelly for an hour, Julia was sure that if they could just get into Qasar, the rest would take care of itself. For now, they would be patient and wait for all the pieces to fall into place. Kelly said she needed a couple of days to pray about it, as well. This, Julia did not understand, but she knew Kelly's faith was an important part of who she was. And if God wanted to help them out, even better.

The next morning, Julia watched Dave holding Mary on his lap as she ate her bowl of cereal, while Kelly spoon-fed a sticky porridge mixture into Samuel's mouth. They had asked for a high chair from the director when the children had first come into camp with Dave and Kelly. They were told that they'd get one. When the moon turned green they'd get one.

Her friends were surprisingly adept at feeding and caring for the small children. Especially Kelly. She had entirely immersed herself in the job of mothering and loving these orphans. Julia liked watching them together.

The adults were washing their cold breakfasts down with hot coffee when Hassan found them, telling them Peter was outside the staff tent, waiting to speak to Dave and Kelly about something important.

"I'll go talk to him, Kelly, while you finish up with the kids," Dave offered, sliding Mary gently off his lap to sit on the bench beside his wife and little Samuel, whose mouth was covered with the white pasty stuff, matching the hardening clumps that had ended up in his curly, dark hair.

"Thanks, hon." She glanced up at her husband for the briefest second before turning all her attention back to the task at hand.

"I can finish up with Samuel, Kelly." Julia moved to Kelly's side, reaching out for the little guy, who looked up at her with wide, wondering eyes, warm enough to melt an ice maiden's heart.

"You sure?" Kelly grinned mischievously at her. "It'll be messy and sticky and possibly end up in your hair."

Julia laughed, taking Samuel from Kelly and settling him into her lap. She reached for the spoon, but Samuel had already grabbed it and, now in possession of the terrible weapon, was launching porridge toward Julia's chin. A large dollop made a direct hit.

"Bingo," Julia said. Then, reaching out her tongue, she managed to retrieve the porridge with it, sliding it into her mouth and making yummy noises.

"Right." Kelly grinned. "You're perfect for the job."

"OK, Buster Brown, let's finish this incredibly disgusting breakfast," Julia said, catching the sight of dimples flickering on Mary's face.

The young girl watched Julia, so obviously an amateur, with interest. Whenever a new clump of food landed on Julia's hair or face, Mary would giggle with glee, making the whole ordeal extremely satisfying for all parties.

By the time Dave and Kelly returned, Julia and Mary were both giggling uncontrollably, and Samuel was the proud possessor of both spoon and bowl.

"Oh, Julia!" Kelly's groan at the sight of them held a hint of laughter in it, but when Julia looked up with a sheepish grin, the sight of tears spilling down Kelly's cheeks stilled whatever she was going to say.

"Kelly? What's wrong, sweetie?" She looked at Dave for an explanation. He just shook his head. His own eyes were misty.

"Peter Kuanen found the children's auntie in camp. He spoke with her. She has a teenaged daughter who was sexually assaulted by the Janja. She wants to take Samuel and Mary to live with them."

"Dave, no, how could she do that?" Julia protested. "Surely she knows that you can provide for them better here than she could out in the camp."

"She wants to care for her sister's children. There's a strong sense of family duty in this culture. It's not just a burden you take on. These children are now considered her own children to raise and nurture. Besides"—Dave stopped to gain control of his emotions—"Samuel is a boy. She doesn't have a son of her own. Getting Samuel means there could be a chance of economic security for her one day, in her old age, in a land where there is no pension plan."

Julia struggled to understand, feeling powerless. There just weren't that many options for orphans and no advocates speaking up for them in a place like this.

Kelly wasn't talking, except softly to the children, as she wiped their faces, hands, and—in Samuel's case—hair. She held back the tears as well as she could, but Julia saw her chin crumpling and straightening out again in an emotional war.

Julia followed the foursome outside into the bright sunshine, where Peter was waiting with a young woman, possibly in her twenties, beside him, holding tightly to the hand of a girl who looked to be about twelve or thirteen years old.

"Mary! Mary!" The shouts of delight and the joy on their faces were unmistakable.

"Auntie!" Mary instantly released Dave's hand and flew to the side of this relative whom she knew.

Dave winced as Mary flung herself around her auntie's waist. Somehow, this seemed to propel Kelly into action. Breaking out of her frozen stance behind Dave's shoulder, she moved toward the young girl, placing baby Samuel into her arms.

"Samuel is your cousin?" Kelly asked, making a show of conversation.

The girl took Samuel in her arms, returning his smile with one of her own, planting a kiss on his forehead, and murmuring to him in their own dialect. Holding him expertly on her hip, she finally looked up at Kelly with great seriousness and replied, "No. He is my brother now."

"We pray their mother is alive. She may come back one day, if God wills it," Kelly said.

The auntie turned hardened eyes toward her. "My sister is dead. I am their mother now."

Dave and Kelly kissed and hugged the children, little Samuel indif-

ferent, but Mary holding tightly to each one, clinging at the end to
Kelly until her auntie grabbed her hand and pulled her away. Then they
were gone.

Standing together, they watched the children being led away, disappearing into an enormous sea of shacks and tents.

"The Lord gave, and the Lord has taken away; blessed be the name
of the Lord." Dave's voice was quiet and hoarse.

"Blessed be His name," Peter echoed.

Julia looked at them in shock. How could they say that? Didn't Dave
care? What about his poor wife—what must she be feeling?

But Kelly had turned away from the rest of them, walking quickly,
her shoulders heaving in her sorrow.

# Eight

❧

Now the fact that God can make complex good out of
simple evil does not excuse—though by mercy it may
save—those who do the evil.

C. S. LEWIS, *THE PROBLEM OF PAIN*

NASSIR SHOULDERED HIS AK-47 AND turned south. It took him forty-five minutes to walk around his new home, Qasar.

When they had sacked the village two weeks before, he had led his men in the shedding of the infidels' blood. When they had finished only a few of the village huts were left standing and some goats and chickens, bounty for the taking. Nassir had taken it.

Abdul, his six-year-old son, ran toward him, past the baobab tree where Nassir had shot three Zurgha. These black Africans were despised by all Janjaweed, so that fact did not trouble him as his son leapt into his strong arms, receiving a warm embrace and kiss before being placed back on the ground with a pat on the behind. All Zurgha were part of the rebellion and, therefore, the enemy of Islam.

Nassir knew the ongoing defiance of the Zurgha left all true devotees committed to destroying the infidels. He had read the Qur'an. Every word of it. Not something many Muslims could boast. He revered and respected the holy book, always ensuring it was in the highest place, above all else in his home. He took what he read in it seriously. Especially the injunctions regarding infidels:

> Those that make war against Allah and his apostle and spread disorder in the land shall be slain or crucified or have their hands and feet cut off on alternate sides, or be banished from the land. They shall be held up to shame in this world and sternly punished in the hereafter.
>
> Prophet, make war on the unbelievers and the hypocrites and deal harshly with them. Hell shall be their home: an evil fate.

Many such verses were in the holy book, but all Janjaweed could recite these.

Nassir knew Allah would give them the victory. He had given the Arabs the riches of the world. It was his will for Islam to conquer. For all to share the one true faith. Fighting was an expression of Nassir's devotion and loyalty. It was his worship. Where there was unbelief, he would remove it. Where there were fires of opposition, he would deal with them harshly, so as to quench them forever. Nothing more, nothing less.

Satisfied with his survey of the territory, Nassir turned toward the largest of the huts. His tea would be ready. Stepping in through the door, his eyes took a moment to adjust from the brightness of the day. He stepped gracefully over the straw mats that covered the earthen floor. Lowering himself with dignity, he sat at ease against his pillows. One of his wives poured steaming hot tea, placed it within easy reach, then retreated from the room without turning her back toward her husband. He barely glanced at her. There was no need; the fragrant tea satisfied his immediate desire and he had carefully trained his wives to anticipate and service his every want.

"The spoils of war belong to Allah and his messenger." Nassir's hard features relaxed as he quoted the Qur'an. He was blessed by Allah, indeed. Brought up in a typical nomadic village, it had been his responsibility as a boy to shepherd the flocks of goats and cattle his family owned. He had found it to be difficult work at first. Verdant pastures had always existed in the southern areas, but the Zurgha had always heavily occupied the south. Nassir was old enough to remember the difficult days, before the Zurgha were driven out of the good rangeland. But that was long ago. Years of plenty had followed and filled his growing years with memories of a full belly and contented flocks. As a young man, it had seemed a natural progression for him to join the Janja. There were still flocks to be controlled and herded, but now they were Zurgha: rebellious, black infidels fighting against the will of Allah. Always the flocks of Zurgha caused difficulty. And sometimes those flocks needed thinning. Like Qasar. He reached for a date and chewed it slowly, avoiding the tooth that caused him so much pain. Out of the corner of his eye, he could see Abdul playing with his stick toys. Abdul, his only son. Four unworthy daughters were born before Allah blessed him with a man-child. What a day that had been! Now this little one was a constant source of delight and pleasure. Bright eyed and intelligent, the boy followed his every move, wanting to be just like his *baba*.

As if hearing his father's thoughts, Abdul looked up from his play and grinned gleefully at Nassir. A quick sip of tea followed the date, burning a path into Nassir's gut but cooling his blood by some reverse law of science he did not understand but knew from experience. Beckoning the child forward with one hand, Nassir stretched comfortably against the array of cushions below and behind him. He gazed solemnly into the liquid brown eyes of his son.

"Tell me the words of the holy book."

"In the name of Allah, the most compass—, companate—" Abdul stumbled with the awkward word and stopped.

"Compassionate," Nassir corrected.

"Compassionate," Abdul parroted. His eyes were intent on his father's face, head tilted slightly to the side as he concentrated on the mantra. "The most compassionate, the most merciful. All praise belongs to Allah, the Lord of all the worlds." He stopped.

"What does it mean, *Baba*, this word *compassionate*?"

"Ah, my son, it is a word to describe how tender the heart of Allah is to his true servants," Nassir answered.

"But if he is Lord of all the worlds, isn't he compassionate to all?"

"But he is, my son. Allah wills that all should confess him as Lord; do you remember the words I taught you?"

"Oh, *Baba*, they are easy." Abdul smiled with confidence and then quoted, "There is no god but Allah, and Muhammad is his prophet."

"Yes, they are easy, Abdul, but many will not say them. Those who refuse do not receive the compassion of Allah. They receive his certain anger and punishment." Nassir spoke heatedly, his fists clenched. "We must never forget why we fight in jihad; it is for this very reason: we must convert the infidel who is ignorant and destroy those who are stubborn and rebellious." He paused in his diatribe. "What is it, son? Why do you look at me so?"

"Oh, *Baba*, you scared me as you spoke. Your face changed, and I couldn't see my *baba* in it. It frightened me." Abdul looked at his father with an uncertainty that had never before been there.

"You speak nonsense, my son. I am always your *baba*. Come here." Nassir opened his arms wide, and Abdul bolted into the safest place he knew in all the world. Soon he forgot all about the fear that he had felt when his father spoke of jihad.

# NINE

و٩

It is an enormous source of human frustration that
our need for intimacy far outstrips its capacity to be
met in other people. Primarily what keeps us separate
is our sin, but there is also another factor, which is
that in each one of us the holiest and neediest and
most sensitive place of all has been made and is
reserved for God alone, so that only He can enter
there. No one else can love us as He does, and no one
can be the sort of Friend to us that He is.

MIKE MASON, *THE MYSTERY OF MARRIAGE*

*FEMALES*, JOEL THOUGHT, WITH uncharacteristic disgust, accelerating
his BMW roadster down an open stretch of road.

The Sea to Sky Highway, one of BC's most infamous, wound
alongside ocean to the west and rugged coastal mountain cliffs to the
east, leaving little room for highway driving of any kind. The Winter
Olympics coming to Whistler Village—the ski resort nestled between
Whistler and Blackcomb mountains—in 2010 had put pressure on the
province to improve this particular highway, but they still had a long

way to go. In the meantime, Joel enjoyed the challenge of the road. Here he was in control. It was dangerous, but he could slow down when he wanted to.

Females, up until recently, were a similar experience for him. Celeste, on the other hand, was proving more problematic than the others. She did not want to let go. She had hounded him. The woman knew no shame. Messages at the office, on his BlackBerry and home phone all ran the same course: "Joel, I'm sorry I upset you. Don't cancel Hawaii until we talk. I know you'll have more fun with me than without me. We can still be friends and have fun . . . Right?" It made him think of the tick that embedded itself into his scalp the summer he was thirteen. He remembered how sickened he had felt at the thought of a bug sucking blood from his brain. When his grandpa had explained the treatment of a hot match to the back of the tick to make it retract its "claws," that hadn't excited him, either. But to try to pull it out by force might leave pieces of the tick in his scalp, possibly leading to infection—not a happy thought. So Grandpa's steady hands lit the match, and the tick, once burned, was eager to leave. What Joel needed to find was a nice hot match for Celeste.

A weekend of skiing at Whistler had brought clarity and focus to his life. He would never meet with Celeste. Eventually she would figure it out and move on to the next sucker. Hawaii was already canceled. It wouldn't be the first time he spent his vacation at the office. He shifted from fifth gear into third, to manage a series of tight twists and bends.

The convertible top was down for the hour-and-a-half trip back into the city. Joel smiled, enjoying the ride. For a November day, it wasn't bad weather. Besides, he liked to drive with the heat on and the fresh air blowing past him. The road worked its way steadily down; he could smell the ocean now and even caught glimpses of whitecaps occasionally. His eyes glanced down at the speedometer: 110 km. The speed limit on this road was 80–100 km, depending on the difficulty of the stretches. Joel's limit was a fair bit beyond the speed he was moving now, but he was taking it easy. He had some thinking to do. He needed to find a match.

Lately, Joel wasn't having any luck finding anything. The Keegan girl was in Sudan, a bit farther than he had thought to hunt for that particular lady. Aunt Rose hadn't had much information about Julia. Other than placing Fred's daughter in Africa, it didn't give him much to go on.

Darfur . . . Joel frowned, considering. It might as well have been Timbuktu. For that matter, maybe it was. African geography wasn't his strong point. In any case, there wasn't much he could do about it. He would do a Google search on her in the next couple of days, make contact with her office, get all her contact info, and find out when she was due back.

He picked up speed as he hit the North Shore Highway, weaving through traffic until he got onto the Lion's Gate Bridge, heading toward Stanley Park, the one hundred-acre emerald that was the city's northwest boundary.

A half hour later, he parked the BMW in the underground garage. He heard the ball bouncing before he saw him.

"Hi, Dominic." He caught the pass and sent it back.

"Hey, Joel. My dad's coming in half an hour. We're going to the IMAX."

"I hear it's a really good one this time." Joel picked off the charge as the boy rushed past him, and then let Dominic steal it back before he headed for the elevator.

"See ya later!" Dominic waved the hand not dribbling the ball. Joel smiled and waved back as the elevator door slid shut. He would personally go and punch the man if he disappointed his son this time.

In the elevator, he remembered the newspaper story. The *Vancouver*

*Sun* had carried it, he was sure of it. He'd had that weird dream about Keegan and then had seen the article.

He searched through the recycling bin for twenty minutes until he found it. Scanning it quickly, he found what he wanted. Someone named John Reese had written it. Another dead end.

Gazing out his window, he looked down on the city lights. It was a brilliant display. *The most beautiful city in the world,* Joel thought, not for the first time. Why a girl would want to leave BC to go to Sudan was a mystery to him. *Face it, Joel,* he told himself, *all women are a mystery to you.* As he listened to the messages on his answering machine, this was confirmed. Helena, his ex-wife, wanted to meet with him on Monday afternoon. Tomorrow. Reasons and explanations were not given. Just a street corner and Starbucks named. Great. Lovely.

Joel sighed. Helena was lovely. Absolutely. Unfortunately, his best friend, Mark, had thought so, too. Granted, they had married young; he had been at law school for only a year when they had met. Mark had invited him to a party at his parents' mansion on Thanksgiving weekend. Somewhat overawed at all the wealth represented on the Addison estate, Joel had walked down to the beach, escaping the crowds and the booze scene. She was there first. Perched on a rock, hair shining with moonlight, blanket wrapped around her, she'd raised a pale face with eyes so large, she reminded him of an elfin creature. They talked. And talked. She had offered to share her blanket with him to keep him warm, and when he walked away from her that night, kissing her on the forehead and promising to call her that week, he knew that he would never be warm without her again.

*What had gone wrong?* he asked himself for the thousandth time. There was financial pressure, granted, but they were in love. They had had fun—all three of them. Joel could hardly separate Mark from the memories of those years. He was a law student as well. But it was different for him. He was being groomed to take his father's place, an established partnership in a successful law firm. Joel was a nobody and needed to work hard to prove himself in a competitive, dog-eat-dog vocation. Mark had had time to play. Joel had studied hard to achieve his 3.0 average. Then studied some more.

One day Helena told him she was pregnant.

He had held her hands tenderly and explained why they couldn't have children yet. It was a mistake. They had both shed a few tears, but eventually, Helena had agreed. She even seemed relieved that he wasn't ready for fatherhood, but after the abortion, things had never been the same between them. He got used to her cold shoulder and flannel pajamas in their bed. But he couldn't and wouldn't ever be able to get used to Mark being there. Unfortunately, neither could he forget it. He shook his head. Things he didn't want to think about. Things he worked hard at not thinking about.

So it stood to reason, he figured when he walked into Starbuck's the next afternoon, that there were dark shadows under his eyes and a knot in his gut like he got just before being punched. It stood to reason because Helena was there before him, sipping her latte and leafing through a magazine. Four years after the divorce, and it still hurt to see her. Squaring his shoulders, he passed the coffee bar and pulled out the empty chair across from his ex-wife.

"May I?" he asked.

She looked up at him, her smile fading rapidly into a concerned frown. "Hi, Joel. Thanks for coming."

"Not a problem." He sat down, his long legs stretched out in front of him, his arms crossed tightly, protecting his heart. "What can I do for you, Helena?" He spoke politely, exercising his best lawyer front. He hated this, but he would die before she knew how much he hated it.

"Nothing." She pushed her long, blond bangs from her face and nervously rolled and unrolled her magazine. "I mean . . . it's just . . . we're getting married, and we wanted you to know."

Uncomfortable silence ensued.

"Mark and I, I mean," she added.

Joel absorbed the punch, clenching his fists, but decided hitting back would not be right. Instead—somehow, instead—he breathed. In and out. He looked into the dark eyes of the woman he had loved once and wondered if anything could hurt more than this.

"Congratulations, then." A stupid thing to say, but all he could think of.

She took a deep breath. "We're having a baby. I'm due in six months." She exhaled like a smoker. Searching his eyes, she seemed to plead with him.

What he read there, he despised. Regret, pity, compassion . . . forgiveness?

He didn't care. This hurt more than it had before. If she was looking for exoneration from him, he didn't have any to give. His eyes narrowed, trying to shut out this reality. He wanted to hate her. He . . . he wanted . . . he didn't know what.

"Joel?" Obviously she was waiting for some response.

Nodding, he cleared his throat. "It's a lot to take in. When is the wedding?"

"Saturday, at the Addisons'. We'd love it if you would come."

Nodding, he stalled. "Yeah, I'll see what I can do." Bombing the place occurred to him, or perhaps arson.

She got up, placed her hand on his shoulder, and added, "I hope you'll come. It's at three o'clock." Then so softly he could barely hear her, "I'm sorry it never worked out between us, Joel. I am truly sorry."

His shoulder burned from her touch, even after she was gone. He rolled and unrolled her magazine, wishing it were a weapon of some kind that he could destroy something with—or everything, for that matter.

When he got home, he realized that the magazine was still in his hand. Placing it on Keegan's solidly made wood table, he smoothed it out and read the title, *Women Informed*. He'd heard of it. A tabloid with a feminist, watchdog mentality, reporting and misreporting on the multifaceted cases of victimization toward females in the world today. He understood why Helena would read it. Smiling cynically at a picture of a beautiful, plastic woman on the front cover, he picked it up to toss it away when he saw the small boxed picture of a skeletal, African baby in the bottom right-hand corner and the name, Julia Douglas, underneath it. *Women Informed*. Of course. Tomorrow, he would read it, too.

But tonight, tonight was made for booze and forgetting. He was determined to forget. If only for a moment.

❦

Joel nursed his very black coffee, his eyes still red from the long, hard night, and concentrated on reading what Keegan's daughter had written:

Unspeakable
(Second in a continuing series of reports from Darfur)
The situation in Darfur is complex and layered. Ongoing struggles between desert nomads and small, sustenance farmers, originally over scarce water and grazing areas, have erupted into a boiling pot of violence and cruelty springing from these and other, more sinister, issues. Deplorable living conditions for Sudanese refugees is the result, especially affecting women and children.

Bekki is a young wife and mother of a five-month-old baby boy named Elias. She lives here at an internationally displaced persons camp, home for 45,000 IDPs. To be a refugee in Darfur means one has escaped a hostile, government-funded militia that systematically annihilates villages, leaving mass destruction behind. Refugees have fled to this IDP camp, hoping for some measure of security, sharing whatever sustenance and supplies the UN or other independent aid organizations have managed to get into the country for relief. This means that there is not always enough to go around. After refugees receive their daily or weekly allotment, it still needs to be prepared and cooked, a simple chore that most North American women take for granted and often begrudge.

JD. How old are you, Bekki, and how old were you when you got married?

B. I am seventeen years old. I got married when I was fifteen.

JD. Why are you living in an IDP camp?

B. Janjaweed came to our village with helicopters and bombed us. Then more Janja came on camels with guns. They looted our village; they raped the women and girls. They killed the men who couldn't run fast enough. If we try to go to another village, we face the same thing happening. If we live here at the camp, it's a little safer.

JD. You say a little safer. Are you still not safe, then?

B. No. Every day we need firewood to cook with. We need to gather the wood from the hillsides, where the Janja wait for us. If they catch us, we are raped and beaten.

JD. Why doesn't your husband go instead?

B. If the men go, they are shot. We have to choose between the possibility of death or rape.

JD. Do you know any women who have been raped by Janja while collecting firewood?

B. There are many. I know many in this camp. I know many who lost their husbands when the men tried to save their wives.

JD. Are there any babies from these acts of violence?

B. Yes, it is very sad. Most women will not keep a Janja baby, and so they are left to die outside the camp or are just neglected until they starve to death. Life is hard here, and so the women make a choice to care for the children from their husbands and ignore the offspring of the Janja.

JD. Bekki, how often do you have to gather wood?

B. It used to be every day, but the camp has given us fuel-efficient stoves that need much less wood. Now we go just two or three times a week.

JD. How many meals do you have in a day?

B. One or two.

JD. When you lived in the village, how many meals did you eat?

B. Two or three. And there was more food in those meals.

JD. Would you like to go back to living in the village?

B. Not as long as the Janja hunt us. Maybe if someone were to stop them, then we could live in peace and safety again.

JD. I hope that will happen one day soon.

B. I hope so, too.

JD. If there was something you could say to the women in Canada and the United States, what would it be?

B. Thank you for everything that is done to help us here. We have nothing, and your countries are doing much to help us. Our lives are full of fear, but it is wonderful and gives us hope to receive a cup of meal or a jug of clean water and know there is enough for one more meal. Thank you.

As with any abuse, be it from an uncle, a priest, or a power-hungry government, there are always things that are too scary to say. What Bekki cannot say and what the volunteer who comes to work here and provide assistance to these hurt and suffering people cannot say is this: several relief organizations have left Darfur due to increased violent activity. Thirty-four aid workers have been killed since 2004, and many more wounded. If they speak out against the crimes, they face suspended visas and travel papers. What they cannot say is that the more than four million people depending on humanitarian assistance for survival in Darfur and now Chad are facing the real possibility of repeated violence and even murder against themselves and their families every day they wake up. If they could, they would tell you that an estimated 200,000 to 1,000,000 of their family members have already been murdered by Janjaweed in front of their eyes. Many more have died from the effects of these atrocities.

In Rwanda, the UN forces were sent into the country to put a stop to the genocide. They were late getting there, and 800,000 people were slaughtered.

What is happening in Sudan is not happening due to tribal warfare, but due to a corrupt government set on ethnically cleansing its populace. This is black African Muslim and non-Muslim fighting together for survival against an Arab Muslim, well-funded government, which may explain the curious absence of the UN forces.

Canadian and American women have seen their countries intervene on behalf of war-torn countries where it was fiscally and politically advantageous to do so, but here in Sudan, with its oil lines and political power, no one wants to get involved.

Hollywood celebrities like Don Cheadle, Mia Farrow, and even the man dubbed the "Sexiest Man Alive" have gotten involved in the Sudan crisis, protesting this lack of intervention. The famous actor George Clooney has gone into Sudan and Chad and is using his platform in the public eye to expose the issues in these places.

Daring to speak out to the UN General Assembly on behalf of these people, he has flown in the face of comfortable politicians, making their seats a little hotter. More than just a pretty boy? What he's done adds up to hero.

Let's not ignore George Clooney's efforts to expose the American and Canadian public to these issues. We have no choice as informed women but to use our voices responsibly to make others aware of this crisis. After all, if we were afraid to gather firewood for fear of rape, afraid to see our homes taken from us violently, afraid to have our men shot down because of the color of their skin, wouldn't we want someone to come to our rescue?

Joel's coffee was cold. He scanned the contact numbers, e-mails, and Web site if one wanted to donate funding for aid or to write a letter to their Member of Parliament. He read her name and the dateline again, *Julia Douglas–Western Darfur*. And he wondered how many days Julia Douglas had left if the wrong people were to read her report.

With that thought, he picked up the phone and called *Women Informed*. He got a recording that gave him several choices of extensions. His first try got him through to the senior editor's assistant, Caroline someone.

"This is Joel Maartens. I am the executor for Julia Douglas's father, who recently passed away."

"Did you say 'Julia Douglas's father'?"

"Yes, ma'am. Fred Keegan left specific instructions with regard—"

"I don't know who you are, mister, but Julia Douglas's father was not Fred whatever-you-said," was the curt reply.

"No, ma'am, actually her biological father, the one who spent most of his days in prison and recently passed away there, was Fred Keegan."

A brief silence ensued. *Better than a loud click*, Joel decided.

"What do you want?" Caroline asked.

"I have a letter for Miss Douglas that her father has entrusted to me. His specific request was for me to see it put into her own hands. I appreciate the highly unusual nature of this request but would someone in your office be able to give me her ETA?"

"Ah, I see. Well, I have no reason to believe that Julia would have any interest in a letter from her biological father—what did you say your name was?"

"Maartens. Joel Maartens, ma'am. But with all due respect, don't you think that she should decide for herself? It was very important to Fred Keegan to have his last wish carried out."

"Well, I'm afraid that I'll have to disappoint you, Mr. Maartens, unless you're a very patient man, since Julia is not expected back for two more months."

"Two months?"

"Her assignment is to send in several reports, journal style, from Sudan. *Women Informed* seeks the aspects of news issues that mainstream media so often overlook or underreport. So you can see that it was necessary for her to be there for longer than a day or two."

*Yada, yada, yada. I don't need the plug.* "Frankly, I've never read anything in your periodical except Miss Douglas's last report, but it was definitely an eye-opener, I'll grant you that." Joel was thinking hard. "The conditions those people live in at those PDI camps—"

"IDP camps, internationally displaced persons." Caroline corrected him as he knew she would.

"Right, IDP camps. I guess it's a good thing the Nile flows right by, so at least they have access to water."

"Sir, I am very busy, so if our conversation is over . . ."

This woman was no pushover. A different tack, then.

"Of course, ma'am. But I noticed that the article never said where Miss Douglas's IDP camp was. I would really appreciate it if you could give me the name of the camp." Direct approaches could work, too; Joel made a mental note to remind himself of that.

"She's working near Zalingei in Darfur. The name of the camp is Hassa Hissa."

"Hassa Hissa," Joel scribbled the information as quickly as Caroline gave it. "Thank you, ma'am. I appreciate it."

"Have a good day, Mr. Maartens."

The next call Joel made was to his travel agent. A flight to Khartoum, via London, with British Airways, was available for Saturday morning. Nothing was happening that day except a wedding. He purchased the ticket, grimacing. At least he was making his office happy.

*I'm going to Sudan. I'm going to find Julia Douglas and give her Fred's letter.* Then, as an afterthought, he added, *So help me, God.*

# TEN

✑

Thus says the LORD: "Let not the wise man boast
in his wisdom, let not the mighty man boast in his
might, let not the rich man boast in his riches, but
let him who boasts boast in this, that he understands
and knows me, that I am the LORD who practices
steadfast love, justice, and righteousness in the earth.
For in these things I delight, declares the LORD."

JEREMIAH 9:23–24

THE LAND CRUISER CREPT ALONG THE rutted road, piercing the morning's quiet with its whining and growling. Hassan gripped the wheel till his knuckles were white, his face a mask of consternation. Julia felt a bit guilty every time she looked at him, knowing that his disapproving conscience was battling heavily with his desire to help Sam and Mary's mom.

Kelly met Julia's eyes and smiled. Before they had set out, Kelly had expressed so many doubts and concerns that Julia had begun to wonder if Kelly would come at all. Now that they were actually on their way, Kelly was, if not lighthearted, then at least peaceful, while Julia herself was beginning to reconsider the whole plan. So many things could go wrong. On the other hand, if it worked . . . well, if it worked, then they would get the information they needed regarding Margaret and her whereabouts. What they could do with that information was not yet completely clear, nor necessarily hopeful, but at least they would have done what they could. To do any less would bother Julia for the rest of her life. She had to try.

They had sent a letter via messenger to Qasar, asking for permission to have an interview with Nassir An-Nur, saying they were from the *Sudan Tribune.* When they received a positive reply, no one was more surprised than Julia herself.

Squinting her eyes, Julia could see the village lying ahead. Too late to turn back.

"Ready?"

Kelly nodded silently, still smiling as she began to fix her burqa about her face, leaving only a small slit, covered with a screen, through which she could view the world. Julia did the same with hers, marveling at the effect of the veil as it blotted out the details of beauty all around them and dimmed the light of the sun. She felt closed in and shut out. This was the uniform of countless Muslim women. And for what they were about to attempt, it suited their purposes very well.

Stepping out onto the road ahead of them, a well-armed guard waved his AK-47 in the air.

Julia looked with interest at the Janjaweed. She knew the title meant "devil on horseback," but this one had no horse under him at the moment. The machine gun held casually in his hands seemed part of him, bespeaking skill and experience. He was dressed in a loose, white robe and a white head covering and was yelling at them in Arabic; Julia could not understand what he said, but his eyes looked hard.

Hassan came to a stop beside the Janja and handed him his travel permit and the personal letter from Nassir An-Nur, indicating his agreement to the interview. The guard took the papers, glanced at them momentarily, then looked up at Hassan with narrowed eyes and a curled lip. Julia held her breath until he finally shoved the papers somewhere inside the folds of his garment, leaned his head to one side, and gave a short grunt, waving the gun to direct them ahead into the little village of Qasar.

It had changed.

Where once had been smoke and charcoal, now neatly raked and tidy paths defined the village. They pulled up under the big cypress tree, beside the only other vehicle in sight, an army truck sporting a large dent on the front right fender. Set back off the path was a large, Bedouin-style tent. It reminded Julia of the large tents at fairgrounds back home with picnic tables set up inside for people to come in out of the baking sun, to eat their onion-covered hotdogs and sip on cold Cokes.

A man stepped out of the large entrance, a little boy holding his hand. Julia gripped her camera, automatically framing the picture she saw in her mind, but knew that protocol said she must wait until they had gone through all the official business of greetings and introductions.

Hassan jumped out of the Land Cruiser and, putting on what Julia knew must be the performance of his lifetime, stepped forward to greet Nassir An-Nur in the customary fashion. *"Ahlan wa shlan,"* An-Nur welcomed them, his voice surprisingly modulated and soft, in contrast to his glinting black eyes. He gripped Hassan's right hand with his own, their left hands tapping each other's shoulders.

Julia and Kelly carried the camcorder and tripod, as instructed, several respectful paces behind Hassan. They would not be spoken to or acknowledged, but in Khartoum, it was not unusual for a woman to have a career as long as she did not use it to flaunt herself in the public eye. Outside of the home, all good Muslim women adhered to the strictest standards of modesty and virtue.

*"Assalaamu Alaikum."* The Janjaweed general greeted his guest with a blessing of peace.

"*Wa Alaikum Assalaam.*" Hassan returned the blessing.

Introductions, so as not to appear hasty, were time-consuming and woven with small talk: how is your health, how is your family, how is their health, and so on.

The soft murmuring voices of the men eventually paused, and Julia and Kelly were directed into the women's side of the tent to partake of the customary hot tea before the real business of the interview could begin. This is where they knew their cover would be most vulnerable.

"I know a lot of the language now, but if we have to really talk, there's no way we can pull it off," Kelly had said.

"If something is really worth doing, it has to have some risk, Kelly." Here was the risk.

They entered a lovely room. Purple and sapphire blue tapestries hung on the white tent walls. A younger woman wearing a thin veil and head covering greeted them, gesturing them to sit, which they happily did. The cushions covering the floor—embroidered with threads to match the tapestries along the walls, Julia noted—were soft and inviting. The girl, all demure, quietly said something Julia did not understand, but obviously no response was necessary from them, since she immediately left the room, returning only a moment later with a bowl of rose-scented water. Handing a towel to each of them before retreating again from the room, the girl shyly glanced up, just once before looking away quickly again, but not before Julia caught sight of the interest sparkling in those dark orbs. What repressed intelligence might lie in that girl's head, Julia wondered, only to idle its way into boredom and finally meanness, all because of a culture that would not allow it to be cultivated.

"I'd love to wash my face, Julia," Kelly whispered as soon as they were alone again.

"We can't chance it. Just do the best you can from underneath," Julia whispered back.

It took a few minutes and was quite awkward, but they managed to wipe down most of their faces, necks, and chests. Feeling much cooler, Julia washed her hands carefully and dried them on the soft towel.

The girl slipped quietly back inside the tent, bearing tea on a wooden tea tray. Kneeling down and placing the tray circumspectly on a low stool, she carefully poured from a china teapot into matching teacups. Old Country Rose. Julia recognized the pattern immediately—the same set of Royal Albert china Aunt Rose used when they had tea parties together. How old had she been then? Ten or eleven? *Once upon a time*, she thought, *in a fairy-tale land where people lived without genocide, starvation, and rape as their daily companions.*

After handing the delicate cups and saucers to each woman, the girl retreated from the room once again. Julia held back her veil and sipped the steaming liquid slowly. It was just what she needed. She was relieved, when they were finished, to realize that no one except the same shy young woman as before, seemed interested in them. If someone came in, talking to them and expecting them to talk back in Arabic, they would be found out. But it didn't happen. They relaxed back into the cushions a bit more, knowing that they would be summoned when the men had finished their refreshments.

Presently, the girl reappeared, stepping almost silently back into the room. Saying something Julia did not understand, she motioned them to follow her.

Following Kelly, Julia stepped out of the tent into brilliant sunlight. They were taken down a short path to a small building. As the girl opened the door, Julia realized the building's purpose instantly. The odor of an outhouse was international. Kelly stepped in, and shortly after, Julia had her turn, too. All necessities of life dealt with, the women retrieved the camera equipment and followed their young guide back to the main outside court under the shade of the cypress.

Hassan and Nassir were seated on comfortable, sling-back folding chairs, one leg slung casually over the other. The women joined the men, standing respectfully to the side, waiting for an indication from Hassan to begin to set up. Soon they had it, and as he waved them forward, he shouted at them loudly, barking rapid orders that they were bound not to understand and making Julia jump. Fortunately, any scowls on their faces were hidden under the burqa, and so, for the moment, they accepted their lot. Julia took encouragement in imagining what sweet revenge she would mete on Hassan once back at camp. The wink that he shot them when his face was turned away from Nassir for a moment mollified her slightly, but only slightly.

Had a Realtor been involved in this recent acquisition of Nassir's, Julia thought, the glowing description would have been: *Complete with its own wadi, chickens, goat herd, and donkeys, this comfy village has it all. Perfect for a growing Muslim family, with lots of room for the in-laws. Recent economic factors make this town a very feasible financial opportunity for members of the Janjaweed. For a limited time, this prime (Sudanese) land can be yours for the taking.*

"Abdul! Abdul!" Nassir shouted.

Julia looked up from the tripod she was putting together and saw the same little boy come running. Cute kid. Maybe six years old, she decided. He jumped up on his father's lap, flashing a dimpled, perfect smile, perfect except for the missing two front teeth. Julia watched Nassir, leader of the infamous Janjaweed, enfold his son in his arms. Struggling with the inconsistency of who this man was and what violence those same arms had brought on countless innocents, she was thankful, once again, that no one could see the expression on her face.

Nassir seemed like the perfect dad. She hadn't expected that.

Never more grateful for modern technology, Julia turned on the camcorder's translation software. She remembered reading that this useful tool had a vocabulary database of more than three million words and could recognize up to fourteen thousand common phrases in the twelve languages it held. The interview, however, only served to solidify what, to Julia, was a huge dichotomy: loving father versus Janjaweed general. *How could a man kill other people for a living and not be evil through to his soul?* Dim memories of her biological father clouded her emotions as she adjusted the camera. She remembered riding on strong shoulders, even the feel of his whiskers as he kissed her goodnight. Some things she could not forget, but she could shut the door to the memories. Or try to.

As Hassan and Nassir talked, she followed their dialogue in English text along the bottom of the screen.

"Thank you for having us here at your beautiful home. Tell us how you came to live here." Hassan jumped right to the point.

"Yes, my family and I are enjoying living here in Qasar. Unfortunately, an uprising occurred in this place that required our attention. As usual the rebels were well armed and we had to deal with them severely."

Hassan nodded. Slowly. "You obviously put yourselves at great risk to contain this rebellion. Tell me, did any of the rebels escape?"

Julia held her breath, hoping against hope. Nassir's eyes had turned stone cold.

"None escaped. I promise you, the rebels who called this place home will never spread their antigovernment propaganda again."

*So Margaret was no more.* Nor any of the other poor people who had peacefully dwelt here only a short time ago. Hassan shifted slightly. Julia wondered how he could keep his control. But after only a short pause, he continued.

"The people of Khartoum rest in the peace of Allah knowing you defend our great city. But you, it would seem, prefer the rural life?"

"Yes, my family have traditionally raised livestock, and I would like young Abdul here to have that same upbringing that I enjoyed."

"You must be very pleased with the success you have enjoyed in your chosen career," Hassan prompted. *He should have gone to Hollywood*, Julia thought. He'd missed a great career as an actor. Now that he was here, he had lost himself in playing his part as a newspaper reporter.

"Oh, yes." Nassir enjoyed being admired; not unlike all the other men Julia had ever known. "I enjoy my life and all the benefits that come with my position. *Allai barik*; it is the blessing of God."

Julia smirked behind her veil. Blessing indeed.

She had attached longer lenses to her camera, letting Kelly take close-ups of Nassir and Abdul. The little boy was especially photogenic. Julia wanted to get the benefit of that. She continued to read the translation on the camcorder screen. *Darn this veil, anyway.* It was annoying not to be able to see clearly through the fine net.

"*Allai barik*." Hassan seemed to agree. "You have much responsibility in the army, I understand. I have heard that you have up to two hundred militia under your command."

Julia knew this was an exaggeration. She waited for Nassir's response.

"Yes, it is a great responsibility, and I take it very seriously."

"So many, but where are they now? Surely they are not all sleeping?"

Nassir chuckled. "They stay at the base a short way from here."

"Of course." Hassan nodded in respect. "There must be many army bases in the region?"

"Yes, yes, there are many. Maybe sixteen in this area, and we will need more before we are finished with this war. Yet I like to think that my men get the best training of all."

Julia slowly let out a breath, fighting an urge to kick and hit this man who could speak so politely about training cold-blooded murderers.

"Tell me, in your own words, how this whole war began, and if you can, when you think it will be over."

"The uprising that started this war began in February 2003. The Zurgha had decided to rebel against the government. We were told to go in and put down this rebellion and stop the fighting. When that finished, there was always a rumor of another uprising somewhere else. It is like those little grass fires that jump and hop from place to place. In the last five years, this is what we have done: tried to stamp the fires of rebellion out one by one." The look in his eyes as he spoke had turned hard. Julia saw Kelly take the shot, her finger firmly pressing the shutter's release. Abdul was no longer on his father's lap.

"Oh, your orders of where to fight the rebellion come from someone else, then?"

"Yes, yes. There are many Janjaweed. Someone must coordinate our efforts. But ultimately, we fight for Allah. This is holy war. The infidel must be annihilated."

"And who is it that coordinates this holy war so brilliantly? Surely you must have a name that we can make mention of?"

"No. I am sorry. Whoever it is does not want to be known. It is the same for all of us; we receive orders, but we do not know the source, only the messengers. But"—Nassir lowered his voice so that Julia could hardly hear—"this is not for the newspaper, you understand . . ."

"Of course. It will remain between you and me. I promise."

"The messengers always come in brand new vehicles. And these vehicles all come from Khartoum."

"I see." Hassan nodded. "Yes, I think that most of us understand that the government of Sudan alone holds the power and intelligence to keep this war alive."

"And will, I feel sure, keep it alive for some time to come." Nassir leaned back, smiling and nodding, his lids half closed. A man completely secure in the ruthless source of power behind his life's effort.

"*Insha'Allah*," Hassan said quietly. As Allah wills.

"Oh, he does. He does," Nassir said.

"Indeed. Well, in spite of the fact that it has been a troubling time for our country, as with all wars, the true heroes of our day have come to the front lines. This is why we are here. We want to give our nation the chance to see the caliber of men who we have fighting for our protection and peace."

"*Al-hamdu lillah*," Nassir gushed, praising Allah for the Janjaweed.

"Thank you, Nassir." Hassan had had enough. "We will not take more of your valuable time; we know you are a very busy man. We wish you and your family peace and health."

Appropriate words were said, more peace and health and blessings, and then they were free to go. Nassir walked with them toward the Land Cruiser, standing at the front end of the truck, which was apparently also leaving. Another Janja was sitting at the wheel, waiting for the engine to warm.

Kelly and Julia carried the equipment and followed Hassan into the Land Cruiser. Julia sat pensively in the back, images of Samuel and Mary filling her mind. They would grow up without their mother. As so many in Darfur did. Her only comforting thought was of the article that would appear in *Women Informed* in just a few days, complete with photos, describing the kind of male arrogance and domination that could rape and murder a village, then settle down with his harem and family in that same village, just a week or so later. She'd be surprised if the magazine didn't feel some shock waves from this one. Just the kind of thing Tabi would eat up.

The sight of Abdul, out of the corner of her eye, distracted her. He was not where he should be, coming toward them, but right behind the truck. She heard the larger vehicle's gears shift into reverse, grind, and connect with the engine turning the wheels. Surely, the Janja driver could see the boy running toward them, she thought in dismay. But the truck kept moving backward as Abdul disappeared from the driver's sight, directly behind the moving vehicle.

"Stop! Stop the truck!" she screamed. Gathering her skirts, she leaped from the Land Cruiser and ran to scoop up the little boy before the truck tires could roll over him. She almost made it out herself. All she remembered afterward was the relief of knowing Abdul was in her arms, a shaft of pain shooting through her leg; then everything went black.

# ELEVEN

❦

The heart of man plans his way, but the LORD
establishes his steps.

PROVERBS 16:9

JOEL NURSED HIS BEER; THE HEAT AND dust of Khartoum gave him a
thirst like never before. This was his second day in the city, and according to the police officer he spoke with, he might have to wait another
week to get his traveling papers. No travel was permitted outside of
Khartoum for a foreigner unless you had the right documents—and
that wasn't the worst of it. Once those documents were issued, you were
legally bound to stop at any and all towns you might happen to drive
through, to register with the local police. The system was full of opportunities for bribery—which was maybe the point. In the meantime,
Julia Keegan, or Douglas, or whatever it was she called herself, had
traipsed off to some IDP camp several hundred kilometers from Khartoum. Joel pulled back on his beer again, thinking with disgust about
how much money he'd be spending trying to find Fred's adventure-
happy daughter. Looking past the room full of marble-topped tables
and rich patrons, he could see the picturesque Nile River through the

large windows. It moved slowly, in a serpentine manner, just like the red tape in this town.

Joel's gaze traveled over the other people in the restaurant, noting with interest the Arabian-style headdresses, called *immahs*, topping off traditional white robes or expensive Italian silk suits. The few foreigners like himself were conspicuous, but no one stood out more than the two women in the restaurant, sitting in the far corner. Definitely Americans, he decided.

One of them would have stood out anywhere, Joel realized, admiring the dark-haired beauty with her ankle, he noted, wrapped in Tensor bandages. A pair of crutches leaned against the wall beside her.

What, he asked himself, would a beautiful, young American girl be doing in Khartoum, obviously injured, at the Grand Holiday Villa? Unfortunately, he decided as he assessed her, she probably wouldn't feel like swimming in the beautiful pool outside.

"You better close your mouth or you'll catch flies."

His reverie broke.

"Hey, Steve, pull up a chair." Joel was surprised that he was so glad to see him. *Unique* and *odd* were the first two adjectives he would use to describe the man he had met on the plane on the way into Khartoum. Steve was from Portland, Oregon, and worked as some kind of missionary. Apparently, quite a few of his ilk worked in this country doing some terribly boring job like digging wells, or building outhouses—maybe it was both. He couldn't remember. Steve was staying at a hotel down the street and had offered to show Joel around the sites of Khartoum, knowing that they'd both be stuck for a few days, waiting for their papers.

"Can I buy you a beer?" Joel already guessed the answer, since the guy had refused all alcoholic beverages on the flight in.

"Nah, that's OK, but I'd love a coffee."

The men discussed their plans. Joel had a rental car waiting outside in the parking lot, but his experience in driving on the left side of the road was nil. The thought of acquiring the skill in Khartoum city traffic was a bit daunting, and he figured that, with Steve at the wheel, he'd be able to learn by observation.

They decided to head to the National Museum first. Joel paid the waiter, glancing one more time at the ladies in the far corner as he left a tip on the table. A man had joined them, a tall, well-built Nordic-type. His hand was resting on the cast-lady's shoulder. Which didn't sit quite right with Joel. Stupid. What primeval instinct made men want to protect vulnerable, beautiful women, he didn't know, but it was annoying. She glanced up and saw him watching her. Joel nodded slightly, just one foreigner acknowledging another in a strange land. He watched her head tip slightly to the side, as if listening to music somewhere, a woman obviously accustomed to being noticed by men, her mouth curving up, Mona-Lisa style, before she turned her attention back to her lady friend.

"That man is staring at you, Julia," Kelly pointed out.

"A lot of men stare at both of you." David winked at his wife. "Which Arab sheik is it this time? I won't take less than forty cows and twenty goats for you, Julia, I promise. That last offer was ridiculous."

"I was so insulted." Julia's hand cradled her cheek as she batted her eyes mockingly. "The shame of it: two camels and twenty chickens. What would my mother say?"

"You two are so funny." Kelly wasn't laughing. Nor was she to be sidetracked. "He's no Arab, honey; he's North American for sure."

"Where? You guys are embarrassing me," Julia sighed. "Fuss, fuss, fuss. You're worse than a pair of Victorian spinsters."

It was true. They had coddled and cosseted her nonstop since the accident. She had come to in a very bumpy Land Cruiser, with each jar sending excruciating pain through her leg. The truck hadn't been going very fast, but Julia's head had a goose-egg sized bump and a migraine competing for preeminence. The little boy, Abdul, was fine, Kelly had assured her. He had suffered a few bruises, but nothing serious. Nassir had thanked Allah for Julia's quick reactions and gratefully insisted that one of his women take care of her until she had recovered enough to travel. Hassan had creatively explained that his "assistant's husband" would not want his wife to receive treatment without his knowledge and approval first. Nassir paused briefly before blessing them again and asking Allah to give them safe travel.

As for Julia's ankle, Kelly told her later how it had been caught between the ground and the back tire of the truck for a moment before the driver had recovered his senses and thrown the vehicle into first gear, relieving the pressure on Julia's limb. According to Dave, who examined her carefully when they got back to Hassa Hissa, it was just a bad sprain, but with a possibility of hairline fractures.

Sequestering themselves in the tiny private office of the camp clinic for several moments, Kelly and Dave had quickly agreed upon a course of action. Julia would be escorted by both of them into Khartoum to get X-rays at the hospital, where she would have access to skilled surgeons if surgery was necessary. It was best, they told her, when she had groaned about being fine and not wanting to leave camp or cause them any trouble. Accepting no argument, they explained that they were long past due for a couple of weeks' reprieve and ended up driving Julia out—a three-hour trip that had seemed like three days—to Nyala, where they caught a plane to Khartoum. At the hospital, the doctor had taken X-rays and determined that she would not need surgery. He told her she was lucky she didn't have a fracture, but the sprain was serious and would require several days of rest, causing Dave to smile smugly, his concerns all justified.

None of them had ever stayed in the Grand, but Nassir An-Nur had been extremely grateful for Abdul's safe rescue and plied them with dinar to help pay for medical expenses. So here they were. Recuperating in the best possible style, compliments of the very well-funded Janjaweed.

"Spinsters, indeed." Dave's gaze lingered over his lovely wife. "I think not."

"Remember me?" Julia waved her hand at her friends. "I'm still here. No getting sidetracked this morning; we have plans for the day. Remember the museum, guys?"

Her words seemed to have their intended effect as, at the word *museum*, Kelly turned away from Dave's enamored focus.

"Right, the museum."

"No fair, Julia. You know her weakness," Dave objected.

"Yup. And I will use it for my own evil purposes as I choose."

"What we need to do with you, Julia, is fix you up with a nice NGO worker." Kelly had already gotten up from the table, obviously eager to get at all those artifacts. "And then you'll have more sympathy for poor Dave."

Julia smiled, recognizing the acronym that referred to people working for organizations such as WFP, CARE, and Doctors Without Borders, all described as non-governmental organizations. The trio headed back to their rooms, ambling slowly to accommodate the crutches.

"Look, Julia," Kelly whispered as they stood in the open elevator of the lobby, waiting for the doors to close, "that's him, getting into that car."

"'Him' who?" Julia asked.

"The guy staring at you in the restaurant!" Kelly said it with just a touch of impatience. "Now there's a good-looking man, if I ever saw one," she added, shooting Julia a wolfish look.

Julia smiled at the uncharacteristic glint on Kelly's face, then laughed as Dave pulled his wife roughly toward him, kissing her before the doors opened again onto the third floor and explaining that she wasn't allowed to notice other men or there would be more of that same punishment.

They had a good marriage, and Julia admired them for it. They reminded her of her great-aunt Rose and uncle Seamus, comfortable companions, but still plenty of spark between them. The only family members on her father's side of the family who had kept up contact with her and her mother throughout her childhood, they had given her many fond memories. For two weeks every summer, she enjoyed home-cooked meals complete with flowers on the table and being read to out loud and prayed with before she went to sleep each night. When Uncle Seamus died, it had never been quite the same. Julia remembered the first time she had gone to visit afterward. The tick-tock from the wooden clock on the mantle seemed louder. The house was too clean, and the smell of Uncle Seamus's pipe had faded. So had Aunt Rose. Sitting in her rocker, working her crochet hook, Aunt Rose appeared completely intact, but when Julia looked into her great-aunt's eyes, she had flinched from the pain in them. Aunt Rose had lost a part of herself, a part Julia wasn't sure she had ever recovered.

Marriages like that were rare, but Julia knew that Dave and Kelly had a similar one. She had seen them in tense situations, tired and irritable with one another, but they never stayed there. It wouldn't be long before one of them, or sometimes both at the same time, would be going out of their way to demonstrate their affection and love for the other. It was a real relationship with pressures and differences of opinion, but it had great comeback-ability, like an Indian rubber ball. Watching Dave comfort Kelly as she grieved over the loss of Mary and Sam had somehow comforted her own heart. Love was not dead, after all. Most of the marriages of her college friends had ended in divorce after a short time. Common law relationships weren't any better, just less hassle to end. Over the years, she had grown more disenchanted with the idea of a "good" marriage, concluding that such a thing was probably no longer possible in this day and age, what with the pressures of dual careers and the difficulties of parenting. But watching Dave and Kelly the last few days, she had found herself reevaluating that theory. If Mr. Right ever came along—a possibility she was extremely skeptical of—she would want a marriage like theirs.

But the guy in the restaurant was not marriage material. Too good looking. Julia had learned that a long time ago: the better looking they were, the less you could trust them. She wanted a relationship with a man she could trust. Trust was important. So far, Julia had never met a man like that. And if there was one, he was probably married already.

❧

"Wanna meet her?" Steve asked.

"Do I—of course I want to meet her. But I'm not going to introduce myself to a stranger halfway across a room, just because she's pretty." They were walking from the restaurant and through the main lobby, the heady scent of the floral arrangements filling the air.

"OK, OK. I agree. I'd never do that, either." Steve clapped him across the back of his shoulders. "But what if I introduced you?"

"What?" Joel stopped in his tracks and stared at Steve. "You know her?"

"No, not the one with the crutches, but I know the other two, or more accurately, I know who they work for."

*The other two?*

"Ah, they're a couple then?"

"Definitely a couple. Or at least they were when I saw their picture in the newsletter that my mom gets from them. When I saw they were with MSF and heading to Sudan, too, I actually read the whole thing. If memory stands me, I think she's a midwife, and he's a nurse."

"MSF?"

"*Médicins Sans Frontières*—Doctors Without Borders."

"Yeah," Joel looked at Steve with raised eyebrows, "I've heard of them, but didn't you say that you dig wells?"

"Basically, that's correct, but MSF doesn't just support doctors on the field; it has a huge contingent of volunteers, all trained in disaster response and relief work."

Joel nodded, impressed but not wanting to show it.

"And the other woman they were with, is she with MSF, too?"

"The one on crutches? No idea. Never seen her before in my life, but like I said, man, I can introduce us anytime, just say the word."

The drive to the museum was surprisingly pleasant. Large, low-spreading trees canopied the older, British-influenced parts of Khartoum. *A big contrast to the drive from the airport*, Joel thought. To say his first impressions of the city were negative would be an understatement. Appalled at the squalor and filth everywhere, he had questioned what he was doing in this place. Garbage littered the wide, dusty streets; buildings were ramshackle, crumbling away in many places. People were too skinny and dressed poorly; most were barefoot. As they had approached the hotel, things had gradually improved, including the makes of automobiles. He had seen Mercedes and BMWs, even a Ferrari. He had paid the cab at the front entrance of the Grand. The red-uniformed valet immediately at his elbow had taken his luggage, following him through the glass doors, past tropical flowers in huge ornate vases. The hotel doors had shut him in, safe from the squalor he had observed through his taxi window.

Now, leaving their air-conditioned car in the parking lot, Joel and Steve made their way through the pillared entrance to the large museum. Filled with relics and artifacts dating back to 2000 BCE, when the Egyptians had called this region Cush, it promised to be worth the visit.

The men walked through room after room of antiquities and pottery, frescoes and murals. It wasn't busy; only a few people seemed to be interested in Sudan's history today.

Steve seemed excited to discover that evidences pointed emphatically to there having been a strong church in Sudan during the Nubian civilization and until the Middle Ages. Stopping in front of the entrance to the Christian Pavilion, Joel was instantly captivated by a large wall mural. He read the placard: *Three Youths in the Fiery Furnace*. Joel walked slowly back and forth, studying the painting carefully. The artist had depicted three men sitting calmly, red flames shooting all around them, with a tall angel standing near them.

"It's something, isn't it?" Steve commented.

"I remember hearing this story as a kid. The fiery furnace. And—do I remember? One was Shadrach, I think; but who were the other two again?" He scrunched up his face, trying to remember.

"Meshach and Abednego." It was crutch-lady. From out of nowhere.

"That's it! Meshach and Abednego." Joel looked at her appreciatively, noting again her tanned skin set off by a very white cotton blouse over a long, linen-type skirt. She wore a wide-brimmed straw hat, which shadowed her dark eyes, but not enough to hide a mischievous glint that caught him off guard.

"But I don't remember the rest of the story. What happened to them?" Joel stroked his bottom lip back and forth with his knuckle, trying to remember.

"I couldn't tell you. I didn't do too much time in Sunday school, myself. I remembered their names because I had a great-aunt who taught me a song about them."

Steve coughed politely. They both turned their attention toward him, and he explained.

"Given the choice to bow down and worship King Nebuchadnezzar or to be thrown into the fiery furnace, the three friends chose the latter.

According to the Bible, Old Neb heated the fire seven times hotter than usual, had the guys bound up, clothes and all, and ordered them thrown in. The fire was so hot that the men who pushed them over the edge were burnt to death."

The man and woman who had accompanied crutch-lady in the restaurant earlier had joined the group and stood back, listening to Steve.

Steve warmed to his story, his arms waving back and forth as he spoke, the excitement of the drama filling him. "Shadrach, Meshach, and Abednego found themselves in the fire, amazingly not getting burnt. Everyone on the outside thought they were toast, but when Neb checked, he could see them walking around with a fourth guy, who looked like some kind of god to him. Nebuchadnezzar came as close as he dared and yelled at them to come out of the furnace. When they did, not one single hair on their heads had been singed. Their clothes didn't even smell like smoke."

"Wow. You have a knack for storytelling. That was good, Steve," Joel said.

"But not, I think, just a story," Steve answered him. He looked surprisingly downcast for a moment, then caught himself, and seemed to shake off whatever had dampened the passion that lit him a moment before.

"Sorry." Steve introduced himself to the couple standing beside him. "I'm Steve, like he said, and this is Joel. I think you two are here with MSF, aren't you?"

"I'm Dave and, yes," he lowered his voice as he continued, "we are with MSF, but how did you know that?"

"My mom," Steve said. "She reads the MSF Newsletter cover to cover and then leaves it in the bathroom for the rest of the family to peruse at their convenience. I remembered you from your picture."

The three volunteers immediately lost themselves in shared stories. Joel smiled at this spontaneous reunion of sorts and then turned to the other outsider.

"Joel Maartens." He proffered his hand to the woman beside him, who took it in a surprisingly firm grasp and answered, "Julia. Julia Douglas. Nice to meet you."

Joel's mouth actually dropped open. Shut. Then fell open again.

"You're kidding," was what he finally managed to say. "I'm here to find you." Then he remembered to let go of her hand.

꧁

"Ah, that's so sweet of you," Julia answered, narrowing her eyes slightly, "but I'm not lost."

Julia maneuvered her crutches under her arms and hobbled over to stand closer to Kelly. This Joel Maartens person unnerved her, and she felt a bit out of her depth. When she had noticed him in the restaurant this morning, she'd figured him for your standard lady's man, superficial and charming. But this person standing in front of a mural of a Sunday school tale was not superficial. Intriguing, yes. A bit silly, maybe, and most certainly charming, but not superficial.

"Julia." He spoke intensely, following her as he did. Any attempt she was making at getting space between them was foiled. "You need to let me talk with you. I came all the way to Sudan to find you. It's a family matter. Please let me have dinner with you tonight. I'd like to explain this properly."

An icy hand seemed to squeeze her gut. "Is my mom OK?"

Out of the corner of her eye, Julia could see Dave, Kelly, and Steve watching them with interest.

"Yes, yes. I don't mean to alarm you. This has nothing to do with your mom," Joel assured her. "It's to do with your father, Fred Keegan, and his will."

Julia absorbed this and let out a breath of air she'd apparently been holding.

"Fred Keegan was never my father."

Dave and Kelly both looked at Julia curiously. She ignored them.

"Fred Keegan was your biological father, and it was his last request that I carry this out."

Joel Maartens's bit of courtroom drama ignited Julia's fury. "If you knew him, you would understand why I don't care. Why I don't want any connection with him, ever." She took a deep calming breath, confident that the discussion was closed.

"On the contrary. I did know him. Pretty well, too, I think. I would say he was probably one of the best men I've ever known."

"You—what?" Julia's mind recoiled at what could only be a blatant lie. Her eyes narrowed as she fought the disgust that rose within her.

Kelly reached out and gently touched her elbow. "Julia. People can change."

That was true. People did occasionally change. Maybe, Julia considered, Fred Keegan had changed at some point in his life. But that did not excuse the legacy of hurt and shame he had left in hers. She sagged into her crutches, her head drooping as she considered the energy and choices she had made up to this moment to escape even a hint of the scandal that was Fred Keegan. Now Dave and Kelly would see her for what she truly was: the daughter of a murderer and a convict. She felt naked and fought the tears that welled up at disappointing her friends.

"Julia," Kelly spoke quietly, "my dad wasn't a good man, either. He beat my mother and us kids black and blue."

Julia's head shot up, meeting the pain and honesty in Kelly's eyes.

"But the best thing that ever happened to me," she continued, "was the day I finally let it go. Through Christ, I was able to forgive my dad. It released me from the cycle of hatred that I lived in. It set me free."

Julia didn't understand all that Kelly was saying. But she understood one thing: Kelly had had a jerk for a father, too. And she was free from hating him. Julia would love to be completely free from her own father. Once and for all.

"I'm sorry, Julia."

She looked up, and then had to look up a bit more to meet Joel's eyes boring into her soul. Eyes full of concern. Eyes that drew her. She stepped back, compensating for the sudden feeling that she was losing her balance, and only half heard what he was saying to her.

"Look, I don't even know you, and I've obviously brought up some painful memories. I sincerely apologize for that. But please," he said and hesitated briefly—clearly a man who wasn't used to being refused—"why don't you let me take you to dinner? To make up for it. We can talk about this in the evening once you've had time to sort out your thoughts."

The invitation was appealing. More than Julia wanted it to be. Emotions churned inside her until a white-hot fury blazed every other feeling in its path. When she finally blurted out a reply, the flames reached out and lashed everyone around her.

"If you think that Fred Keegan was one of the best men you ever knew, then you must have been royally conned or maybe you have a warped sense of what a good man is."

"Julia—" Kelly said with rebuke in her voice. Julia wasn't listening.

"I don't need time to sort my thoughts. I already know that I have no desire to talk about this, nor will I have dinner with the friend of a man who I have every reason to despise." Turning on her good heel, with a shove and an awkward turn of the crutches, she hobbled away, tears burning in her eyes.

Where she went, she didn't remember afterward, but by the time Kelly and Dave found her, she had composed herself enough that they were able to make small talk the whole way back to the hotel, avoiding any discussion about the incident at the museum. Julia begged off their invitation to join them for iced tea on the veranda, using the headache that was building as an excuse.

Two hours, one nap, and a shower later, Julia stretched languorously on the lounge chair by the pool, enjoying the breeze blowing off the Nile.

A little crease wrinkled her brow as she thought over the things she had said to Joel Maartens. It was just that, for as long as she could remember, she had believed her father to be a monster. Had, in fact, built her life around the impression that since her father had been the instigator of evil and pain in people's lives, she needed to do what she could to expose evil and eradicate pain. Hence, a career in journalism and a focus and commitment that some called obsessive. But she never thought so. If anything, she felt behind. Like there was always something more she could or should be doing. Even when she finished a project, sometimes it would take her months to stop worrying about the things she'd left unsaid in an article, wondering if she had truly helped a situation or merely exploited it.

Now to have someone tell her that her father was a good man—what was she supposed to do with that?

"Hi."

Joel stood, looming over her, holding two glasses of what looked like ice-cold lemonade. He offered one to her.

"May I join you?" he asked.

She accepted the glass, nodding as she did, trying to think of something intelligent to say but coming up completely blank.

Joel sat down on the chair beside her, apparently, by the look on his face, perplexed by the contents of his glass, which he kept jiggling back and forth.

Julia smiled, in spite of herself. This man had a little-boy vulnerability about him that somehow was emphasized rather than hidden by a strong physique and an afternoon shadow about his jawline.

"You're staying in this hotel, too, aren't you?" Not intelligent, but all that she could think of.

"I am," he answered, then continued, "Julia, I want you to know how sorry—"

"No, please, don't," Julia interrupted him. "I overreacted this morning."

They both sipped lemonade for a moment, the space between them filled by the calls of parakeets overhead and monkeys chattering in the nearby treetops.

So the loud, slurpy noise of his straw draining the last of the lemonade didn't seem right at all. She looked up at him in surprise. The grin he flashed her confirmed the "little boy" thought she had about him, flanked as it was by two adorable dimples.

"So," he asked, "do you think that you might have pity on my terrible manners and reconsider my invitation for dinner? Maybe even teach me how to drink out of a straw without slurping?"

Julia cocked her head to one side, considering. He was a flirt. Obviously. But she liked him in spite of it. Maybe it was his messy hair. Maybe it was the earnest look in his eyes . . .

"Unless you're busy already—we could meet in the morning, instead, if that works better for you."

"No, it's fine." Julia reached for her crutches, handing him her empty glass as she did. "Dinner would be nice. I'll meet you in the dining room at seven."

The boyish glee that lit up his sea green eyes as she said it would not leave her thoughts for the rest of the afternoon. Her normally efficient and straightforward wardrobe choices were unusually difficult as she laid out the one blue sundress she had with her, then beside it, two skirts—one white, one brown—capris, two short sleeved blouses, and one longer, orange cotton smock-top with bead work around the square neckline. Eventually she settled on a pair of white, loosely flared capris, a white crocheted cotton tank-top, and a short-sleeved turquoise shrug. Her Tevas would definitely not work with the ensemble. Her brown leather slip-ons would have to do. Refusing to admit to herself how much time she was wasting on this simple decision, she scolded herself for thinking about sea green eyes.

By quarter to seven, she was only slightly more composed. Before she went to the dining room, she stopped and knocked on Kelly and Dave's bedroom door. No one answered immediately, so she knocked again. And waited. When Kelly finally opened the door, Julia realized why it had taken so long. Red-rimmed eyes, disheveled hair, and outside on their patio, Dave, with his back turned to them, his head down, minus a friendly greeting. Unbelievable. Dave and Kelly fighting?

"Kelly. Are you OK?"

"I'm fine." She sniffed.

"No, that's not fair, Kelly," Julia said gently. "You guys nurse me and hound me with your concern, but when something's troubling you, you pretend everything's OK?"

"Honestly, we just—why are you all dressed up?"

"I'm meeting Joel Maartens for dinner."

"You what? I thought you were determined not to give him one minute of your time."

"I know, but we bumped into each other down at the poolside and, you know, I think I misjudged him. It was just so weird to have my biological father's past brought up here in Khartoum. I didn't expect it, and it just kind of sideswiped me."

Dave had joined them and stood with his arms crossed, looking a little disconcerted, but Julia noted with relief that at least he hadn't been crying.

"Be careful, Julia. That man is smooth. After you ran out of the museum, he told us that he was your father's attorney. He might be sincere, but he is also one smooth lawyer."

Kelly pulled her into the room, closed the door, and proceeded to give her a list of dos and don'ts: listen and try to understand what Joel had to say about Fred Keegan; don't make any hasty judgments; try to relax and enjoy the evening. Sudan was not the kind of place you could afford to throw away a chance of light-hearted entertainment, even if it was in the guise of dinner with the lawyer of one's estranged and deceased father. A good point, and one that made all three of them smile.

"I know it's true. I'll be careful; I promise. And when I get back from supper with all the juicy details, I want to know what's happened to upset you two."

She smiled as she rode the elevator down to the main floor, glad that she had friends. Her smile faded into a concerned frown as she mused over what it was that could be troubling them.

# TWELVE

The integrity of the upright guides them, but the
crookedness of the treacherous destroys them.

PROVERBS 11:3

"DRAT." ROSE SIGHED, GLANCING AT her watch again. Where was that
woman? Not known for being punctual, Julia's mother was now twenty
official minutes late. She would wait only five minutes longer. Then she
would have the waitress phone a cab. Wasted money and wasted time,
that was Annie to a T.

The last time Rose had seen her must have been at least ten years
ago. At Julia's graduation from university. Annie had been dressed in
something incredibly tight and inappropriate. Rose shook her head,
remembering. How that lovely girl had been raised by such a brash
female was one of God's mysteries, was all she could think. The two
weeks or so that Julia had spent with her in the summertime when her
mother needed her "breaks" could not account for it. And the child had
come less often over the years, until now it was only every six months
or so that they had tea or lunch together. No, Rose had no real hand
in helping to raise Julia to be the fine woman she was, except to pray

for her. She still prayed. Rose knew that Julia did not like to talk about
God or religion. She had long ago decided that her best tack would be
to show the child God's love as much as she was able to.

"Don't preach at me, Aunt Rose," Julia would say. "I'd much rather
talk about something of interest to both of us."

Gracious and polite even in her dismissal of God. That was Julia.

"I'm so angry, I could spit."

*That*, Rose thought, looking at the florid face of a woman who was
not quite fat and had been very pretty many years ago, *is Annie.*

"You're late," Rose welcomed.

"I had no control over it. No control. I stopped to get directions, and
some idiot told me to go the complete opposite way. I ended up having to stop and ask again in the worst part of town; it's a miracle I'm
here and not raped and murdered over on Georgia Street, somewhere."

Rose's eyes narrowed. Disapproval seethed. Her tongue was not tied,
but for the Lord's sake, she was biting it so that she wouldn't say what
she wanted to. *What had poor Fred ever seen in this female?* she asked
herself, not for the first time and probably not for the last.

"Well, that's a fine, sympathetic hello, Aunt Rose." Annie plopped
herself down in the seat opposite. "I thought we pagans would know
you Christians by your love, but I see that isn't so with you today, is it,
Auntie?"

The woman could make her feel so many strong emotions simultaneously. None of them good.

"You asked me to meet you, Annie, and here I am. What's this
about?"

Annie opened her menu, flagged the busy waitress—who was walking by with a tray load of heavy dishes—asked what the specials were,
and informed her they were ready to order. She emitted an extended
*humph* when the waitress politely explained that she would return as
soon as she was able.

"They are so slow here. We should have gone to that nice new place over by Costco, but no, you had to have your way, like you always do. Oh, well, I don't mind putting up with this for you, Rose."

Rose's ice cube stuck in her throat. Coughing and sputtering, her hands trembled as she set down her water glass, carefully wiping her mouth with her napkin.

"That other place is a bar and grill, which, I am sure you remember, I do not patronize. Alcohol has certainly not been your friend over the years, Annie, and I will not make it mine."

Defiance and triumph mixed on Annie's face as Rose came as close to losing her temper as she had in the last ten years. Since the last time she'd had a conversation with Annie, in fact.

"Alcohol and me aren't friends, Rose, but we're not enemies, either. There's been lots of times it helped me forget what hurt too much to remember. Especially about your nephew."

"And it's because he died that you called me to meet with you, isn't it?" Rose deflected.

"Partly that. But mostly I wanted to meet because of Julia."

This Rose hadn't expected.

"Have you heard from her? Surely she's OK." Rose's concern replaced her irritation.

"I got an e-mail from her a few days ago. She never tells me much. Just not to worry and she's fine. You know, the normal stuff," Annie answered.

Rose did not know. She did not own a computer and so could not receive e-mails, and Julia's form of communication was always through e-mail while she was on assignment. No, she waited for the phone call once Julia came back home. That filled her in and let her know her niece was safe. During these calls, Rose always invited Julia to come for a visit, and sometimes she did. Those were cherished times.

"No, Julia's fine. It's her future I'm worried about."

Rose raised one brow.

"I've become aware of the fact that Fred left an estate behind when he passed on. Did some furniture building or something on the side that ended up being quite a tidy little business and never spent much money—didn't even gamble, I'm told. Anyway, there's been no inheritance passed on to myself, which of course, I would never expect. But I would think the man might leave his money to his child, wouldn't you? Or possibly to you?"

"To me?" Rose asked in disbelief. "What on earth would I want with Fred's money?"

"Well, there's been no lawyer or executor paying me a visit, Rose, so I just wondered what Fred could have been thinking, passing by his own daughter like that."

The lawyer man. He'd been looking for Julia. Polite and respectful, if somewhat obtuse, she remembered. No gardener, that was for sure. And now Annie was trying to get information about Julia's inheritance before she had even had a chance to receive it. There could be no reason for it, unless she was hoping to bleed the money from Julia for herself.

Rose nodded. That was it. Annie wanted to know the money was there before she started pressing her daughter for it. She would not stop until she had power over every last penny. And Julia would give into it. She didn't need the money, herself. She did well at her career. But she was a little too codependent with Annie for Rose's liking—habitually sympathizing with her and accepting all the lies her mother filled her head with regarding poor Fred. Fred had done wrong. Rose admitted it to herself time and again. But Annie had been cruel in cutting off all contact between him and Julia. The man had nothing else in all the world to live for except his daughter, and Annie had effectively erased her from his life.

It had made her wonder: when the lawyer had spoken of it, he'd said something about Fred finally having something of value to give Julia. Could he have meant the money from the furniture business? Rose had hoped, probably a little unrealistically, for something more. Well, it wasn't her business. And it definitely wasn't Annie's. What Julia's father had left to her should be hers. And would be if Rose had anything to do with it.

Annie finished her steak sandwich (the most expensive thing on the menu, Rose noted), sipped noisily from her straw, and leveled a narrowed gaze at Rose.

"Has anyone contacted you? Anyone official?"

A direct question, needing a direct answer. But please, Lord, not the truth, not to this woman.

"Annie, I guess if someone contacted me, I would let the right people know about it, wouldn't I?"

Annie's pursed mouth and shrewd gaze did not look pleased, but it was all Rose was revealing.

She wasn't that surprised when Annie suddenly looked at her watch.

"So sorry, Auntie, but I'm already five minutes late for my dentist appointment." *More like a drinking appointment*, thought Rose, immediately chastising herself for judgments she had no right to make but was seriously struggling with in regard to Annie's behavior. "You don't mind picking this one up, do you? I have absolutely no cash on me. There's a love. And please, let me know if you hear anything." Annie's meaning was obvious.

Rose watched her walk away, the heavy fragrance of her perfume dissipating somewhat as she left, just like the emotionally charged atmosphere.

"Lord Jesus, I am a sinful woman. Sometimes I think I'm not so bad. But I am, and today reminds me of that fact." Rose's confession was silent, but every word was sincere. "I have no love in my heart toward Annie Douglas. You will have to help me want to love her, Lord, because I don't. And Lord, I need Your love and patience for her, because I have none of my own."

Rose shook her head back and forth in the cab the whole way home, her emotions still in turmoil.

Stepping out of the cab onto the sidewalk in front of her house, a thought came unbidden and full of humorless irony.

*No wonder Fred had become a criminal.*

# Thirteen

There be three things which are too wonderful for
me, yea, four which I know not: The way of an eagle
in the air; the way of a serpent upon a rock; the way
of a ship in the midst of the sea; and the way of a man
with a maid.

PROVERBS 30:18–19 KJV

JOEL NODDED AND LISTENED WITH interest as Steve explained the history of how the triple cities of Khartoum, Khartoum North, and Omdurman had grown into what was now a sprawling metropolis with more than two and a half million people living in it. He had talked Steve into getting a predinner drink with him—to pay him back for being such a good tourist guide earlier that day—and, after ordering a beer for himself and a Coke for Steve, found himself listening, but also wondering about him.

A bit younger than himself, not unattractive, no wedding ring, yet spending his life in the middle of nowhere: there was something about this guy that Joel just didn't get and that always aroused his "lawyer" suspicions. Occasionally in his career, he had known he didn't want any more information than he already had about a client, but it was his job, and he owed much of his success to the fact that he always knew about the things his client couldn't or wouldn't say. That way, there weren't surprises waiting in court, or even if there were, Joel would have his backup plan ready and a better chance of winning the case. Now his instincts were in overdrive. Steve was, for all appearances, just a regular good guy. And that was the problem. As far as Joel was concerned, that particular animal was almost, if not completely, extinct.

Joel leaned over and offered him a cigarette, which Steve, unsurprisingly, refused.

"Yeah, I'm going to quit again, myself. It's a stupid habit." Joel squinted with distaste at the cigarette, trying to figure out how to ask the question that was burning to be asked.

"So, why are you really here, Steve?" The direct approach, Joel decided.

"Where? Here with you? I guess 'cause there was no one prettier to sit with." He smiled at his joke. Joel nodded, smiled, tilted his head back slightly in his best "it's all in confidence" manner, and asked again.

"No. Why are you here in Sudan? I mean, I know what you do, with the wells and that, and it's great. I really mean it. You're making a difference in a tangible way to so many people who need help."

"Exactly!" Steve was nodding seriously, but there was a twinkle in the back of his eyes that perplexed Joel.

"Couldn't you do that at home with less discomfort? Why do you have to come so far to help people who can never repay you? I mean lots of people at home in the States and Canada need help. Look at New Orleans after the hurricane. How many men and women worked for years afterward cleaning it up?"

"You don't know the Lord, do you, Joel?"

Where did that come from? What did that have to do with anything?

"I'm sorry—what?"

"Know the Lord. You don't, do you?"

"I guess I don't. I have no idea what you're talking about."

"Well, it's the answer. The answer to why I do what I do. I don't do it for me. I do it for my best friend, the Lord Jesus Christ. He's the reason why I'm here."

"You know Him?" Joel crossed his arms over his chest and tipped back in his chair the way his mother didn't like. He was surprised to discover that Steve was a religious fanatic. Unusual, since he was pretty good at reading people most of the time, but he'd definitely missed this one. For Pete's sake, the guy was a university graduate. No one who graduated from university remained Christian, did they?

"Yeah, I know Him." Steve spoke quietly, wonderment softening his rough features, while Joel figured his head had to be even softer. "It's the same for me as for the three guys in the furnace. I know why they would not bow down to Nebuchadnezzar's golden statue. I know why they told him that their God was able to save them and rescue them from the hand of the king. And I know why they said that, even if He didn't save them from the furnace, they would still not bow down or worship the idol."

Steve paused, lost in thought, gazing out toward the Nile. Joel followed his gaze and watched as a heron swooped down, scooping a fish from the water, leaving only a ripple where his long legs had skimmed the surface.

"I know," Steve said, finishing his thought, "because I serve the same God they did."

There was a surety about him, Joel decided. As Joel listened to and watched Steve talk—with his tousled hair, whiskery chin, steady eyes—he knew it. Steve was telling him the truth. That realization, more than any of the other white-coat possibilities he'd conjectured, left him unnerved. He stubbed out his cigarette; the taste had turned sour in his mouth.

The Nile was beautiful, reflecting back the colors of the setting sun. Joel pondered it without really seeing it. He had no response to what Steve had said, truth or not. But the emptiness that sometimes surged and threatened his ability to enjoy the pleasures of his life—the fast cars, the fast women, the fast career—that emptiness felt worse now than it had for a long time, and he didn't like it.

"Yeah, well, I guess I better get ready for my hot date," he reminded them both.

Steve tilted his head and raised his eyebrows. "I'm surprised she changed her mind. She sounded pretty sure about not wanting to spend time with you earlier."

"Yeah, but I had a chance to chat with her by the pool this afternoon. I found out she likes lemonade."

"Ah, of course, lemonade. That explains her complete change of mind," Steve said, smiling. He then added on a more serious note, "Purely professional, right, Joel?"

"Absolutely," Joel said, not feeling at all professional.

"Good. For a minute there, I thought maybe I'd get chivalry points by being a third party—saving the damsel from a fate worse than death, and all that."

"Not necessary. I'd be a pretty bad fate, but probably not worse than death. Besides, I get the strong impression that Julia Douglas can handle herself. She'd be like her dad in that."

Steve nodded in agreement. "And a good thing, too. She's a beautiful woman."

"Did you think she was beautiful? I kind of thought she had funny ears."

"Did I say beautiful? I meant in a big-nose kind of way. You know, Sarah Jessica Parker . . ."

Joel focused on the facial features of his dinner companion later that evening and decided that Sarah Jessica Parker's and Julia Douglas's nose had nothing in common. Julia's was perky and cute, with a smattering of freckles. Her ears sparkled with simple diamond studs, two on one side and three on the other. Her dark hair was swept back and up, with loose tendrils and wisps escaping to frame her face. Her chin had a little stubborn tilt to it, which was evident as she explained how she had hurt her leg. She was feisty and independent, a complete contradiction to his earlier vulnerable-and-needing-protection impression, but much more interesting.

"Tomorrow I go back to the hospital to have one last check, and then I'm free to return to the IDP camp," Julia explained. "It's the waiting around that's been hard on me."

"So what do you do here in Khartoum all day?" Joel asked her after they placed their order with a Sudanese waiter, whose dark skin was accentuated by his white pants and white jacket.

"I work on my laptop and catch up on my reading."

He asked her about her work, enjoying the flush on her cheeks as she grew animated, explaining how much her career meant to her, not to mention the satisfaction she had in seeing a story published that challenged the status quo, reminding those who picked up *Women Informed* of others less fortunate.

"It's been nice to get to know Kelly and Dave better here in Khartoum. They are the real heroes. People like them, who give so unselfishly of themselves to help others. They have been so good to me, treating me like a queen and taking me on little tourist jaunts, like today."

"So Khartoum's Grand Holiday Villa is quite different than life in an IDP camp, I guess."

"You have no idea," she answered dryly.

Appetizers were set in front of them. Julia had chosen an Asian salad with rice noodles, sprinkled with sesame seeds. Joel worked his way eagerly and carefully through a plate of prawns, dripping with capers and lemon juice.

"Yeah, I'm relieved I can bypass the camps, actually." Joel expertly speared the pink fleshy meat from the crustacean's skeleton with a tiny fork, then dragged it through the sauce before placing it in his mouth. "I had prepared to go in if that's what it took to find you, but now you've gone and gotten yourself injured, saving me all that trouble," he added.

Julia's face was impassive. She was listening to him, but not giving away a single response she might have to anything he was saying. He pushed on, wondering if her reaction was positive or negative. "I just don't see the point," he said, trying to explain his reaction to the poverty he had seen in Khartoum, "of getting all worked up about thousands of poor people in a world full of suffering. We can't help everybody, and it's too big a problem to fix with one simple solution. I know I'm a privileged person to live the way I do in Canada, but I also know I don't have answers for the world's problems in my back pocket."

"I don't think anyone has all the answers," Julia agreed, wrapping cold, clear noodles around her fork, then stabbing a baby corn with it, "but I don't think anyone has the right to turn their eyes away, either. We share our humanity with these people. We share the earth with them." She waved her fork in the air, making Joel wince in expectation of flying noodles. "If you were living in an IDP camp after your town had been slaughtered by your country's paid militia, and your family was surviving on handouts provided by first-world countries and NGOs, wouldn't you be grateful that someone, somewhere—someone, anyone—knew and cared about you enough to provide those handouts?"

The waiter returned, breaking the tense atmosphere with the arrival of their dinner specials: Blue Nile perch with fresh scallops, served with grilled leeks and wild rice and smothered in a lemon-garlic sauce. He carefully set the hot plates down in front of them.

"Enjoy," he said, smiling broadly at them with brilliant white teeth.

The food was delicious, and they both ate well. *Too well*, Julia thought, the twelve extra pounds she'd packed on in the last year nagging her conscience as she sipped a dessert coffee between spoonfuls of creamy, cold, mango-coconut Italian gelato. Joel was working his way through a custard dessert and drinking espresso, black. Utterly stuffed, she sighed in contentment, wishing the meal could last longer.

Joel was smart and charming. Surprised, she realized that she felt relaxed with him and even enjoyed the conversation. It was too bad that her accident prevented him from visiting an IDP camp. The best way she knew to understand the situation of desperation that the Sudanese people were suffering under, especially in western Darfur, was from the inside.

Thoughtfully, she finished the last delicious spoonful of gelato. When she looked up from the empty dish to an expression of complete amusement and something else unfathomable on Joel's face, she was suddenly overcome with self-consciousness.

"What is it? Do I have ice cream on my face?" she asked, swiping randomly around her mouth.

Joel had tilted back his chair but now let it drop forward. Leaning across the table, she grew very still as he traced the corner of her lip with his finger.

"No, I don't think you had any on your mouth at all." He grinned, his complete honesty disarming any offense she thought she should probably feel.

Maneuvering the conversation and atmosphere back into safe territory, she asked him about his career and life story, hoping to divert attention away from her flushed face.

He told her about growing up on an apple orchard in BC. About how school had always come so easily and how eventually he found himself studying to be a lawyer and enjoying the city life in Vancouver. And he told her about Helena.

"Actually, that's partly why I'm here now. I mean, I'm here for Fred, definitely, but I just found out Helena's getting married again—correction—gotten married, by now." He took a sip of espresso. "Our marriage seems like a lifetime ago, and I don't feel bad. I'm actually happy that she's happy. It just took me by surprise, and I knew I wanted a change of atmosphere."

"Whew," Julia blew softly, "when you change your atmosphere, you really change it, don't you?"

"Yup, I guess so. But I also owe your dad."

It was Julia's turn to lean back in her chair; crossing her legs and arms, she regarded him with a wary expression.

"He kept a picture of you taped up in his cell, you know."

"I don't think so, Joel." She shook her head. He was mistaken; he had to be.

"It's true. It's a picture of you as a little kid, two pigtails in your hair, and you have missing teeth. You've grown up since then, and I, for one, could not be more delighted with the end result, but that kid was definitely you."

Julia ignored the flattery, focusing on her father.

"You have no idea what it was like growing up, moving from place to place, trying to protect your reputation, hoping that no one would connect you to a convicted murderer. I've often felt sorry for my mother, knowing how she struggled to hold onto jobs and how one day, inevitably, she would go to work and everyone would look the other way and the boss would fire her with a lousy excuse . . ."

"That was wrong, I agree, but that wasn't your dad," Joel interjected.

Julia put up her hand, silencing him with the motion.

"The worst thing was living in a kid's world and knowing something was terribly wrong with you, but never really understanding what. Trying to imagine what dark and dirty deed your dad had to have done to bring the disapproval of your teachers and the silence from your friends, until one day, you finally learn the truth. He shot a sixty-five-year-old grandma in the head, robbing her corner grocery store in an act of such selfishness and stupidity I can hardly think of it without gagging." Tears filled her eyes as she spoke, turning them into pools of darkness.

Silence filled the air. Joel reached across the table and took her hand, his thumb moving back and forth slowly across her wrist, offering the only comfort he knew to give. What he said next stilled her, adding a crack in the wall of her defensiveness.

"I know. He told me. He lived with it and regretted it every single day."

"He told you?" she echoed.

"Yes, he did. He said he deserved everything he got, and more. But somewhere along the line, Julia, he changed. He got an education in prison, something he'd never had before. He learned to read, and his shelves were full of books."

Julia's eyes widened in surprise and interest—and just maybe a spark of sympathy.

"Then why," she finally whispered, "why didn't we know?"

But Joel didn't need to answer. Julia realized the truth for herself. She and her mother would never have opened a single letter or returned one call if they thought it was him. She chewed on the inside of her cheek, her chin moving up and down slightly as she pondered the past, the shadow of her thoughts darkening her pale face. "But now he's gone."

"Yes. He died in October. But before he died, he asked me to give you this."

Joel reached down into a soft case beside his chair and laid a large manila envelope beside her coffee cup. Someone had written her name across the front with a black marker, in bold slanted letters. It said *Julia Keegan.*

She reached for it, but halfway across the table her arm froze in mid-air. It felt like she'd hit a brick wall. Pushing her chair back suddenly, she stood up and looked at Joel, wishing she could explain, hoping she wouldn't cry and that he wouldn't think she was a complete idiot.

"I just can't, Joel." She shook her head back and forth. "I'm sorry." And then she fled—or more accurately, hobbled—as fast as her crutches could take her, away from Joel, from Keegan's letter, and from emotions she could not control and did not understand.

She did not get very far.

"Hey, hey, hey, what happened, honey?" It was Kelly. She and Dave had camped out in the hotel foyer, like anxious parents waiting for a daughter after a first date. Filled with several small groupings of arm chairs and low lighting, the foyer was the perfect place to talk. Julia gratefully sank into an empty chair beside them.

"No, way. You two first. What happened to you earlier tonight?"

Kelly and Dave exchanged a look and a nod. Kelly took a deep breath before she spoke.

"We can't have children of our own." Her eyes brimmed with tears. "We'd been waiting for some final test results to get back to us that we'd taken a few months ago on our last leave. When we got home from the museum, Dave checked our e-mail, and it was there. Conclusive. It was our last hope."

"What? No! You guys, I can't believe it." And she didn't. Dave and Kelly were the perfect parents. They were made for family. They practically had *Ma* and *Pa* tattooed to their foreheads. Julia reached out and gripped Kelly's hand. "I'm so sorry." What could God—if there even was a God, like these two believed—possibly be thinking to let this happen to such a wonderful couple? Her mind struggled to accept, could not accept, and searched the alternatives. "Adoption?" She said it as she thought it, but instantly wished she hadn't as Kelly's and Dave's faces filled with anguish. Blurting things out before she thought how people might be affected was a weakness that she had struggled with all her life. And one of the reasons why she preferred to communicate with written words. Written words could be revised and edited. Words falling out of your mouth just vanished into the air, unretractable.

"I'm so sorry. That was completely insensitive."

"No, it's alright, Julia," Dave quickly said. "That's pretty much where our conversation was when you saw us earlier tonight. We spent a lot of time with Sam and Mary at camp. Really bonded with them, you know. If we could adopt them, we would in a heartbeat.

"As far as adoption itself, well, we still have a lot to learn about and to talk over before we make any decisions. Right now, I think we just need to adjust to the fact that we can't have our own children." Dave's voice was tired. His arm rested on his wife's knee, his shoulder leaned into her. Her fingers were woven together with his.

They were all silent for a moment.

"And dinner?" Kelly asked finally, a little smile of hope hovering across her face.

"Talk about a dose of perspective. You guys have just put my life in its place." She couldn't remember what had upset her so much earlier.

"So? Come on Julia, we're starving for some romantic relief here. Delivery, please," Kelly begged.

"Right." Julia looked into the tired eyes of her friends and made a decision. She would embellish. "We were completely swept away with one another. He wined and dined me, and quite honestly, I found myself wanting to swim away in his eyes." Julia paused, not sure if that was quite the right way to have worded it, but encouraged by Dave and Kelly's expressions, she carried on. "It was love at first—or rather second—sight but then I ruined it. When the moment came and he asked me if I would marry him and keep his kitchen clean forever and ever, I lost it. Overcome with emotion, I had to run away. How could I speak with such passion in my breast? What he couldn't and must never know is that I would gladly lick his shoes clean every day if I could only be his housewife—mend his socks and iron his shirts— but now it's too late," Julia moaned, thumping her chest with her hand dramatically. Dave was grinning broadly at her humor, but Kelly actually giggled.

"Seriously," Julia admitted, "the man is quite intriguing . . . but then he started to talk about my father and tried to give me that letter and, I don't know—I want to scream and shout and yell at my father first. Not read a letter. I mean, one day, I guess I'll have to. But for now, I need time to get used to the idea of him. Anyway, suddenly I couldn't talk. So I bolted." Kelly and Dave were both shaking their heads. *Good listeners*, Julia thought, so caught up in analyzing her own feelings that she missed their cues. "I mean, Joel makes me feel so alive, like a blast of fresh air, or cold water—but in a good way—then this thing with my father comes at me sideways, and it's cold water, too, but not in a good way, you know?"

Kelly's mouth had fallen open. Julia recognized the look. It was often on the faces of people to whom she expressed herself freely. She was not prepared to hear Joel's voice from just over her shoulder.

"I want you to know that I would never ask you to lick my shoes clean." Julia froze as her words played back to her in baritone. "Ironed shirts are very nice, but you would never have to mend my socks. I do, however, require a clean kitchen, but I don't mind helping out sometimes. So, as they say, all is not lost."

Julia went very cold, then quite warm all the way to the roots of her hair. Squinting her eyes up, she turned toward this man whom she had just confessed—what feelings had she confessed for him?—and who, at that moment, had dropped to one knee beside her chair. If she hadn't liked him enough before, she liked him enormously for what he did then. Taking her hand in his, he kissed the back of it lightly, smiling sweetly the whole while.

"Good night, sweet Julia. May your dreams be filled with clean dishes and sparkling faucets, but not too much cold water." With a flourish of a cap that wasn't there, he stood up, turned on one heel, winked broadly at her, then walked away.

"Smooth. I told you he was smooth." Dave was thoroughly enjoying the moment.

Kelly's eyes had grown enormous, and tears of laughter streamed down her cheeks.

"I'd marry him," she giggled. "Sorry, honey, but he's way cuter than you are."

"Excuse us, Juliet—oops! I mean Julia, I must take my own sweet woman to our room. It's very late, and she doesn't know what she's saying anymore."

But Julia barely heard him or noticed them leaving as she held her forehead in her hands and moaned softly to herself, wishing that she had no tongue.

# FOURTEEN

~

Again I saw all the oppressions that are done under
the sun. And behold, the tears of the oppressed, . . .
and there was no one to comfort them. And I thought
the dead who are already dead more fortunate than
the living who are still alive. But better than both
is he who has not yet been and has not seen the evil
deeds that are done under the sun.

ECCLESIASTES 4:1–3

SITTING IN THE HOTEL'S BEAUTY SALON the next day, Julia felt slightly
better. Dave and Kelly had gone away, with a million unnecessary
apologies, for a day by themselves, so she had decided to get a much
needed hair trim. The young and exotic stylist snipped and snapped
expertly while Julia contemplated her face in the mirror and played
with the idea of sticking her tongue out as far as she could. The scissors might do her a huge favor and save her from a lot of trouble. Her
ability to say the wrong thing at the wrong time was becoming increasingly annoying. Her Arabic and the stylist's English weren't compatible, so Julia's sighs and the scissors carried on the only conversation

until the opening of the door set off a muted tone indicating a new customer.

A woman in full Muslim dress entered. She was greeted instantly by another hairdresser, who emerged silently from a room somewhere at the back of the salon and assisted the new customer with the removing of her burqa in the privacy of what Julia divined must be a "women's only" shop. Underneath the burqa was a woman dressed to kill, beautiful in a pale skin, too-much-black-eyeliner kind of way, that emphasized unusual blue eyes. She wore her hair in long curly tresses that had been dyed a warm chestnut shade with lots of highlights. Julia wondered briefly what she could possibly be getting done to herself when she looked so . . . finished, already.

"Adila, it is always good to see you, come and sit down." The patroness embraced her new customer, something, Julia observed, that she herself had not merited when she came in that day. Much older than Julia's stylist, this one had had black hair once, but now it was streaked heavily with white and pulled back into a tight bun.

Adila obediently sat, crossing her legs as she did, her short white skirt exposing what was an indecent amount of leg even in North America. The other woman either didn't notice or didn't care.

"What shall we do for you today, darling?"

Julia wondered if the other woman felt like a pet, the way her hair and hands were being stroked.

"I don't know, Sufia. I'm sick of it all. Let's cut it really short, shall we?" The woman spoke clearly, with the Queen's crisp English. Probably educated in Cambridge or Oxford, Julia decided, watching Adila wave her hand back and forth rapidly in front of her face, her blood red, manicured nails acting like exclamation marks.

"You know Ahmad will not allow me to do that, Adila." Sufia shook her index finger back and forth, her brow knitted in worry mixed with something else. *Maybe pity*, Julia thought. *Or disapproval.*

"I hate him," Adila spat out, with complete sincerity. "He does not treat me like a wife; he treats me like a . . . possession, as if I am one of his fancy cars or a silk shirt. I am not a person to him. Just something to be used and to use up. I hate it, Sufia."

Julia's trim wasn't done, but she felt awkward, as if she should get up and leave a very personal situation that she had accidentally stumbled into, except that she was trapped in the chair, forced to eavesdrop as the scissors continued to cut away.

"He's cruel. He hurts me and then tells me to shut up when I cry. I can't bear it any longer. I think I want to end my life." Sufia had started to brush out the long hair, using slow, gentle strokes. Caresses.

"Adila, you know that he treats you well. He's just a man and doesn't understand your feelings. Men and women never truly understand each other; you know that. Weren't you just telling us about your trip to Paris and all the lovely shops? And what about little Rashid?"

"Yes. There is Rashid. But for how long? He is four years old. His father will completely dominate his life in another year or two. What little pocket of affection he has for me will suffocate in the world of men he will lose himself in."

"Now, now. You don't know what will be. Maybe there will be changes, hmmm? Until then, we must accept. Accept our lives as the will of Allah."

"Sufia, I am so tired. Too tired."

Julia watched in fascination as Adila's face slowly began to relax, losing some of the hard lines in response to the soothing brushstrokes. She couldn't be that much older than Julia, probably in her mid-thirties somewhere.

Adila suddenly opened her eyes and met Julia's stare.

"Are you married?"

"No." Julia, surprised at suddenly losing her spectator status in this conversation, had nothing meaningful to add.

"Don't ever marry. Men are pigs. They will use you, then discard you after they find a prettier toy. But the worst thing, the worst thing is that they never truly care about anyone but themselves. The only people who care about me are Sufia and my sister, Jasmine."

Even *Women Informed*, not known for its love for the opposite sex, but still, the main source of information for relational tips in Julia's life, didn't print such scathing advice. Until now, she had not considered what life might be like for Muslim women. Muslim women who did *not* live in IDP camps apparently still faced abuse from wealthy, "civilized," Muslim men.

This was probably not a good time, Julia decided, to mention the nice dinner date that she had enjoyed last night with one such "pig." Maybe North American men were different somehow. Intrinsically rooted in family values and apple pie and all that.

"What is your name?" Adila asked.

"Julia. Julia Douglas."

"Where do you come from, Julia Douglas?"

"Canada. Vancouver, British Columbia." Then she added, feeling the need to explain, "I'm in Khartoum, visiting friends."

"Of course you are." Adila's expression had changed. Where there had been absolutely no personal interest or more concern than one would show to a fly or an inanimate object, she now looked at Julia with sharp intelligence. With an idea.

"You don't know how nice it is for me to talk to a foreign woman. Why don't you come and visit me this afternoon? I will serve you proper tea, and we can get to know one another. I know you think I must be a terrible person. But I'm not. Or I didn't used to be. I'm just a bit bored. You would be good medicine, I think. You can tell me about life in Canada and cheer me up."

Sufia's brushing had paused during this conversation, then continued, not as gently as before, her lips pursed and eyes lowered.

The reporter in Julia woke up. An opportunity to see the inside of what was probably a harem in Khartoum? Absolutely.

"I'd love to. When should I come?"

"No, Sufia, I don't want that." This to a hot curling iron being proffered. "Just a shampoo and massage today." Turning back to Julia, she added, "Let's say three, shall we?"

Julia's stylist had finished. The cape was removed from around her neck, and her crutches were brought for her.

"Yes, I would enjoy that, I think." She turned to leave, then back again. "I don't know your address."

"Tell the taxi driver to take you to the house of Ahmad Barak. He'll know."

⚜

The house of Ahmad Barak was nothing less than a mansion concealed from outside eyes by high walls. The taxi entered the estate through an electric gate that was opened for them by a guard who first demanded to know their names. Waving them through, they continued down the driveway. Julia's vision was sated with a tropical Eden. Palm trees and flowering shrubs she did not recognize shaded both sides of the lane that led them around a rotunda dominated by a huge water fountain. The taxi stopped at the front entrance. Overwhelmed by the opulence that surrounded her, Julia almost forgot to ask the taxi to wait. When she turned to open her door, she found that a man in full "Arab sheik" dress had already opened it for her. *The Khartoum equivalent for Jeeves*, Julia thought, amused. Which he evidently was, she decided, as he beckoned her to follow. Passing through arched mahogany doors, they entered yet another beautiful garden with a second fountain in the center of it. Peacocks were displaying themselves in the sun while several parrots scolded loudly from their tall perches.

The garden grew inside a square-shaped courtyard surrounded on four sides by a two-storied apartment complex. Patios ran along the front of the rooms on the main floor and a covered balcony, supported by arches, repeated the pattern on the second floor. Glimmering like burnished gold in the afternoon light, the columns and arches lent beauty and grace with their height and decorative facings.

Julia followed the "butler" up a curved staircase with wrought-iron balustrades onto the right-wing balcony above, then down a hall until he stopped outside the fifth door—another arched mahogany doorway, but on a smaller scale than the ones at the main entrance. He knocked and waited, his features completely unreadable. When Adila opened the door, he bowed his head curtly, then left.

Adila took Julia's arm and pulled her into a room tastefully appointed in luxurious Persian rugs and leather furniture. The room was rich with warm colors: rugs interwoven with threads of scarlet, gold, and deep blue, and heavy gold brocade curtains tied back to let the light in. Adila sat down on the burgundy leather couch, Italian made—Julia was sure—and indicated for her to sit on the chair across from her.

"Adila," Julia gasped, "this place is fantastic. I feel like I'm in a Persian palace or something."

"I'm glad you came. You can't imagine how boring my life is." Adila poured steaming tea into dainty tea cups decorated with emerald green clovers. She had changed from her previous outfit into American designer jeans and a T-shirt that said OXFORD, answering Julia's earlier question.

"And you hope to alleviate this boredom by making your husband angry for inviting me here?"

Adila looked intently at Julia for a moment, apparently reassessing her, before handing her the tea cup.

"Yes. That is exactly what I want to do. You don't mind?"

"I don't think I really understand, Adila. It's so beautiful here; your home is like a palace. Women in Canada would kill to live in a place like this. And shopping trips to Paris? For most women in my country, that could never happen in their entire lifetimes. Can't you just enjoy what you have? The way I see it, there are no perfect marriages anywhere, anyway, so maybe what you have isn't that bad, after all." Julia sipped. Delicious. She loved Earl Grey. The cookies on the coffee table looked like Scottish shortbread. She sampled one just to make sure.

"We have everything we want except freedom to *really* live," Adila said. "I had two girlfriends I went to high school with. One was murdered by her husband for getting involved with another man. The other one committed suicide last spring after her husband brought his fourth wife into his household. We're supposed to find all our happiness in pleasing husbands who are distracted continually by their younger wives. If that fails—and it does—we are told to find fulfillment in our children, who have no affection for their mothers who can give them nothing, but who adore their fathers who spoil them rotten."

Julia knew that Adila was not making it up. She had watched *Oprah*, had heard the accounts of women who had run from the confines of their Muslim culture only to take on anonymous identities in America in hope of escaping severe retribution and even death at the hands of male family members. She knew that these things happened to Muslim women. She had just never imagined them being women with so much luxury.

She carefully brushed the crumbs from her shirt and took another sip or two of tea, trying to collect her thoughts into rational questions.

"How many wives does your husband have, Adila?"

"I am his second wife; he has eight altogether."

Julia tried not to register her shock. "But you're so young!"

"And younger still are six other wives."

"How many children does Ahmad have?"

"Thirteen so far, but only one from me, hence the great degree to which I must go to receive any attention from him. You begin to understand."

"Oh, Adila. I'm sorry. I had no idea. Goodness, what does your husband do to afford such a household and on such a scale as this?"

"He works for the government. He is the minister of finance to President Omar al-Bashir."

Julia nodded twice, taking this in. The minister of finance knew everything. He knew how many billions of dollars Sudan was getting from its vast oil resources, oil resources from land that two million southern Sudanese had been forced from or killed. Julia remembered reading the background of southern Sudan and the civil war that had raged there. Adila's husband knew how much of Khartoum's money was funding terrorist regimes in Sudan and other countries and who Sudan's private endorsers and supporters were. Most sinister of all, this man would know how much money was being used to support the Janjaweed with the funds and resources they needed to continue their genocide on Darfur. This man controlled the piggybank.

"But you must tell me what you do, Julia, and all about your life. In Canada and the United States, women seem so independent and powerful. What is that like?"

Julia had prepared herself for this moment and gave a half truth. "I'm a writer."

"Are you a novelist?"

"Well, I've been working on a novel"—that part was true—"but mostly I write short stories." Also, technically true.

"What degree did you get from Oxford, Adila?"

"I majored in history with a minor in English; I hoped to be a teacher one day, but my husband would never allow one of his wives to take a job or study at a university. My degree is wasted and I must never mention it to anyone because it would be an embarrassment to my husband. I envy you your writing career, Julia, with so many stories in the world to tell; your job is the perfect vehicle to explore and discover with."

As she spoke a look of such yearning washed over her that Julia's heart was filled with sympathy.

"You know you could even write about me. Although, I guess no one really wants to read a story with a sad ending."

"Why does it have to be a sad ending, Adila? You're young. There are so many things you could still do with your life."

"No! That's what I've been trying to tell you, Julia. My life is over. I can do anything as long as it doesn't take away from my primary job of being an ornament in Ahmad's household. An ornament, I might add, that must not cause trouble or annoyance of any kind. If it does, it will be disciplined. If it does not reform, it will be discarded.

"My problem, Julia, is that I have to choose precisely how to be discarded, for an ornament I cannot and I will not be."

"What are you saying, Adila? Are you talking about taking your life?" Julia's mind was racing, searching for words of hope or comfort that might encourage this woman. "Surely you must have loved Ahmad and he you at one time. Isn't there any way that you could rekindle that love? Perhaps gain his friendship instead of provoking his animosity?"

"Do you think that I haven't tried that?" Adila's voice rose sharply. "I loved him so much once. He was the sun and the moon to me. I was sick with love for him. I would spend my whole day trying to find the perfect outfit and the perfect hairstyle that would make him think I was the most beautiful woman he had ever known. I spent hours studying politics and current events so that I could talk intelligently with him about his job. If I didn't see him during a day, I felt like I wasn't breathing properly.

"So many lonely nights I would cry myself to sleep, agonizing over which wife he was with and imagining delightful ways to kill her. I have exhausted myself over the last six years trying to be the most desirable wife. I have given my soul for this. Every moral and immoral thing he has asked of me, I have done for him. But it's left me so cold, Julia."

Adila's gaze bored into Julia, and the strange, clear light of her eyes revealed depths of pain that left Julia feeling dizzy and sick. "Now he rarely seeks me out anymore—and it's certainly not for friendship when he does. The worst thing is I'm all alone with this burning hatred inside for him and for myself. I hate him for crushing the light of goodness and hope that I once possessed.

"I'm lost in this place, Julia. I have no desire to stay any longer."

Adila spoke with almost no emotion. No trace of tears. Julia supposed there were none left.

"Adila, I want you to take my e-mail address." She was writing it on a piece of scrap paper she had pulled from her purse. "Surely there must be some way that you can get away from here. I have heard of women who have been successful in leaving and finding sanctuary in other countries. Couldn't you do the same?"

"I would like to e-mail you. It feels good to talk to someone who will really listen to me. But there is no way I could ever escape. Ahmad is the minister of finance. He has power. He would find me and kill me wherever I went. No. I have thought it through. I know what will happen." The richly hued room, warmed by the golden rays of the afternoon sun, was suddenly cast into shadow. Someone had passed by outside on the balcony, blocking the sunlight. Julia shivered involuntarily. Adila's tea cup and saucer clattered as she set it down and reached to take the e-mail address, which she stuffed into her jean pocket.

The door opened unceremoniously, and Julia knew, without being told, that the man who entered was Ahmad. He was of medium height, maybe only a few inches taller than Adila, but his body was lithe with well-defined muscle under a silk shirt that he wore untucked over his jeans. The man moved like a panther. Quietly and smoothly, he strode across the room to stand beside his wife, who was visibly trembling in his presence.

"You bring an infidel woman into my home to pollute it? What are you thinking?" His sharp slap made Julia jump.

His eyes never left his wife's face, now burning red on one side, as his hand flicked impatiently at her guest. "Get out!" he ordered Julia.

Adila was obviously terrified, despite her calm words of self-destruction. But Julia remained frozen in her chair. Face to face with brutality, she had not expected it to be beautiful. This wasn't the face of a monster, but a finely sculptured Greek god.

"Julia, please leave me now," Adila said. Her long, beautiful hair had fallen around her shoulders and half hid her face, but Julia still saw the tears drop.

She got up and walked away as if in a nightmare where one does the worst possible thing and knows it the whole time. She turned to shut the door, looking back one last time. Adila still stood beside her chair, her right hand tucked in her jean pocket, the one where she had put Julia's e-mail address. Glancing up, she saw Julia, locked gazes with her, then looked down at her pocket and smiled, her lips barely lifting. It was enough. Julia knew that if at all possible, she would hear from Adila again.

Fear rose up in her throat and choked her as she retraced her steps, the crutches slowing her to a quick hobble when every instinct was telling her to run down the staircase and past the peacocks and the water fountain, through the doors, and back into the security of a Khartoum taxi.

"The Grand Hotel, please." Her voice shook, but not as much as her hands did.

When she knocked on Dave and Kelly's door and it opened, she was so relieved to see them, her knees immediately turned to Jell-O. Dave, always quick to assess a situation, moved a chair quickly beside her, which she collapsed onto.

She told them what had happened and how she had left Adila. She told them who her husband was. They exchanged worried glances with each other, but Julia pressed on.

"We need to do something for her. We need to get some police there or something."

"In this country, the police are on Ahmad's side, not Adila's, Julia," Dave reasoned.

"But surely as a prominent wife in society there must be some protection for her?" Julia insisted.

"Her protection is only in her husband. Her protection and her discipline are both up to him to provide. Thus is it written in the Qur'an, and therefore she is legally at her husband's mercy, or in this case, lack of it."

"But—"

"Julia," Kelly interrupted, "think for a minute. This is the same country that pays its military to kill entire villages, maiming and killing women and children. Those orders come from the government here in Khartoum. Just because there's a cloak of wealth over Adila doesn't mean she gets diplomatic immunity. She is a Muslim wife in a Shiite government. The law is on the side of her husband. She has no protection. But"—Kelly paused and moved beside Julia's chair, taking one of her hands in her own and one of Dave's in the other—"we can do something to help her."

And so Dave and Kelly prayed. They prayed for protection over Adila and power from God to overcome the evil there. They prayed for some things that Julia didn't quite understand, but when they stopped praying, she realized so had her shaking.

It was only later on, as she was finally falling asleep, that Julia remembered to think about Joel and wonder what he had done that day. Dave and Kelly wanted to head back to the IDP camp as quickly as possible, and Julia wondered if she was likely to even see him again. After the events of her day, she felt much less concerned about that possibility than she had twenty-four hours earlier.

# FIFTEEN

❧

Sudan is indeed where all the world's worst atrocities
come together, like a perfect storm of horrors.
War, slavery, genocide—you name it. But particularly
genocide. Beyond the Sudanese government and
other perpetrators of mass atrocities,
however, the "bad guys" in this story are apathy,
ignorance, indifference, and inertia. It is up to
us to overcome them.

JOHN PRENDERGAST, *NOT ON OUR WATCH*

JULIA'S HEAD BOUNCED AND NODDED, finally jolting her awake. Dave
was driving the Land Cruiser, with its large, red crescent—the Red
Cross' alternate symbol in Muslim countries—emblazoned on the
door and hood, over an almost impassable, pot-holed excuse-for-a-
road. They had flown into Nyala last night, then decided to take
a quick survey of a refugee camp just across the border in Chad.
They had underestimated the damage to the road from the floods.
They had also underestimated the amount of repair that hadn't been
done. They left the hotel in Nyala, with its cold showers and hard,

thin mattresses, at sunrise, hoping to make it back to Zalingei before dark.

The sun blazed from high overhead, reminding Julia of her parched throat. Drinking from a warm water bottle wouldn't be so bad, she thought, if she'd never tasted ice-cold Coke.

Sometimes she wondered how she had gotten here. Canada seemed like another lifetime. And Khartoum? Well, that wasn't quite another lifetime, but it was fading fast. She was surprised to realize that it had been only two days since she'd said goodbye to Joel. He hadn't asked for her phone number. She really hadn't expected him to, especially after how silly she must have sounded to him in the hotel foyer that night, but secretly she was disappointed. Joel was the perennial playboy, charming, but only interested in enjoying the moment. He'd kissed her goodbye lightly on the cheek as casually as some men shake hands. It shouldn't be too hard to forget Joel Maartens, she told herself. Unfortunately, she could still feel the tingle of his lips against her face. She gritted her mind against that track. She was not a kid in high school, and she would not behave like one.

Her experience with Adila had left her shaken. She had checked her e-mail every day since then, but had not received anything from the Muslim woman. It was hard not knowing if Adila was all right or not. Julia wondered if Ahmad had beaten her . . . or worse. Her vivid imagination was not her friend on this matter, and she spent her nights tossing and turning. Remembering the peace that she had had when Dave and Kelly had prayed with her over the situation, she tried the same thing on her own—not with as much effect—but better than nothing.

"OK back there?" Kelly yelled over the whine of the engine.

"I'd like a cold drink, air-conditioning, and paved roads, but other than that, everything's grand."

"Right, then." Kelly turned to Dave. "She says she could go another five hours."

Julia stuck out her tongue, making sure they both saw her from the rearview mirror.

She was actually glad to make the trip to Chad, having heard reports about the terrible conditions there, reports that said that more than two hundred thousand refugees had fled into Chad, with hundreds more pouring into the country every day. The refugee camps were overflowing.

Dave and Kelly had prepared her for what they might see at the border crossing. Trucks from the refugee camps came to the border, where women and children would pile in. Fathers and brothers would surround the trucks and run alongside as far as they could, arms outstretched, reaching for one last touch.

Every camp could take only so many refugees. Every truck could hold only a limited number of people. But for every refugee who made it across the border into Chad there were ten more waiting to get in. Sometimes the refugees at the borders waited for days before another truck came by. So the men would load wailing women and children onto the trucks, in hopes of a safer existence for them, and in the process, separating themselves for months, if not forever, from their families. The probability of reuniting with loved ones in the chaos of paperwork and the scores of camps that existed, when—and if—the men themselves found refuge was difficult, if not impossible.

They drove on, passing a continuous stream of Darfurians on the road. Taking just the rags on their back and a plastic gasoline jug—if they were lucky enough to own one—to carry water with, these refugees were headed for the same place: a place where they could be safe, a place to find some food, a place to stop running.

"I'm going to pull over up there by that grove of trees. I need to get out for a bit," Dave yelled.

Julia could see a group of skinny trees up ahead. Grove was too generous a word.

They pulled up and climbed out of the vehicle, stiff legs and backs creaking and complaining. Julia stretched as unobtrusively as possible, seeing dark eyes watching her with curiosity. They looked like a family, but without any males. Just a group of women and children, sitting and resting in the sparse shade. Kelly went to talk with them. Dave had gone a short distance away, looking for some privacy.

Sitting back on her haunches, African style, in the shade of the Land Cruiser, Julia took out her camera and changed the lens, hoping to get some shots. The outer sheet-like garments the women wore were multicolored, bold prints, providing a cheery contrast to the bleak desert landscape around them. Julia caught Kelly's eye and lifted her camera slightly toward the group. Kelly turned and said something to the women. Immediately giggles and cackling issued forth from the younger females of the group. Women were the same everywhere, Julia thought; the idea of getting their picture taken was always met with, "Looking like this? But I'm a mess!"

Kelly turned, a grin lighting her face, beckoning Julia to come.

Julia started shooting, marveling at the beauty of these people. Striking, noble features, high cheekbones, full lips, skin like midnight. The camera loved them. And they loved the camera, laughing with delight when Julia turned it around for them to see the picture displayed on the back. Suddenly, the walls between them were down, the children chattering at her a mile a minute. A young girl, about nine, obviously a clown, crossed her eyes and pulled her mouth at the corners with her index fingers, making Julia laugh. Kids were so fresh. So innocent. Yet she knew that these particular children had in all likelihood witnessed their fathers and uncles being murdered, their mothers and sisters being beaten and worse, and their homes being torched to the ground.

Two of the smaller children were noticeably paler of skin than the others. The eyes of one of them, a little girl about five years old, perhaps,

were light brown, almost tawny. The smile on her face was huge, showing a gap where her front teeth were missing.

"You can't take them home, Julia," Dave commented, chuckling at
the antics the kids were performing in order to see themselves on the
camera's screen.

Julia sighed. It was sad, but true. The thought of how she would
walk away from everything here and pick up like normal once back in
Canada was beginning to trouble her.

Kelly distributed packets of chips and fruit snacks from the supplies in the Land Cruiser amidst shrieks of delight and thank-yous, one
woman putting her hands together prayer style and bowing to them.

With a buck and a roar, they set off again, heading due east. They
had stopped for only twenty minutes or so, but it humbled and sobered
Julia to think that what they had given, casually and easily, meant so
much to someone else.

"Those people were refugees from Touloum Camp in Chad," Kelly
informed them once they were back on the road. "They said there are
over fifteen thousand people there, but some of them are coming back
to Darfur now."

"But I thought—"

Kelly didn't let Julia finish. "There's been a coup in Chad. Those
women think the Janjaweed are behind it. Now even some of those
camps are under attack. The violence is everywhere."

Dave geared down, pulled the Land Cruiser to the side of the road,
cut the engine, and looked at his wife.

"They've fled from Chad to Darfur because they think Darfur is
safer?" he asked incredulously.

"Nowhere to run; nowhere to hide," Julia whispered to herself.

"I know; it's terrible." Kelly shook her head sadly. "Those women and
children were separated from their husbands on the way into Chad;
the men sent their families ahead, due to the limit on refugees they're

allowing through. They have no way of finding them now, no villages to go home to, just another overcrowded IDP camp."

"I think we ought to reconsider the wisdom of going into Chad," Dave said.

"Me, too. Besides which, we have the information we were looking for," Kelly replied. "Chad needs aid workers as much, or possibly more, than we do."

"Right, then. We're turning back."

"Out of the fire, into the pot," Julia encouraged.

But her friends didn't laugh.

They drove without conversation, making only one stop again in Nyala at a gas station to empty their bladders and fill the Land Cruiser's tank. Julia noticed the equivalent to an Internet café (one solitary computer of some ancient pedigree) on her way to the bathroom, in the back of the tiny store. After using the grimy and primitive facilities very carefully, trying to touch as little as possible, she headed to the front counter, where Kelly waited. Wordlessly, Kelly handed Julia antibacterial hand disinfectant.

"Yes, please!" she said, rubbing the stuff onto her hands and fingers. "I'd like to use the Internet access here, Kelly. It shouldn't take long— maybe ten minutes or so."

"No problem. I'll be waiting outside."

The proprietor of the store spoke English well. He told Julia a little defensively that of course the computer was hooked up to the Internet, then charged her too many dinar for fifteen minutes online, and, after a bit of persuading, threw in three cold Cokes.

The computer was slow. Finally it found its server. Touching the dirty keys gingerly, Julia went to an English search engine and checked her online mail. An e-mail from Adila. She was fine, just sorry Julia had been forced to leave on such an unpleasant note and hoped they could have a visit again—somewhere else—sometime. Julia replied in the affirmative, then dealt with a couple of questions from Tabi about the article she had written after the interview with Nassir. Done. And so was her Coke. Glad to have gotten the articles sent, and even more thankful for the drink, Julia left the store, oblivious to the dark eyes that watched her from the back of the room.

Back in the Land Cruiser, she smiled at her friends and handed them their drinks.

"Good thinking!" Dave commended her. He almost drained the contents in one gulp.

"Isn't that Nassir An-Nur?" Kelly was squinting hard at a figure on the opposite side of the road, deep in conversation with another man.

Julia drew a quick breath. It was indeed Nassir. Suddenly, she yearned for a burqa. She knew he had never seen her before, but it didn't help her feeling of exposure.

"If it is, he's probably with them," Dave observed with a frown, drawing their attention to a large transport truck parked a short way off.

Julia could see men sitting inside the truck. They carried a full arsenal, obviously prepared for action. She shuddered, knowing what she knew. The people they would be setting out to murder and destroy would be completely unprepared. Completely unarmed.

"Don't look at them," Dave cautioned, his voice sounding uncharacteristically harsh, and his hand, Julia noticed, shaking slightly as he turned on the ignition.

"Turn your faces away," he ordered, pulling out of the gas station and maneuvering the Land Cruiser back onto the main road. "We don't want any attention."

"Aren't you being just a little overly cautious?" Julia asked, noticing that Nassir had finished his conversation and was now watching them from across the road. "We're obviously relief workers." After all, they were in a Red Crescent vehicle. Surely they had asylum from these men, barbarians that they were.

"I don't think so, Julia." Dave's voice was emphatic; his eyes looked straight ahead. "Tell her, Kelly."

"Tell me what?"

Kelly looked at her husband, sadness tingeing the corners of her mouth. Sighing heavily, she turned toward Julia and explained.

"It's gotten out of control in the last several months. NGOs are told to enter Darfur at their own risk. There have been attacks at IDP camps, and aid workers have been abducted and killed. The Janja think we're spies against the Sudanese government. We used to be able to move from town to town, show our papers, get a friendly wave, and pass on. Now we get glares and suspicious looks from the local police force. We are the bad guy. We are the Zurgha."

"I know that you face danger here and that there have been attacks in the past on aid workers and camps. Is that threat seriously escalating, then?"

"Absolutely, Julia. Our value in the eyes of the Janja is no greater than the 'rebellious' ethnic Sudanese victims of this genocide. It's not talked about. Even among the NGOs. You rarely hear the word *rape* used among us. It's too accusatory. We're the ones dealing with the trauma of the victims, bandaging up their wounds and trying to help them, yet we're afraid to vocalize the reality of the situation."

Julia shook her head. "I guess Darfur isn't the most desirable location for the average aid worker."

"No. But what happens if they kick us out? Who will be here to help if we're sent home? It's happening all the time. People who try to bring Sudan to the attention of the outside world are not granted travel visas. Sometimes they just disappear."

Kelly paused, gazing northward toward the mountain ranges looming in the distance. "We have become codependent; we stay silent, enabling the tragedy to continue, in order to offer a bit of assistance to more than two million homeless and hungry people. It's a terrible situation that we can't talk about. We have effectively been gagged."

Kelly leveled her clear blue eyes at Julia and spoke with an earnestness that sent a shiver down Julia's back. "But you can, Julia. You can use your voice for us. You'll be home in a few weeks. Say what we can't."

"I will," Julia promised, looking steadily at Kelly. "I will."

## Sixteen

꩜

A basic fact of life is that any of us may suffer and
all of us will die. . . . Another basic fact of life is that
countless human beings live in abject daily fear of evil
and the brutal people who abuse power and oppress
them. For much of the world, evil is—and always has
been—a daily fact of life.

OS GUINNESS, *UNSPEAKABLE: FACING UP TO THE CHALLENGE OF EVIL*

"WHAT'S WRONG WITH HER?" JULIA felt the hair on her arms rise at the
sound of Bekki's wails. Hassan clutched his wife tightly in his arms,
his face a blank mask. He was trying to coax her to go with him, but
she wasn't moving. Finally, he scooped her into his arms and carried
her toward the clinic, away from the prying eyes of the crowd that was
gathering.

They'd driven back into the IDP camp less than an hour ago and
immediately scavenged a few sandwiches and sodas from the mess tent.
Julia felt fatigue begin to hit in the form of a headache as she struggled to take in the scene unfolding in front of her. Turning to Kelly to
ask for clarification, she discovered Kelly had disappeared. The people

gathering around her were tense, shifting from side to side. Strange behavior. No one would meet her eyes. No one was talking. What was happening?

"Come with me, Julia." It was Peter Kuanen.

Relief filled her when she heard Peter's voice. He had earned a special place in her heart as she watched him caring for young and old alike, helping confused and traumatized people wade through the myriad complexities of life in a refugee camp, settling disputes between adults who lived in too close proximity to one another, between children who often acted out in violence toward one another as the frustrations of the emotional burdens they carried spilled over, even between women bickering over firewood and food rations. All this, Peter did with a soft word and an understanding ear, often with an arm over the shoulder of those he sought to help, cajoling people toward compassion and tolerance.

Julia and Peter walked together, past a couple of the Sudan Liberation Army trucks, toward one of the empty picnic tables. With their mounted machine guns and young boys in tattered clothing carrying AK-47s, the SLA was the official, Khartoum-sanctioned defense for the millions of homeless and terrorized Darfurians. Julia knew their numbers were pathetic, with only around seven thousand in their force, and that was on the decline with each passing day. One young boy walking beside a truck flashed her a shy smile. Julia couldn't help fearing for this kid, up against trained and organized Janjaweed.

"It is hard to understand, these problems our people face every day, yes?" Peter said.

Julia nodded.

"These boys fighting for the SLA found Bekki outside the camp an hour ago. She was unconscious and hurt badly."

"What happened?" Julia whispered the question, not sure she wanted to hear the answer.

"I am an old man. I have seen great evil under God's heaven, but this thing that has happened to Bekki . . ." Peter stopped. His large, black hand covered Julia's small white one.

"It was Janja. Bekki went out to gather wood with some other women today. Janja attacked them. The others were able to get away, but Bekki was taken. It is a horrible thing . . ." Peter's eyes had filled with tears.

Julia began to understand.

"No, not Bekki." She shook her head, tears welling up in her own eyes.

"She was found a short time ago. Unconscious. Now—" He broke off, trying to compose himself. Trying to say the words. "Now she is remembering."

"Julia." Peter reached over, touching her cheek tenderly where tears had dampened it. "You must make the world understand. This is what our women face every day. We have no defense against this evil but the light of God's truth. Please tell your world the truth."

Julia hung her head in horror. He was right. It was her job—why she had come to this place. She wanted to inform the world. Not just for information's sake, but to create change. When people knew the truth, they would help. This was the dream she had comforted herself with. But suddenly, in the midst of the reality, she knew it for what it really was: only a daydream. The women who read her magazine articles would talk about the shocking stories, would discuss it over Starbucks and sushi. Some of them might send money to a relief organization, or write a letter, or even join a protest rally. But afterwards most would probably turn on the TV or go shopping to try to forget, and the world would ease them seductively into a state of numbness. Alive to manicures, perms, designer labels, and TV shows; numb to uncomfortable truth. They might hear the horror stories that their fellow women across the world endured on a day-to-day basis, but they wouldn't let it affect their own comfort zone. Nothing would change.

Withdrawing to her tent, she threw herself down on her stomach and covered her head in a vain attempt to stop the pain. She was a professional journalist. She had borne witness to a fair amount of injustice and tragedy in her lifetime, but Darfur confounded her with the terror its multitudes lived in every day. Darfur made everything else seem like a domestic quarrel. Darfur did not have an easy solution.

Julia imagined Aunt Rose sitting in her quaint little kitchen, the epitome of domestic tranquility and all things cozy. If she could talk to her right now, Julia knew exactly what Aunt Rose would say: "Talk to God about it." Aunt Rose was always talking to God—or telling other people to. Soaking her washcloth with tepid water from her bottle, Julia wiped down her face and arms and chest in an attempt to cool her skin. Until she met Dave and Kelly, Julia had always thought prayer was just a lonely old person thing to do. Certainly not something *she* should do. Besides, even if she did talk to God, she knew He wouldn't talk back. So what was the point?

Lying perfectly still on her bed, she let the tears trickle freely down her cheeks.

Sleep overtook her sore spirit and gave her peace for twenty minutes.

"Julia." Dave's voice was low and quiet, calling from the other side of the tent wall.

"Hi, Dave."

"Kelly asked me to come and get you."

A fist of fear clenched Julia's chest, even as she reached for her notebook and camera. The tools of her work, usually filling her with a sense of satisfaction, felt like a ball and chain.

"Is it Bekki?"

"Come with me, and I'll show you."

Julia stepped back out of her tent and followed Dave as he led her past the medic tent and through the gates of the relief area. They walked down one dusty lane after another until they had gone deeper inside the camp than she had ever been before.

Finally, they stopped at a large, cleared opening where most people were squatting back on their heels. Someone was playing a drum. Women's voices were singing low and deep, their harmony haunting. One man walked to the center of the loose circle and spread his arms open wide, speaking toward the sky. Julia realized he was praying.

"What is this Dave?" she asked him. "Is it a meeting?"

Dave nodded, smiling gently at her. "It's important that you see this." They walked along the outside of the circle, found Kelly, and slipped in beside her. Reaching over, she gave Julia's shoulder a squeeze, smiling a teary smile at her and humming along with the music.

Julia was struck by the beauty of it all: the slow, rhythmic music, rising and falling; the bright colorful clothes that undulated now to the tempo of the song; the ebony faces of the men and women, upturned and full of light as the afternoon sun touched them. She could see Peter Kuanen, moving and waving his arms, spry for such an old man. He saw her watching him and smiled back. The joy that lit his smile surprised her. This was the man who had already sorrowed and suffered for so many . . . and now for Bekki. She hadn't expected smiles.

Then she saw Bekki, herself. She was leaning heavily against Hassan as they moved into the middle of the circle. Not looking up, her face was closed, devoid of all expression.

*What were they doing here?* Julia wondered. Was this some kind of shunning, like she'd witnessed in the Amish community she had reported about? She glanced over at Kelly and Dave. Surely they would never be part of such a shameful thing. It was obvious, looking at them, that they knew what was happening. Their faces were peaceful and hopeful, as if waiting for something good. Something about it reminded her of sitting beside Aunt Rose in the little church she attended with her when she got to stay there in the summers. Except everything was different.

There was no building. No pews to sit on. No announcements made. Seven women and men from around the circle stepped forward to stand with Hassan and Bekki. Placing hands on their heads and shoulders, they began to pray. Julia could not follow the prayers spoken in the local dialects, but the ones spoken in English jarred her soul.

"Father in heaven, we love You. All we are is dust. But You are God, and we love You . . . Visit us with Your peace, Father. Take the dirt of the enemy from our mouths and hearts, now. Rest Your Holy Spirit over Bekki and Hassan and open their eyes to Your loving hand. Help them to believe again in Your goodness. Strengthen them. Touch them. Heal them from the scars of bitterness and hatred. Do not let evil win today."

"Who are they?" Julia asked Kelly, wondering what kind of cult this might be.

"They are Christians, like Bekki and Hassan, who have suffered in the same way."

Soft moanings and prayers were spontaneously breaking out around the circle, quietly adding to this choir of petition. Some people were lying on the ground, overcome with the pain of life that they lived each day. Others knelt in the dust or stood.

Julia jumped when Kelly suddenly raised both her hands. Tears were rolling down Kelly's cheeks. Both of Dave's hands were covering his eyes; his head was bowed. Julia felt strangely detached. After all, she was a professional, and although she had never seen anything quite like this before, she knew what it was. Religion was simply man's way of coping with his problems and troubles. Just look at the history of the African Americans. Under the stress of slavery, some of the greatest spiritual songs the world had ever known were born. Revival camps had been common, where everyone went to get religion. It was a drug. It put a bandage on a wound. It helped people get past today and live for the hope of one day getting to heaven. Wherever that was.

Julia had studied the phenomenon of religion. It was important to her that women be empowered to effect change in this world, but she understood the chains and weights that Christianity tried to foist onto her sex—and she rejected them. There would be no submission to a man as if he were some godlike creature, no spanking and abusing children, no apron tied around her waist in a futile attempt to be the perfect image of virtue and domesticity. The world was wiser now. Women had choices. Bekki had a choice. She didn't have to come and be gazed at in the midst of her pain, like some kind of stage show. She could receive good counseling and coping strategies from the volunteer psychologist in camp. Julia would speak to her later and make sure that she was aware of this support and that it was made available to her.

Julia liked Dave and Kelly; she liked Peter and Bekki and Hassan. They were good, well-meaning people. They were just simple and locked in an old system that kept them bound from discovering the power of self-enlightenment. She shook her head sadly, gazing out on the pathetic huddle at the center of the crowd.

Hassan and Bekki knelt side by side. Half leaning against each other, Hassan's arm protectively covered Bekki's shoulders. Lifting his other arm, he motioned to speak. The crowd hushed, listening hard as he prayed, too.

"We trust in You, Jesus. Though You slay us, we trust in You. We accept what You have given us. Help us to be obedient and increase our faith . . . help us to forgive our enemies . . ." Julia swallowed hard. "Help us to want to forgive them. These ones who hurt us and kill us all day long. These men who are slaves to sin and evil deeds. Help us forgive them. Teach us Your ways. Not ours."

Bekki's head was thrown back, her arms straight up like Kelly's, and she sang. Tremulously at first, then growing stronger, more certain. The words played havoc with Julia's philosophy:

We know God is strong and He will save us
It is well, It is good.
His way is truth, His way is life.
We know God is great and He will keep us
It is well, It is good.
His way is safe, His way is sure.
We know God is love and He will heal us
He is good, He is good.
His way is peace, His way is joy.

After Uncle Seamus passed away, Julia had walked in on Aunt Rose kneeling by her little chair, her hands lifted up in the same way Bekki's were now. She had been singing, too.

But how could they? It didn't make sense, yet others in the group had begun to sing it with Bekki, the song gaining volume and voices, like a tornado, threatening to . . . She dashed tears from her face, embarrassed to have let the moment overwhelm her. Maybe she was PMSing. Whatever it was, she didn't know, but she'd had enough. Turning and moving among the crowd of people that had grown since she'd first stood in the circle, she stumbled and groped her way through, emerging finally on the outside. Gazing ahead and setting her jaw, she made her way down the bleak, dusty path.

# Seventeen

Since you believe that God is always with you,
no matter what you may be doing, why shouldn't you
stop for a while to adore Him, to praise Him,
to petition Him, to offer Him your heart,
and to thank Him?

BROTHER LAWRENCE, *THE PRACTICE OF THE PRESENCE OF GOD*

POURING THE BOILING WATER INTO the ceramic teapot just to cover the bottom, like her mother had taught her, then slowly pouring the water out, Rose pondered what she should make for supper. She had three potatoes left. She loved baked potatoes. That would do the job nicely. There was still a tomato on the windowsill, a little overripe, but it would be good with the potato. Throw on some chives and voila! She would eat like royalty.

But first a cup of tea. She waited for the water to come back to the boil and then poured once again, adding the tea ball full of aromatic black tea leaves as she poured. She carried the pot in its cozy over to the table that sat in a sunny nook, looking out into her back garden. The yard was definitely in its winter state. Leafless trees reached stark, empty branches to the sky. No flowers bloomed. Everything was lying dormant, waiting for spring. But she knew that, no matter when spring finally came, it would be a long wait.

Pouring milk into her empty cup first, adding the tea, and finally stirring in a heaping teaspoon of sugar, she watched her feathered friends. The bright red birdfeeder was busy today. Nuthatches and chickadees were cheerily feasting on their evening meal. Bird watching was a great source of enjoyment to Rose. She spent more money than she should on expensive bird feed, hoping to lure the rarest types. To date, evening grosbeaks were her favorite, their yellow and black markings such a contrast to the brown sparrows. But the flash of those yellow wings was seldom seen, compared to the faithful visitations from her plain little friends. Birds were, to an old lady, what sports were to young men: a fascinating and entertaining pastime.

Perfect tea. Perfect company. She pulled her well-worn, brown, leather-bound Bible toward her and opened it to the book of Isaiah the prophet, chapter 49. She read through the whole chapter, meditating on the ancient words, letting them speak peace into her heart. Something about the last few verses jumped out at her. Years of communing with the Creator God had taught Rose good listening skills. She read them again and waited, knowing that God had something to say. *"Can the prey be taken from the mighty, or the captives of a tyrant be rescued?"*

She didn't expect it to be Julia. The verses didn't seem to fit. Had she heard wrong? No. It was Julia. She needed to pray.

"Father, You know that Julia is not saved. She is willingly listening to the Deceiver. Open her eyes to truth. Help her. Set her free from her captivity.

"For thus says the Lord, 'Even the captives of the mighty shall be taken, and the prey of the tyrant be rescued: for I will contend with those who contend with you, and I will save your children.'

"Yes, Lord. Deliver Julia. Bring her into saving knowledge of Jesus.

Your arm is not weak that it cannot save. Reach her, and push down the enemy of her soul.

"'I will make your oppressors eat their own flesh, and they shall be drunk with their own blood as with wine. Then all flesh shall know that I am the Lord your Savior, and your Redeemer, the mighty One of Jacob.'"

The presence of the Holy Spirit filled Rose's heart and mind and body. She prayed, tears rolling down her cheeks, suddenly overcome with longing for her niece to come into the kingdom. Time slipped by, unnoticed. Prayer was nectar to her soul. Here she shared God's heart and mind, finding fellowship and communion that was better than any she had ever known in her life. Here she sometimes, like now, was moved for the lost sheep for whom the Good Shepherd had laid down His life. Here she was alive, the sweetness of heaven visiting earth, filling her with joy.

The song slipped out of her aged vocal cords without forethought. An old song, sung to her King:

> The king of love my Shepherd is
> Whose goodness faileth never
> I nothing lack if I am His
> and He is mine forever.

After that one, there was another song, then another. The tears fell again, washing her face, but this time tears of joy. There were no words to describe the delight and desire that mixed together and filled her, to be fellowshipping with her Savior but still hampered by her frail flesh.

She woke from a deep, refreshing sleep, utterly content.

The room had grown dim, the sun dipping out of the sky. Rose turned on the lamp beside her, a rosy glow filling the room with light. She got out of her chair, her old bones creaking, and carried the teapot back to the counter. After turning on the oven, she picked up a potato, scrubbed it with a well-worn scrub brush, poked holes all around it with a fork, then wrapped it in a piece of used foil. Placing it in the warm oven, she carefully shut the door, remembering to turn the timer on for an hour.

It was a good thing she did set the timer, because Ella called, upset and anxious, needing some reassurance. Charles, her husband, had had a second stroke a month ago but hadn't bounced back like he had from the first one. Ella didn't know what to do. It was getting too hard to care for him by herself, and their grown children lived in other provinces. So Ella agonized over the decision of whether she should put him in assisted-care living. Rose usually spent a half hour with her on the phone every day, listening to her friend's concerns and praying with her for God's peace and clear direction.

When the timer rang, Rose realized how hungry she was and, after a few unsuccessful attempts, said goodbye to her friend, assuring her that God did, indeed, care about each detail of their lives.

"Remember what the Bible says, Ella: not one sparrow falls to the ground apart from the will of the Father. And even the very hairs of your head are all numbered. So don't be afraid; you and Charles are worth more than many sparrows."

They prayed together, then said goodbye. Rose placed the receiver very gently on its cradle before turning to take care of her supper.

The potato was perfect. Butter melted into the mealy white flesh, causing her mouth to water. She set her plate down on her round, maple table, bowed her head formally, and asked her dear Friend to bless the meal, to protect Julia, and to strengthen Ella and Charles, and to give Ella the wisdom she needed for the days ahead. Then she raised her head, looked up at her ceiling, feeling and knowing the Person who never left her side, and said, "I love You so much."

# Eighteen

A Heaven on Earth; for blissful Paradise
Of God the Garden was, by Him in the
East of Eden planted.

JOHN MILTON, *PARADISE LOST*

*COME ON SAFARI WITH US!*

As Joel pushed through the door of a little shop advertising African adventures, a bell over his head jangled to announce his entrance.

He had found Julia Douglas more quickly than he had dared to hope, attempted to fulfill Keegan's request, and failed. Sometime when they were both back on home soil, Joel knew he would try again. Keegan's daughter had gone back to the IDP camp, but the impression she had made on him hadn't lessened a bit.

He was in Africa and had no intention of going home to Canada before he had taken in some of the sights. Joel perused his options. Red Sea and Nile River explorations—those included scuba-diving excursions. *A possibility.* An exploration of the ancient pyramids and kingdoms that Sudan proudly boasted. *No, probably boring.* The eight-day camel trek, he decided, would only leave him aching and sore. He ruled out a hunting safari after discovering that the game he had the highest chance of bagging would be gazelle, sheep, or rabbit. He could only imagine how that would go over with the guys at the office. *Look guys, I caught Thumper.* Not a chance.

But the next one had definite possibilities: "Hike and explore Jebel Marra, rising to ten thousand feet above sea level, the highest mountain in Sudan. Situated in the province of Darfur, it is home to monkeys, rabbits, kudu, and various birds. Spend four days and three nights enjoying the most beautiful area of the western Sudan, filled with lush vegetation, waterfalls, fruit trees, and more."

So, Jebel Marra in Darfur or scuba diving in the Red Sea.

Darfur. Where Julia and her friends work. *Not that I'd see them.* But hiking and exploring a mountain—that was more like it.

He bought the ticket, was given instructions as to what kind of clothing he'd need, and was told to be ready in his hotel foyer by eight the next morning.

Joel left the safari office and walked across the road to the Acropole Hotel, where Steve was staying. They had agreed to meet at the restaurant beside the hotel for lunch at one o'clock. Joel was late, but Steve didn't look like he minded, from the smile on his face and the warm handshake, with the Arabic shoulder pat he had coached Joel in.

"Hey, not bad, my friend. That wasn't bad at all." Steve sat back down at the round marble table. "I was beginning to think you weren't going to show up to wish me farewell."

"Hey, sorry about that, Steve. The taxi arrived a few minutes early, and I wandered over to that safari-trip place across the road." He reached into the bowl of *ful-sudani* on the table, crunching down on the well-toasted, salty peanuts. "You know I'd never forget to say goodbye to you, my only friend in Sudan." Joel loved peanuts; he scooped up another handful, dropping them in his mouth while explaining, "It's just"—here he had to stop and swallow—"I ended up buying one."

Steve, bemused and smiling at Joel's ability to eat like a pig and maintain a perfectly white shirt, became suddenly very serious.

"You did what?"

"I bought a safari trip—well, not a real hunting-type safari. This one is more like a hiking-camping thing." Oblivious to Steve's concern, Joel picked up the menu and stared. "What the heck is *kakaday?*" he asked.

"It's an herbal tea, Joel. But listen, where does the safari take you?"

"Nah, I don't want tea. Maybe wine. Would you have a glass of—No you wouldn't; I should know that by now." He focused intently on the menu. "Hey, do you know what any of this food is, Steve?"

"Joel, where does the safari go?"

Joel sighed, lowering his menu and looking over the top, for the first time noting Steve's worried look. "Darfur, my friend, and don't worry, I'm not going to try to find Julia. You were right about her. She needs time to work through her issues—what's the matter?"

Steve had let out a groan, his forehead dropping into his hand in exasperation.

"Joel, what are you thinking?" Then, in undertone, "Going into Darfur is like crossing a land mine. The fighting is going on all the time now, and no one knows where it will hit next."

"Hey, this place seemed very reputable. They took Visa. I'm sure they wouldn't run their trips into areas where they were putting themselves into serious danger."

"Were they Black Sudanese or Arab Sudanese? The people who sold you the ticket, what color were they?"

"Steve," Joel's tone was disapproving, "you know I don't notice things like that."

"I didn't, either, until I came to this place. But here it makes a difference to a lot of people." Steve leaned across the table and whispered, "Especially a certain group of people with machine guns, whose name I won't mention here."

This got Joel's full attention. He was quiet for a moment—reconsidering his trip, Steve hoped.

"Arab Sudanese. Definitely; so I guess I'm safe."

"You are not safe. You're a sitting duck. They will do nothing to help you if—" He broke off and mouthed the word *Janja*. "If they decide to pick on you. They know which side their bread is buttered on. You are at best an infidel and most likely a spy in the eyes of those people."

"Yeah, OK, I get it." Joel did get it. There was a definite element of risk to this trip. If he went, he could get into trouble. On the other hand . . . "But what about you, Steve? You're going back in. Why is it OK for you and not for me?"

Steve didn't answer right away. Joel's thoughts wandered back to the unintelligible menu again, and he caught tantalizing aromas of spices, onions, and meat as other people's meals were carried past him.

"It's different for me," Steve finally answered, "because I'm here under my Boss's orders, and He told me He would protect me. And"— Steve shot Joel a particularly piercing look—"even if He doesn't, I will still do the job He sent me to do."

"You're a spy?" Joel's left brow was up, doubt written all over his face.

"I'm a Christian."

# Nineteen

Whether we adore our bodies or loathe them, it is
still shame that is the master. For shame, essentially,
is the guilt and condemnation the soul naturally
experiences for having robbed its God, for claiming as
its own what is rightfully His. For the body . . .
is the Lord's. It is for Him to bear the shame of it,
and for Him to have the glory.

MIKE MASON, *THE MYSTERY OF MARRIAGE*

JULIA FOUND HASSAN AND BEKKI'S tent with difficulty. Walking through the gates of the aid compound, she had passed lines of people waiting to register or to get medical attention, and then had entered the camp proper. Following Dave's directions, she crossed into the main camp territory, sure she could find Hassan and Bekki, looking for familiar landmarks along the way. There weren't many.

Finally, feeling certain she was in the right place after wandering around and retracing her tracks twice, she stood in front of a shelter covered with a white plastic sheet. Three children sat on their haunches in descending order of size, watching her.

"Hello," she said.

"Hello, miss. Sweetie, please," they said in unison, holding their hands out and giving the standard response at the sight of an American.

Julia knew camp policy, knew that sweeties were forbidden as casual handouts to children, but it seemed like such a minor thing. She reached into the pocket of her cargo pants and felt four hard candies. Pulling three out, she carefully put one in each small, upturned hand, causing their young eyes to grow round with delight.

*So this is how the ice-cream man feels*, she thought.

She watched them peeling the wrappers off and popping the candy into their mouths, with more pleasure than she thought possible, enjoying the moment.

"Do you know Bekki or Hassan? Is this where they live?" she asked finally, pointing at the tent behind them as she asked, and immediately three young dark heads shook no, while their mouths sucked busily.

"Do you know them, Bekki or Hassan?" Two heads shook a negative, but the middle-sized child, a little boy about seven years old with a very runny nose and a ripped and dirty red T-shirt, responded. "Bekki, I know."

"You know Bekki?" Julia's question met with a nod, quick and sure.

"Could you take me to her?" She was smiling with relief. "Can you show me where she is?"

"I take you, miss." He took her hand in his own very grimy one and led the way. A fleeting thought of hand sanitizer passed through Julia's mind, but she held onto her young guide until he deposited her at the front of another plastic-sheeted shelter.

Bekki was sitting outside on a small piece of cardboard, nursing her baby. She looked up in surprise at the sight of Julia, a shy smile lighting her face.

"Julia, it is good to see you again. You look very well."

"It is good to see you, too, Bekki. I'm glad you are here because I was hoping to speak with you. Is this a good time?"

"Yes, please, it is a good time." Bekki started to get up, shifting the baby slightly in her arm. "I will get you a stool."

Julia knew from the last time she had come here that it was useless to refuse; the honor of these people was tightly woven together with hospitality.

Bekki and baby disappeared briefly, somewhere behind the tent.

Julia noticed a small group of children gathering on the other side of what, for lack of a better word, was called a road. She smiled at them and waved; several of them waved back and called hello. A few brave ones were calling for sweeties.

Bekki returned with the same hand-hewn stool Julia had used before.

"No camera or recorder today, Julia?" Bekki gestured to Julia's empty hands.

"Not this time." Julia paused, gathering her thoughts, wanting to speak, yet not sure how to begin.

"Something is troubling you?" Bekki asked.

"No, no, not that," Julia assured her, "but how are you, Bekki?"

A flash of pain flitted across the young woman's face and was gone. In its place a calm remained.

"I am truly well, my friend. Thank you for asking about me." Bekki looked down with a self-consciousness that hadn't been there three weeks before. "But I am, truly well."

Julia nodded as Bekki spoke, not wanting to directly confront what had to be some kind of denial.

"Have you been to see Dr. Morgan yet?" Julia asked.

"No, I would not go there. She tells women to kill their babies."

"She tells you to kill the babies?" Julia's disbelief came through loud and clear. This could only be some kind of superstitious lie.

Bekki was nodding her head vigorously. "It is true, Julia. Women who are hurt by Janja and are taken to Dr. Morgan are told to kill the babies."

Abortion. Bekki was talking about abortion. But that wasn't the same as killing babies . . .

"I see," Julia conceded, "but even your own women take the Janja babies out and let them die. You told me that in our interview."

"Yes, some do this thing. But not those who love the Lord Jesus Christ and follow His way." Her expression was implacable.

"But Bekki, what if . . ." Julia hesitated to say it.

"You mean what if I am pregnant from Janja?"

"Yes."

"I am not afraid. At first, yes, it was terrible. A bad dream I could not leave. But God's people have prayed over me, and His healing work has begun in my heart, Julia. It was different with Hassan. He did not know what to think at first." Sorrow from the difficulty of the decision, the difficulty of surrender, shadowed Bekki's eyes as she spoke. "It was harder for him. But he prayed to let God's will be done. Three days passed before he spoke about it again. Then one night as he prayed a blessing over the *kissra* and *ful*, as is his custom, he asked God to bless the baby that might be growing in me, as well.

"Later, when I lay in his arms, I asked him what had changed. He said if we were to have a child because of this terrible thing, we would raise it for the Creator, who alone can form a new life. He said if I am to have a child, we will trust Him to turn to good what was meant to harm us."

Neither woman spoke for a time. Bekki was seemingly lost in the memory she'd shared. And Julia, pondering the sweetness and quiet joy on the face of the African woman in front of her, longed for her Nikon, thinking she had never seen anyone so beautiful before.

From somewhere distant, voices were shouting excitedly. Young voices. Lots of them.

Julia looked at Bekki, not comprehending. Bekki, in turn, seemed puzzled, then suddenly got up, grabbed Julia by the arm, and started pulling and tugging her rapidly down the dirt street.

"What is it?" Julia finally managed to ask, trying to keep up with the fit young mother carrying her baby. "What's wrong, Bekki?"

"You gave them sweeties, didn't you, Julia? You can't do that."

"Sweeties?" The utter unexpectedness of the accusation shocked Julia to a stop. "We're running because I gave them sweeties?"

"You must stay close to me." Bekki's face was deadly serious. "Don't let me go, whatever happens. I will try to get you back to the aid station before it gets worse."

"What? Worse than what?"

But Bekki didn't need to explain. A swarm of young children came running, turning a corner just behind them, voices screaming in excitement. Julia took one look at what must have been hundreds of kids all calling for candy, turned heel, and fled, clutching tightly to the hand of her friend. They were about to be mobbed.

"Run!" The women ran hard. They were bigger but not faster than many of those who pursued them. Julia could see young boys running alongside her, almost even with her. When Bekki saw the gates, she yelled and screamed at the guard, who took one look and jumped to his feet, knocking over the little stool he sat on. As the women sprinted inside, the guard threw the gate shut and slid the bolt home. The herd of sugar-deprived boys and girls on the other side yelled and screamed in a frenzied craze.

Bekki turned to Julia, sweat beading her upper lip and brow, and said, "You can't give them candy. They swarm. This could have been very bad. There is almost no way to reason with them or escape if you are surrounded. You would have been mobbed."

"Yes," Julia panted, the humor and relief of the situation setting her off in uncontrollable giggles. "I see that"—she doubled over, holding onto her knees—"now." Seeing Bekki's frown, she fought for and gained control. For a moment.

"Bekki, I am so sorry to have put you in danger. I am ashamed to have caused this." Then glancing over at the calming riot on the other side of the gate, mirth engulfed her again.

Bekki stood looking at Julia, a frown of consternation troubling her normally smooth brow. She shook her head at the Canadian journalist. "I do not understand you. But I know what might help get rid of your giggles," she told Julia, who was still doubled over. Bekki waited for a moment until Julia could speak coherently.

"What? What can help?"

"You should go and see that Dr. Morgan person you came to tell me about today. I've heard she can fix women with many unwanted conditions."

Julia heard it. Then she understood. She looked up in surprise, only to see Bekki wink at her, silencing her giggles more effectively than any touché.

# Twenty

For with hearts like an oven they approach their
intrigue; all night their anger smolders;
in the morning it blazes like a flaming fire.

HOSEA 7:6

KELLY DIDN'T SEE THE YOUNG SLA fighter until he was standing right in front of her, staring at her as if to will her to stop. She didn't see him because she was exhausted after a busy morning. Three women had delivered babies before lunch, after laboring all night long. She had not had a wink of sleep and now was concentrating on putting one foot in front of the other. She had given herself small goals. Shower. Eat. Sleep.

But this boy was in her way. He wore a casually wrapped turban around his head, cut-offs with frayed bottoms, and an button-up shirt that used to be white. His machine gun was slung behind his back. His feet were bare.

"Hello," she said, moving to go by him. He spread his arm out blocking her way. Hazel green eyes burned with urgency into hers.

"Lady, I speak with you, please. Your man, he is Dave, yes?" the boy asked, pointing toward her chest.

"Yes, Dave is my husband," she said. *My husband whom I haven't seen in almost two days and I miss*, she thought.

"I have message for you."

"Oh." That was odd. Her brain was muddled. Why would he send a message?

"He says, you come with me, please. We go fast, yes?" The boy grabbed her elbow as if to lead her away, but she stood rooted, icy fear tickling her neck.

"Is he hurt? Is my husband all right? Should I bring medicine?"

"It is not necessary. No medicine. Just hurry."

As they spoke, he had taken her elbow again, firmly, almost roughly, and was guiding her toward a Jeep. Tired and alarmed, Kelly climbed in, concern and confusion boosting her adrenaline.

They drove as quickly as was manageable through the overcrowded camp, the smoke of the cook fires drifting past them, along with the makeshift, tarp-covered hovels that eventually disappeared as they swung up onto the main road and headed northwest, toward Nyala.

Kelly observed her young chauffeur. He looked to be a young fifteen, his bones showing under his skin, making his features seem sharp. Why would a child be fighting this war? Why would any boy risk his life daily to challenge a government-supported army to defend the innocent victims that same government was betraying? Openly betraying, with nothing more than a casual glance behind to make sure nothing moved.

As she studied him out of the corner of her eye, a look of pure hatred flashed from those unusual green eyes. It unnerved and alarmed her. This boy was so young to know such hard hatred. She watched him, studying him when he wasn't looking her way. His skin was lighter than the other young SLA soldiers she had seen in camp. He was definitely not a typical African Sudanese, unless . . .

"Where did you say Dave is?"

"Not far from this place, not far, lady." He turned and shot her a quick, easy smile. Just a little boy. She was silly to suspect anything.

She hadn't meant to sleep. But after a half hour or so of warm desert, monotonous and flat, she succumbed to her exhaustion, sleeping dreamlessly, but starting awake, with a catch in her throat and a weight on her chest when she realized that they had stopped. She slowly raised her head off the seat rest—oh, she was stiff. Her throat was parched and dry, her eyes and nose and ears thick with desert sand. Wiping herself off as best she could, she saw three men sitting under the baobab tree a short ways off. Her driver was one of them. Dave was not. Three camels tethered beside the Jeep ignored her imperiously as she marched over to the men.

"Where is Dave?" she demanded, looking directly at the boy and ignoring the others. "I thought you said he was here waiting for me."

"Yes, lady, maybe we get lost?" Turning toward the man beside him, he laughed and held out his hand to Kelly, opening his fist and displaying a wad of cash. "Now I have to go. So sorry. But my job is over."

With that, the green-eyed boy was gone.

*Heavenly Father, help me. Hide me. Defend me and protect me, I pray.*

Turning to the other two, still sitting calmly under the tree, she saw them appraise her like a camel at market. Crossing her arms, she suddenly felt self-conscious in her khaki pants and short-sleeved, cotton blouse.

"Do you have water?" she asked them. Water was, at the moment, the priority. Realizing that Dave wasn't here had actually given her a sense of relief. For some reason she was not cognizant of, someone had wanted to trick her away from the IDP camp, but for now, there was nothing she could do about it. Oddly enough, this gave her a strange sense of calm.

"Water?" she repeated.

The men glanced at one another, then up at her again, expressions blank.

"Water." This time she mimicked drinking out of a canteen.

This met with an element of success, as they both began to get up and walk toward their camels. Kelly followed them. No other options were available.

The taller of the two Arab men took a canteen of water from under the saddle flap of one of the camels. Kelly took it from him, past caring about how long it had been boiled, and glugged greedily, only to meet with extreme disapproval when she finally lowered her head. Roughly grabbing the canteen out of her hand, he screwed the cap back in place with obvious disgust and dropped it into the saddle pocket, motioning her to get on. Tilting her head and sizing up the height of the camel's back, her own five-feet, two-inch frame coming only somewhere to its middle, she shook her head. Not possible. Apparently reassessing the situation himself, the Arab looked hard at her, then made a series of clicks with his tongue. The camel immediately got down on all four knees. Kelly straddled the saddle, finding it very unstable. At least this was a one-humped camel. Was that a dromedary? She couldn't remember but ceased to care as the creature began to rise up jerkily onto its feet.

"Ohh, ohh, oh, oh!" she squealed.

And then it was over. She looked down from her precarious perch at the two Arab men who were in all likelihood Janjaweed and guilty of crimes she couldn't, and didn't want to, imagine and who, at this moment, were laughing at her.

*Not much of a life, is it guys?* she thought dryly.

Following third in line in their short caravan, she slid and jostled and bounced, asking the Lord to help her not fall off. In spite of the saddle, she decided that camels were not made for ladies. She also decided that God was sparing her from having to field any unwanted attention from these men. For this she was thankful—definitely nervous and a bit scared, but thankful. And somehow, she found, being thankful was not compatible with great terror.

Occasionally her eyes would droop in fatigue, in spite of the dis-comfort, and she would start falling, clutching at the saddle's hand-grip to stay on. It didn't help that every few minutes this particular beast turned her lovely, long-lashed, brown eyes back toward Kelly and gnashed at her with teeth that had not seen a toothbrush in a very long time.

"Well, I don't like you, either," Kelly snarled back.

When they finally clumped into town, Kelly didn't immediately rec-ognize it, one small African town seeming pretty much like all the oth-ers. It wasn't until they rode past the huge cypress tree, in the middle of the settlement, twined with bougainvillea, that she knew for sure she had been brought to Qasar.

Dave lifted the girl's frail arm tenderly; she was barely more than a skeleton.

"Hi, I'm Mr. Dave," he said gently, wondering where in this tiny frame he would be able to insert a needle to begin an IV drip. She would be dead of dehydration within twenty-four hours if she didn't get one. Dave saw it every day.

With more than four million people in Sudan dependent on inter-national aid for survival, and with half of those having been forced to flee their homes due to Janjaweed attacks, the needs were over-whelming. It was said that Janja were responsible for the murders of several hundred thousand civilians. Dave knew it was much higher. Indirectly or directly they were responsible for every person whose health was compromised from life as a refugee. The child he held in his arms now, too weak to resist as he inserted the needle, would not likely survive. Starvation would take many, and the living conditions in the overcrowded camps, often lacking sufficient water and producing

a sanitation nightmare, causing frequent bouts of malaria and chol-
era, would take many more. Finally, there would be those who died
because there just wasn't enough aid being provided. Many organizations refused to work in Sudan because of the high risk, and now,
with the Janja directly attacking IDP camps and international workers
themselves, more would leave.

Dave shook his head sadly. He had no medical hope for this little
one staring hopelessly at him. But he knew his God delighted in healing the sick. Bowing his head, he prayed over the girl, asking for a miracle, once again. Raising himself up from her mat, he turned to see
Jonathan Edwards, the camp's director. Jonathan often came down to
the clinic, and Dave wasn't surprised to see him.

"Hey, Jonathan, how are things up your way? A little better than
what you're seeing here, I hope." Dave nodded toward his patient.

"Actually, Dave, I need to talk to you. Privately." Jonathan spoke
quietly, his eyes meeting Dave's directly.

"OK, privately it will be." Dave led the way out of the clinic, pausing to wash up as he did.

"What's this all about, then?" he asked over his shoulder as he
scrubbed and sanitized with disinfectant.

"Do you know Nassir An-Nur, the general of the Janjaweed in this
area?"

Dave began to shake his head. "I don't really know him, but I know
who he is."

He told Jonathan about Julia and Kelly's visit to Qasar. An idea,
he assured him, that he had not been thrilled about at the time. He
explained how they had pretended to be reporters from the *Sudan Tribune*. Having talked Hassan into going along as the main interviewer,
they had convinced Dave that they would be practically invisible as
modern Muslim women dressed in full burqa and posing as camera-
women. Secretly, Dave admitted, he had hoped that it would distract

Kelly from the grief of having to give up Samuel and Mary to their aunt's care.

In a way, it had worked. They had ended up going into Khartoum with Julia after her foot had been so badly sprained. For Julia, Dave had thought, it had probably been a bit boring, being a journalist and used to a lot of nightlife, which in Khartoum was practically nonexistent. But for Kelly and himself, it had been like a second honeymoon. They welcomed the break from the IDP camp, and their stay at the Grand Villa, compliments of Nassir An-Nur, was icing on the cake. So yes, he actually owed Nassir An-Nur his thanks for footing the bill for the best holiday he'd had in a long time.

They had been walking while they talked, Dave following Jonathan's lead until they arrived at the picnic tables, where he was surprised to see Julia, Peter Kuanen, Hassan, and Bekki. The four stopped talking and watched Dave and Jonathan's approach. Something funny was going on here; Dave could see it on the faces of his friends. Jonathan placed a hand on his shoulder, gently pushing him down toward the bench, seating himself directly across.

"Dave," Jonathan said, clearing his throat, "we received a letter from Nassir An-Nur today."

Dave nodded, trying to think what ramifications this might have on the camp and wondering where Kelly was. It was odd that she wouldn't be part of a group discussion among these people. They were used to standing in as consultants on occasional camp issues that arose. Hassan was trusted and respected as an IDP who knew and understood the difficulties of both the relief organization and the refugees themselves. Peter had wisdom and godly discernment and had grown in status outside the walls of the relief base as much as he had inside. Dave and Kelly provided the medical expertise that was usually needed. So where was Kelly now? Likely too tired to join them after a couple of lengthy deliveries. Almost two days ago, his wife had been called to assist at the birth of one of the camp women, and a second call had come shortly on the heels of that one. Just as he opened his mouth to ask Julia if she had seen Kelly recently, Jonathan spoke again.

"Nassir has taken Kelly, Dave. He's holding her hostage."

The world tilted. Dave actually felt it tilt. He could see everyone's mouths around him moving and knew they were speaking to him, but he couldn't hear. Squeezing his eyes shut hard and shaking his head, he tried again. That was better. He could hear what they were saying, but his ears were ringing.

"Kelly!" he finally managed to call out. "No! Why? Hostage for what?"

Julia's head sagged down suddenly as if she were praying. But Dave knew she didn't pray.

"It's OK, Dave." Jonathan put his hand on Dave's fist, squeezing so tightly that the knuckles showed white. "I'm sure she's all right. We'll get her back."

"But why? Why would Nassir take Kelly? I don't understand!" Dave's words shot out like the last words of a drowning man. Desperate and too fast.

"We received a message from Qasar. It came by a kid everyone assumed was with the SLA. But now we think he must have been one of Nassir's Janja," Jonathan explained.

"I'd like to see it, please," Dave asked.

Jonathan took the letter out of his shirt pocket, handing it silently to Dave, who read it over three times before he understood:

> We have something that belongs to you.
>
> We know she is valuable to you and hope you will agree to what we ask for in exchange for her return.
>
> You are harboring a female journalist. This woman has published insults and false accusations against the Sudanese govern-

ment. When her apology to Khartoum and statement of retraction is published, your medical man's wife will be returned.

Until then,

Nassir An-Nur

When Dave looked up from the letter, he saw that every eye was on him.

"What can we do?" he asked.

Peter Kuanen had the answer.

"Now we must pray."

Julia hardly heard what was said. All she could think about was Kelly. What was happening to her? Would they hurt her? They wouldn't kill her, if they could believe what the letter said, but Janjaweed were not known as men of honor by any stretch of the imagination.

This wouldn't be happening if not for her. Julia couldn't forget how nervous Kelly had been before they went into Qasar in disguise as a reporting crew from the *Sudan Tribune*. She felt responsible for this terrible situation. Kelly did not deserve to suffer because of words that she, Julia, had written. How could this trouble fall on them when all they had wanted was to help people? And—the real question—how was she going to fix it? Because she would fix it. She must fix it. She would not rest until Kelly was home safe and sound.

# Twenty-one

What is the one passion of your life that makes
everything else look like rubbish in comparison?
Oh, that God would help me waken in you a single
passion for a single great reality that would unleash
you, and set you free from small dreams, and send
you, for the glory of Christ, into all the spheres of
secular life and to all the peoples of the earth.

John Piper, *Don't Waste Your Life*

Joel sipped a rum and Coke, watching the Nile slip from sight and
the Sahara desert spread out ahead as far as the eye could see. *So far,
so good*, he thought. No danger, no guns, no worries. Steve would be
pleased. The plane trip would take only about forty minutes before
touching down in Nyala, according to the tourist guide.

The steward conveniently reappeared just as the contents of Joel's
glass disappeared.

"Yes, please," Joel said, placing the cup in the hand that was proffered, "I'd love another one."

After an unusual delay, Joel looked up to see, not the steward, but Steve, holding his still-empty glass.

"I don't understand how you drink this stuff, Joel. Don't you know what it does to you?"

"Yeah, it gives me terrible hallucinations of missionaries on airplanes."

"Who else do you fly in planes with? Happy to see me?"

"Happier if my drink was filled," Joel said dryly as Steve took the seat beside him. "So what are you doing here?"

"Well, I got my travel papers, but then found out that there was no one to come get me. I wondered how much longer it would take to get to camp via a safari with my good friend Joel Maartens, than it would waiting for all my other travel arrangements and possible hold-ups at police-unfriendly little towns. Wanna guess at it?"

"Faster, eh?" Joel hazarded.

"By two days, eh." Steve attempted to mimic the Canadianism.

"Whoa."

"Uh huh. So. Here I am."

"But I didn't see you in the airport or getting on the plane."

"I was the late one, the guy they held the plane for."

"I remember now." Joel thought for a minute. "You held your back-pack in front of your face when you walked past me, didn't you?"

"What can I say?" Steve grinned. "I like surprises."

Joel looked at his empty glass. He would have to adjust his drinking plans, but overall, he was quite pleased to see Steve again.

Going on safari with him, he suspected, however, might be like going on a safari with Julia's great-aunt Rose. In a word, tame.

A Land Cruiser met them at the airport in Nyala, squeezing six excited safari-goers with their gear into the vehicle. After various bags were strapped onto the roof, including supplies for the trip, they were off.

Besides Joel and Steve, there were Anita and Mark, a young Australian couple whose goal it was to backpack and hike the highest peaks of Africa. So far, they had already been up Kilimanjaro and Mt. Kenya. Making their way west after this, they intended to climb the Atlas Mountains. The other two were Robert and Bill, a father and son, respectively, who were using the safari as an opportunity to visit the place where Robert had been born to British colonists, fifty-seven years before.

The Land Cruiser stayed in four-wheel drive for the entire two-hour trip. Passing through a sparse savannah, it geared down for the ascent into rocky foothills covered in patches of grass and low shrub-like trees, gradually turning greener as they climbed, until it seemed like they were in a Mediterranean-type Scotland.

"It's amazing that this lush, green mountain range springs up out of the middle of the desert," Joel commented.

"The safari guidebook says Sudan has an annual rainfall varying between four and seventy-two inches, depending on what region you're in. It rains here every day," Steve informed him.

"Every day?"

"Yup, and I thought Portland was bad."

"Yeah, well Vancouver's national flower is mold." Joel made his old joke with a wince.

"That was bad, Joel."

"Yeah, it was," he said smiling, "but if it rains that much up here, why isn't it raining now?"

"It's a tropical rain; it pours down for an hour or so, usually shortly after noon, and then suddenly it's over, the sun is shining, and you didn't have to put sprinklers out on the grass after all."

"You read that little book from the safari place? The whole thing?"

"Hey, I like books," Steve said.

The road switchbacked up, higher and higher. Joel nodded off several times, only to be repeatedly and violently jolted awake. Finally he gave up and became absorbed in the passing scenery.

Craggy and creviced, the mountain range was rich with lush vegetation growing thickly on every side of the narrow road; vines and huge broad-leaved plants reached right through the windows, occasionally slapping their faces and arms.

Veering off the main road, they jolted their way down what could only be an elephant trail, Joel figured, until they suddenly left the thick, heavy jungle behind them. Driving over a none-too-sturdy-looking wooden bridge, they crossed a small, rapidly flowing river and entered a sun-drenched clearing. Covered in green grass and sprinkled with round, thatched roof huts, it was like a little Eden.

The Land Cruiser cut left and pulled into a parking lot overlooking the flowing river.

"Wow!" Steve swung open the door and jumped out. Then again, "Wow!" as he surveyed the safari camp. Slowly, he turned in a circle, enthusiasm lighting his face.

Joel, eager to get settled and go exploring, picked his bag out of the neat pile the driver had made of their luggage and swung it over his shoulder.

An official-looking person, wearing a khaki shirt with Jebel Marra Camp emblazoned on it, announced, "Welcome to everyone. My name is Eddy. I am a Jebel Marra safari guide and have worked here for seven years."

Anita and Mark were completely ignoring Eddy while he spoke, their backs to him as they sorted through the luggage.

"Your attention for a short moment, please."

Immediately everyone turned to listen.

"We know you are tired, and we have a delicious meal ready for

you, which will be served shortly in this main building." He pointed
behind the group toward a large hall with screened walls, through
which Joel could see round tables covered with white tablecloths. The
place had obviously been a popular destination once upon a time. A
large thatched roof dominated the building—*a good place for a spider
or a snake to live*, he thought.

"But before dinner," the guide continued, "we would like to orient
you to Jebel Marra Camp."

He stood with his back to the river, pointing to the large waterfall
on his left. "This waterfall is forty-three feet high, falling into a natural pool carved out of the rock that is pleasant and good to swim in.
We do not recommend swimming in the river, however. It has a strong
current. It would not take more than a few moments to be swept away
down the face of the mountain."

Here he gestured, and everyone looked to Eddy's right, turning
slightly to see that the river did, indeed, bend farther down, turning at
the elbow due east, where the mountain obviously dropped away, leaving them a spectacular view of the valley below.

"There is a map of the camp on the sheet that I will now give you,
when I call your name. It also has the number of your cabana circled
at the top. Joel Maartens and Steve O'Hara," he began. Joel took their
directory, studying it carefully as he did so. They were in number ten,
beside the waterfall.

"You will also find many hiking trails marked out on the reverse
side. Again, we would like you to note that the trails marked in red are
restricted unless accompanied by a safari guide. Dinner is served at five."

They found their cabana—a round hut, with thatched roof, screened
walls, and canvas curtains to keep out the cold night air. Two rooms
were divided down the center, a double bed on each side. Two lounge
chairs sat invitingly on a small veranda built on the riverside. A prime
sunset-gazing location.

It didn't take long to find the bathrooms and showers, conveniently located behind their hut. This building was attached to a long, open, activity center. Poking their heads inside, Joel and Steve turned to each other with eager smiles, realizing the room was full of game tables: table tennis, pool, foosball, and hockey. Someone had thought of everything, including the huge, wide deck facing the view and dotted with rattan patio furniture.

Waiting for Steve to finish up in the bathroom, Joel started unpacking his bag, putting his clothes away in the dresser provided and laying out his toiletries on top. Shaking out the contents of his bag, making sure he had everything before he stuck it out of the way under his bed, he spotted a book. It was old and green: Fred's diary.

Joel looked at the book quizzically. Why was this here? He didn't remember packing it. He must have, though, since here it was. Shaking his head, he went out to the porch, sank into the soft cushions of one of the rattan chairs, and began to leaf through the journal.

It was strange to think that if it weren't for his friendship with Keegan, he would never have come to Jebel Marra. Funny, how life was so fickle. Little things people didn't even seek after could change their whole future.

"Joel, you look strange." Steve bounded up the porch steps, threw his kit and towel in the general direction of his room and bed, and came back to gaze thoughtfully at him. "You have a book in your hand and a solemn countenance. I can only conclude that you are thinking."

"Even me, Steve, even me," Joel said dryly.

"Well, can I help?"

"It's no big deal. It's just—well, this is Fred Keegan's journal, his diary. You know—Julia's dad. I have no memory of packing it, but here it is. I guess it reminded me about him and made me realize that I would never be here, if it weren't for knowing him. It's funny."

"Why funny?"

"Well, it's little things, really, that change our lives. The big things that we have planned often just fizzle away, but little things we don't even think about—they can turn you completely around."

"Wow." Steve looked impressed. "You're deep, Joel. Actually, I think you're onto something, but we've got to go get food." He rubbed his belly. "I am so hungry."

"Right." Joel tossed the journal onto the chair, and the men headed to the dining hall.

The waiter's name tag said Arnold and he asked if they preferred the roasted kudu or grilled bream, fresh from the river. After taking their orders, he turned to go.

"Excuse me, Arnold, this dining room seems pretty empty with just the six of us. How many people do you usually have here?" Steve asked.

"Ah, sir. This is a good question. I only have worked here for two years, but it is never very busy. Some of the older staff, they say that before the trouble got so bad, here in Darfur, there would be sixty to eighty guests here at once, but that hasn't happened in a long time."

"So this is a normal turnout for you?"

"Oh, yes, sir. This is very good. Sometimes many weeks pass in a row with no guests. Then we have no work, and that is very bad."

They feasted on roasted kudu, a local antelope-like animal tasting a lot like venison. It was delicious and followed by a caramel pudding, running with syrup. The coffee was all right, but Joel suspected it was instant. In Sudan, he was discovering, it was usually safer to order tea, which was always pretty good thanks to all that British influence, but coffee, if it was Sudanese, instantly added hairs to his chest, it was so strong. If you got "American" coffee, it was usually instant. Oh well.

He leaned back, a little too full, and smiled at Steve. "That was good."

"Delicious," Steve agreed. "You know what you were saying before about how it's the little things that direct our paths, not our big plans?"

"Yeah."

"Well, it reminds me of a verse from the Bible, and I quote: 'The heart of man plans his way, but the Lord establishes his steps.'"

"So you're saying that the little things are really God?"

"I think God puts us where He wants us to be, using whatever He wants to accomplish it, be they little things or big things," Steve answered.

"I planned to be married and have a family by now, but my wife left me, I became good friends with a convict, and now I'm single, having dinner with a missionary bachelor in Sudan," Joel said. "Do you think God actually planned all that?"

"Emphatically," Steve answered him, "and I think that He does it with our greater good in mind. 'For I know the plans I have for you, declares the Lord, plans for welfare and not for evil, to give you a future and a hope.'"

"Is that the Bible again?"

Steve nodded.

"So His plans are for our good?"

"Yes." Steve nodded again.

"But if He plans it all, how can there be so much tragedy in life, including here in Sudan? No, I decided a long time ago that if God exists at all, I don't think I like Him."

"Let's go for a walk, Joel. I want to show you something."

They left the dining hall, heading toward the mountain's edge. The sun was setting behind them as they stood looking out over the valley to the east. Slanting rays of pink and orange filled the scene below with a luster that beautified what otherwise was an unremarkable stretch of desert.

"When you look down there, what do you see, Joel?" Steve asked.

"I dunno. Desert, I guess. It looks pretty barren."

"Yeah, that's what it is. Barren. And it gets worse the closer you get.

The more you find out about the people there and what's happening, the harder and drier it is. That's the place God has clearly directed me to be. At first, I thought it would be terrible: all that pain and misery and violence. But then I found out that it's in the darkness that God's light shines brightest; it's in despair that hope is valued; it's when facing death all day long that life finally comes into focus. Now it's the place I want to be, Joel, more than any other."

"Was it hard to leave North America and all your stuff?" Joel asked.

"I fought it for a long time. I figured I was getting a good income back home, working as a plumber. I had my own business, owned my own house." Steve's light brown eyes reflected the golden dimming of the valley below as he spoke. "But God started moving all the little things around me, directing me to this path. I wasn't sure I wanted it. I hesitated." He looked directly at Joel, almost as if assessing him. "Then I couldn't hear His voice anymore. It was like the sun turned off."

"His voice?" Joel asked. "How do you hear His voice? Is it like really loud, or what?"

"You know that journal, that one you were reading on the porch earlier?"

"Keegan's journal?" Joel nodded. "What about it?"

"Well, when you read it, you can hear Keegan talking, can't you?"

Joel considered this, but finally nodded slowly. "Yeah, I guess I do."

"Well, it's just like that for me. When I read God's Word, the Bible, I hear Him. The amazing thing is that He really wants to talk!" Steve threw out his arms, indicating the valley below, the sky, the mountain. "Look at what He's saying. There's no way He could shout it louder if He tried."

Joel deliberately stepped away from Steve, just to be safe, eyeing the embankment a bit nervously.

"OK, I can see you think you really hear Him, Steve," he affirmed, nodding politely. "That's good, and I'm glad for you. I really am. But my ears must be a bit on the deaf side." He winked while he said it, in a failed attempt to defuse Steve's intensity.

"No, they aren't, Joel. You're an intelligent person; what's happening right now, as the sun is setting?"

Nodding slowly, a doubtful look on his face, Joel answered, "It's getting dark?"

"Exactly!" Steve warmed to his subject. "Every day, God puts the sun in the sky, and every day it gives us light to live our lives by. And at night when it's gone, we universally climb into our beds because we can't work and play without it. It's a picture of Himself. A lot of people have worshiped the sun literally, believing it to be God. It isn't; it's just part of His message that He's left all over creation." He paused, took a breath, his face growing increasingly dim in the evening light. "And then there's water. What does water do?"

"It, uh, waters?"

"It waters everything. Nothing would be alive without it. When we get thirsty, we crave it; if we ignore our thirst, we die."

Joel felt the tiniest glint of interest.

"But there's more. Water keeps us alive, and it purifies us. With it, we wash our dishes, our hands, ourselves. It keeps us clean."

"So you're saying that God is like the sun and the water? That He's trying to show us who He is?"

"All the time, my friend, all the time."

"Is there more?"

"Is there more?" Steve echoed. Taking a deep breath, he continued, "I could go on forever. Look around at the details. He didn't have to give us color, but He did. Why? 'Cause it makes life interesting for us. Think of how He painted the world for us. It's beautiful here. He didn't have to make a rose smell so good. Or garlic and lemon taste so yummy. He didn't have to give us the pleasure of sex. He didn't have to, but He did. Why?"

Joel listened intently.

They had started to walk back toward the cabana, the sounds of the waterfall and the cicadas growing louder with each step.

Steve stopped. Gesturing around them, he explained, "If I wanted to buy a piece of property and turn it over for an investment, would I look for commercial property or residential?"

"Money no object?" asked Joel.

"No object."

"Commercial. Always."

"Right. But if I wanted to really impress the one woman in the world whom I loved and wanted for a wife, should I buy the same thing?"

"Nope. For her, you'd be out-of-pocket, paying too much for a piece of park somewhere."

"Right again." Steve continued, "But if I really wanted to impress her—"

"Money still no object?" Joel interrupted.

"Not even an issue."

"Then," Joel continued, sitting on the steps of their cabana porch, "you'd put in expensive landscaping, a statue or two, a water fountain, a pool, maybe a pond with white swans—the sky's the limit."

"And that, my friend," Steve's voice had grown quieter, "is exactly what the Creator did. There are waterfalls and peacocks and oceans and angel fish and butterflies and mountains and flowers and . . . and . . ."

"I think I get it."

"You do?"

"Yeah, I think I do. It means He likes us, after all."

"It means He's crazy for us," Steve agreed.

They stayed on the deck for a while after that. Neither of them said anything. They just listened to the sounds of the African night, watching the moon's beams reflecting like diamonds in the waterfall's cascade and the glow of it bouncing off the pool below. There was nothing to add.

# Twenty-two

⚜

It was in Gethsemane that Jesus sowed the seeds
of victory on Calvary. I will be faced with countless
Calvarys, and the only way I can prepare for them is
to go through Gethsemane.

W. GLYN EVANS, *DAILY WITH THE LORD*

JULIA HAD KEPT THE BURQA ON A HUNCH. Now it was serving its purpose well. It kept her hidden completely, even from the eyes of her
friends as she walked past them toward the relief base's parking lot. For
this, she was relying on luck and probability. How many workers left
the keys in the ignition of the vehicles they borrowed and used on a
daily basis? She was about to find out.

Two. *A little disappointing*, Julia thought. Out of twelve vehicles in
the lot, the only ones with keys were a supply truck and a car with
UN insignia on the back plates—apparently Jonathan had important
guests. Well, this was the wrong time to start stealing from the UN,
she thought, and she wasn't about to drive a supply truck. Turning to
go back to her tent and square one, she heard an approaching vehicle.
It was a Land Cruiser. She watched as the driver jumped out of the

vehicle, glancing her way with a smile and a nod as he walked past her into the supply building. She nodded back, fighting an impulse to kiss him for leaving his keys, and slowly, with the grace and patience of a Bedouin shepherdess, she approached the vehicle. Hopping in, she turned the ignition, shifted into reverse, then first, pulled out of the parking area, and drove out of the station.

It would be an odd sight for some of these people, perhaps, to see a woman in a burqa driving a Land Cruiser out of camp. Julia decided she'd have to take her chances on that one. Enough oddities occurred in an IDP camp that one more would probably go unnoticed. She hoped.

The road to Qasar had not gotten better in the last few weeks, but Julia found her way back without any trouble. The same guard barked at her in Arabic. Handing him the note that she had picked from Jonathan's vest pocket, she waited silently. Whether he actually read it before handing it back to her or just recognized Nassir's signature, she had no idea, but it worked. He waved her on, and she drove past, parking under the big familiar cypress tree.

As soon as she turned off the ignition, two armed guards stepped up beside her, asking her questions she did not understand. Again, she silently handed over Nassir's note, after which they began to argue heatedly in Arabic.

Finally, they waved their guns forward for her to walk ahead of them, past the cypress, past the tent where she and Kelly had waited, sipping tea, while Hassan had talked with Nassir last time she'd been here.

They ushered her into a smaller building, shining brilliant white in the afternoon sun with what had to be fresh paint. After a few moments of utter blindness, her eyes adjusted to the dim light.

Nassir sat at a desk, working at his computer; he was wearing the traditional *jellabiyya* and *immah*, held to his head with a broad black band. The guards didn't speak, so neither did she. Finally, Nassir looked up at the three of them. His eyes betrayed no surprise.

"*Oh, Kef ya Mustafa?*" He asked the guards if everything was OK.

"*Oh, Kwaiyis,*" the bigger guard replied, gesturing toward Julia with his gun. "*Ma batal,*" he added.

Handing the note that Nassir had written a few days earlier back to him, the guards waited respectfully for him to read it, which he barely did, glancing at it in recognition and then back up at his guards, and finally, with more attention than he had given her yet, at Julia, herself. A discussion followed, in which she could make out only one or two words, but she knew that it mostly had to do with her, going by the chins and guns pointing in her direction.

She knew she should not speak unless she was spoken to first, but it took everything for her not to interrupt them before they were finished. Watching the three of them, she decided that Nassir was definitely the intelligent one of the bunch. The big guard, whose name seemed to be Mustafa, made her uneasy for some reason. The other one was shorter, around her own height, and was too young to be intimidating.

Nassir turned to her.

"I assume you are the journalist lady, come to visit us?" He spoke English with only a slight British accent, his tone polite, his eyes steel.

"Yes, I am Julia Douglas," she replied.

"And what do you think you accomplish by coming here, Miss Douglas?" Nassir asked, studying her Islamic dress.

"Mr. An-Nur," Julia decided that it was now or never, "we have met before."

"Is that so?"

"Yes," Julia forged ahead, hoping against hope that her gamble would pay off. "I am the woman who pulled your young son, Abdul, away from the tires of your work truck before it could kill him."

The steel in his eyes melted ever so slightly.

"So," he finally sighed, "I suppose that explains why the *Sudan Tribune* never printed an article with photos about Nassir An-Nur."

"Precisely." Julia decided to be as truthful and direct with this man as possible. "But it also explains why you still have a little boy and why"—she took a breath—"you owe me a favor."

"That favor being?" He exhaled the words slowly.

"I would ask for the release of Kelly, the American woman whom you took. I will also agree to print a retraction of what I have written about the Janja, apologizing publicly for slandering your government."

Nassir leaned back in his chair, studying her with interest. The guards were also studying her, but she knew their interest was not the intelligent kind. Once again, she felt grateful for the potato sack of a burqa that she wore.

Leaning his head toward one side, Nassir sighed and finally replied.

"Julia Douglas, I suppose I am grateful to you for saving Abdul. You would not have been in such a position, however, unless Allah willed it. So I am really indebted only to him. Besides which, I distinctly remember giving to the man who was with you several hundred dinar to cover any medical expenses that may have been necessary. Were there any, by the way?"

Julia cleared her throat. "Well, it was actually a very bad sprain, but after staying off it for several days, I was fine."

"I see."

Julia saw, too. He didn't really owe her anything. He wasn't the sentimental type. Nor overly appreciative. She was at his mercy. But he wanted a retraction. What he did next was not a scenario that she had envisioned.

Standing up from his desk, he moved slowly and with grace to stand in front of Julia. Then with a swift move, he yanked off her headcovering and slapped her. Once, twice, three times. Hard, across her cheeks. She sucked in her breath, momentarily voiceless, tears welling up in her eyes.

"How dare you!" She spoke low, her voice shaking. She struggled to keep her hands at her sides instead of cradling her burning cheeks.

"I ask you the same question, Miss Douglas. How dare you? How dare you insult a Janjaweed general with a masquerade intended to deceive and gather information? How dare you think that you have some kind of authority over me or my decisions, that you would come here again, shaming the Islamic way by wearing our women's clothes? How dare you?"

Turning to the guards, he spoke to them in Arabic, issuing an order that Julia feared but did not understand.

She was shepherded with guns, none too gently, back outside into the blinding light of day. They walked her toward a truck, maybe the same one that had almost run over Abdul; she couldn't tell. Gestured by guns to climb into the back, she did, and was followed by Mustafa, steadying his machine gun on her as the younger guard jumped into the front and drove away from Qasar. Julia looked back once, to see Nassir, standing like a ghost, his white *jellabiyya* billowing out around him, holding Abdul by the hand—a smaller, exact replica of his father.

## TWENTY-THREE

The greatest cause in the world is joyfully rescuing
people from hell, meeting their earthly needs,
making them glad in God, and doing it with a kind,
serious pleasure that makes Christ look like the
Treasure He is.

JOHN PIPER, *DON'T WASTE YOUR LIFE*

JOEL COULDN'T SLEEP. HE'D TRIED to get back to sleep for the last hour, but the sound of the waterfall and the steady humming of the cicadas or geckos or whatever they were was driving him a little mad. The digital clock on his nightstand said 3:38 AM. After tossing and turning with no success for another twenty minutes, he gave up. Swinging his legs over the side of the bed, he felt gingerly along the wooden floor until he found his sandals, which he picked up and shook out before slipping them on. Spiders. One never knew. Steve had put the heebie-jeebies into him with stories about scorpions and tarantulas that people inadvertently disturbed when they put on their shoes in the morning. Now he checked every time. He didn't like spiders.

Grabbing his mini flashlight off the nightstand, he opened the screen door, trying to keep it from squeaking too loudly. Unfortunately, when he let it go, he forgot about the spring mechanism. It snapped back into place with a bang. He froze, waiting for Steve's yell, but the sound of gentle snoring was all he heard. Good; he didn't want to disturb the guy's sleep.

Sitting down in the lounge chair, he propped his feet up on the railing of the porch in front of him, crossed his arms over his chest, and took in the night's beauty, breathing deeply of hibiscus and jasmine, the sound of the falls resonating through him. It was an amazing spot. But uncomfortable. Joel reached down the side of his seat cushion, pulling out Fred's hard, sharp-cornered journal. He hesitated for a moment, feeling the book, firm and smooth in his hand, before he turned on his flashlight and opened it up. His eyes fell on the entry of July 14, 1999:

> I have come to a strange state.
>
> Nothing is different; I live in a jail cell surrounded by other criminals, their sounds, their smells, their hate. Nothing is different, but everything has changed.
>
> I can almost touch it, it's so real. Life has come to me. Life and its fullness. Before, I was alone. Now, He's with me. Before, I couldn't see light or beauty. Now, everywhere I look shimmers and glows. All I had before was hate. Now all I have is Love.

Joel was surprised by this poetic side of Keegan. A softie, through and through, yes, but poetic? And who was with him? He wrote that someone was with him, but Joel had always known him to be a bit of a loner. Sure, the other inmates liked him well enough, but they also paid him due respect. He'd earned it. A long time before Joel had known him, Keegan's fighting and brawling had landed him in trouble with prison guards and prisoners both. By reputation, he was not someone the other guys wanted to upset. But a cellmate? Joel didn't think Keegan had ever had one.

Obviously, this person made Keegan's life seem a bit brighter, and that was good. Joel had often felt guilty leaving him alone in a dark cell, heading back to his fancy apartment downtown, amid all the lights and . . . well, freedom. He flipped ahead a few pages, looking for clues as to who this person was that had lived with Keegan.

No date on this page. Just more poetic writing. No—verses from the Bible, from the looks of it:

> "I will never leave you nor forsake you." So we can confidently say, "The Lord is my helper; I will not fear; what can man do to me?" Remember your leaders, those who spoke to you the word of God. Consider the outcome of their way of life, and imitate their faith. Jesus Christ is the same yesterday and today and forever (Hebrews 13:5–8).

Keegan had believed that *God* lived with him.

Joel flicked off his flashlight. Sitting up in his chair, he absorbed this thought. On the one hand, it would be great if there really was a God who liked people. Steve almost had him believing it last night. But a God who wanted to live with people? A powerful Creator who would bend Himself down to man? Yep, it was a good idea. A good dream. A dream, for sure, Joel decided with a bit of regret, but a good one. On the other hand, it seemed like believing it wasn't necessarily a bad thing. Keegan had been a great guy. Joel liked him better than almost anyone else he'd ever known. And Steve was a good guy. A little intense, maybe, but a good guy.

So maybe it was OK to believe it. Believe that God lived with you and talked to you? Yeah, they believed God talked to them, too, Joel was sure about it. But how they were able to believe it was beyond him.

He tried. For a moment, he actually tried. No. He opened his eyes, saw the hard book in his hands, the wooden porch, and the waterfall streaming down in the moonlight and it was all so solid and . . . real. He shook his head, stood up, dropped the book on the chair, and stepped down off the porch.

Walking along the stone-flanked path, his flashlight shedding light ahead and the moon lending some of its own, he made his way toward the pool at the bottom of the waterfall. Joel loved the water. He'd been drawn to it all his life. He lived in an apartment with a view of the ocean, for Pete's sake, never regretting the extra fifty thousand or so he had paid for that view.

Not really thinking about it, he loosened his sandals, and pulled his T-shirt over his head. Walking into this pool of moonlit water in the darkness of the night just seemed like the right thing. He swam back and forth several times, figuring one length to be about two standard pool lengths. The water was like silk. Turning straight toward the waterfall, he cut through the water, stroking hard as he reached the bottom of the cascade to dive underneath it and then resurface on the inside of the curtain of water crashing down. Clambering up an embankment of rough rocks hidden behind this curtain, he sat on an outcropping to catch his breath. The air was misty and damp, and the thundering water roared in his ears.

The morning had just begun to dawn, shedding a glimmer of light through the veil of water, but Joel still had to sit patiently for several minutes before his eyes adjusted to the darkness that blanketed him. Carefully groping, half feeling, half seeing his way, his hands felt along the rock wall behind the falls, guiding him toward the other side of the pool. And then there was nothing. Joel stopped, slowly moving his feet and hands forward, inches at a time. The cave wall had turned sharply northward. Joel realized he was feeling the outline of a yawning, pitch black cavern. Tucked in behind the falls, it was well concealed. Joel felt around the edges of the opening with his hands. It was half his height, but quite wide. Shaking his head at himself and whatever this was he thought he was up to, he decided he needed his flashlight to investigate. It was back on the grassy embankment beside his shirt and sandals.

Diving beneath the falls once again, he swam back toward the bank, but stopped to tread water when he saw people moving about.

Apparently forced from their beds, Joel's fellow tourists huddled together in the early morning dawn. Men wearing *immahs* and carrying AK-47s stood guard over the bewildered group, yelling at them. Were they Janjaweed? What were they doing here? Steve was turning his face cautiously from side to side.

Joel knew Steve was looking for him, wondering where he'd gone. But he couldn't catch Steve's attention without attracting the guards, as well. The thundering waterfall would surely drown out his voice so that even if he tried to call out, it was unlikely his friend would hear.

Carefully swimming away from the middle of the pool, Joel moved as smoothly as possible into the shadows of the bank where he could avoid detection but still see what was happening.

Anita and Mark looked surprisingly calm, but Robert, the father of the father and son duo, was obviously distraught. He kept trying to approach the guards with offers of "money or liquor or whatever they wanted," but only got a machine gun waved in his face. Bill was shivering. He looked scared.

The harsh rattle of machine-gun fire broke out by the bridge. A fist of fear clenched Joel's chest, and without deliberation, he started to pray.

"God, I don't know if You're really there or not, and we've never talked before," he whispered, "but I think Steve just might be right about You. If You do like us the way it seems maybe You do, this can't be what You had in mind. So we need some help now, God; a bit of a break would be really good. Please soon, God. And oh," he added, suddenly remembering, "amen."

The gunfire had escalated. It sounded like a war had broken out. Joel noticed the men guarding the tourists were craning their necks, trying to see what was happening over at the other end of the camp. When another man, dressed the same and obviously part of the AK-47 wielding party, came running down the path from the dining hall, shouting and gesturing, the guards sprang into action, racing toward him, away from the group, guns at the ready to rejoin the rest of their contingent.

The tourists stood frozen in fear. Joel could not figure it. What was going on? Where were the camp workers? Why hadn't they been brought out with the tourist group? Joel didn't have any answers, but didn't feel at all comfortable about waiting for the gunmen to come back in order to ask polite questions. No. They had to get out of here.

# Twenty-four

❧

Be strong and courageous.

JOSHUA 1:6

"STEVE!" JOEL BELLOWED AS LOUD as he could, hoping to be heard above the roar of the falls.

Steve's head swiveled toward the pool.

Reaching up onto the embankment, Joel heaved himself up and out, yanked on his sandals, and grabbed his shirt and the flashlight. He scrambled the rest of the way up the path, finally reaching his companions.

"We need to get out of here before they come back." All eyes fastened on Joel. "There's a tunnel behind the waterfall I think we could hide in for a while. I don't know how big it is, but there's at least enough room for all of us to sit there while we wait this out." Joel indicated, with a tilt of his head, the stutter of machine-gun fire coming from the bridge. "It's not the Hilton, but I think it's better than the alternative."

"Let's do it!" Steve prodded them to action. "Come on, guys!"

Hastily they slipped, one by one, into the water behind Joel, who carried the flashlight between his teeth. Following his lead, they edged around the pool instead of cutting through the middle, and then ducked under the waterfall, Everyone except Bill emerged on the other side. Joel handed Steve the flashlight, then swam back out into the pool to find him. Surfacing into the cool morning air, he saw him. Bill stood shivering at the water's edge, oblivious to the fact that a soldier stood directly behind him, holding a machine gun pointed at his head.

"Hey!" Joel splashed and yelled. "Over here! You—Janjaweed!" Too late, Joel considered that diverting the guard's attention from Bill onto himself was not necessarily a good plan. Pushing himself back under the water, he headed toward Bill's feet, which he grabbed, felling the teenager and pulling him under the surface of the pool. Bullets whizzed past them in the water. Joel could feel the bubbles left in their wake vibrating his ear.

Surfacing for one last gulp of air before going back under the falls, Joel saw, like one last, suspended freeze-frame, the Janja who had been shooting at them pitch forward onto the ground, while another soldier, a young boy, stood triumphantly behind him. What was forever cast into Joel's mind was the look on the young soldier's face: absolute, unsatisfied revenge. His enemy was dead, but the hate wasn't. Just before Joel went under, the boy's gaze locked onto his own. He had seen them.

The clatter of the guns was drowned out as Joel fought the powerful pull of the waterfall. His arm muscles were straining, dragging Bill's limp body through the water as well as his own. Finally emerging inside the curtain, Joel yelled for help, but Robert was already there, pulling his son from the water. Steve immediately started trying to resuscitate Bill. Joel searched for bullet wounds, but the boy had none.

Finally, Bill coughed, then heaved and threw up while his dad supported him. "He doesn't know how to swim very well," Robert explained as tears slid down his cheeks.

Joel nodded, patted Bill a few times on the back, and then heaved a sigh of relief.

"I think we're safe for the moment," Steve said, assessing the situation. The soggy group of tourists crouched on a ledge together, looking at the backside of a waterfall, and hoped they were hidden from the eyes of an enemy they didn't know. Early morning sun filtered into their hiding place, dancing on the rocks and filling the damp, misty cavern with shimmering light and rainbows.

"I, for one," Steve announced, "could really go for some bacon and eggs right about now."

A couple of chuckles eased their tension a bit.

"Yeah, and I was thinking about a Starbucks espresso," Joel replied, deciding that he should maybe keep all that he'd just seen on the embankment to himself for now, "but I'll settle for a look inside this cave." He pointed his flashlight toward the rear wall, where the opening of the cave was all but invisible, hidden in the shadowy recesses.

"Interesting," Robert said, running his hand along the dark, moist rock. "These mountains are well-known for their caves and waterfalls, but I've never seen anything like this."

"Did you actually grow up here, then?" Anita asked.

"We lived in a little village not far away from here until I was eight years old. I used to roam these hills with my village friends, who knew them inside out. Many of these mountain caves tunnel for a long ways. Stories around the evening fire told of people actually disappearing inside them, never to be found again."

"Spelunking," Steve interrupted. "It's called spelunking, isn't it?"

"Yes," Robert agreed, "I believe that is the correct term."

"What is spelunking?" Mark asked, trying to follow the conversation. "I don't think we have that in Australia, do we, Nita?"

Anita shrugged. "I never heard of it."

"Exploring caves," Joel clarified, "is called spelunking, which we are all now about to do." And encouraging this group of people to move farther into the recesses of the cave, away from any hostile eyes was what Joel wanted to do. He turned on his flashlight, illuminating the hollow they stood in. It was a cavern. They ducked through a low passageway and found themselves in a room with a ceiling height of at least fourteen feet. It was long, almost the length of a tennis court, and veered farther west, he thought, remembering the sunset. He walked its length, feeling against the back wall, wondering. It was there.

"Hey, Steve, come here." Joel called his friend over from where he was trying to cheer up Bill by discussing the different possibilities of breakfasts that none of them would enjoy this morning. Steve tore himself away with obvious regret.

"What we need to do when we get back to Khartoum," Steve informed him, "is demand one of those food vouchers from the travel agent for the meals we'll have missed while they get this mess under control."

Joel smiled and shook his head, admiring Steve's ability to focus so intently on one thing.

"Look at this." Joel knelt down, pointing his flashlight into a small alcove. "I think there's a tunnel here."

"Really?" Steve immediately dropped down beside Joel, reaching his hand inside the opening and waving it around. "What about . . . ?"

"Spiders?" Joel asked, swallowing.

"Yeah," Steve winced. "I mean, men with machine guns are one thing, but—"

"I know what you mean," Joel agreed. And he did. Still, maybe this was another way out of here. A way that would get them out past the fighting. It was something they needed to find out.

"Steve, there's something I need to tell you."

"I'm not going anywhere fast, Joel."

"Right. Well, when I went back for Bill one of those gunmen was about to shoot Bill, but then a younger fighter came up behind him and killed him."

"What? Are you serious? You saw this happen?"

Joel realized that he was trembling. The shock of everything was beginning to set in.

"Yeah, I saw it. But we got away and we're okay, except for one thing."

"I hate 'one things.'"

"Me too. But here it is: the young guy who killed the other guy—he knows we're in here. He saw me, looked straight in my eyes just before I went under the waterfall."

"So. No big deal. He has to be on our side, 'cause he killed the other guy, right?"

"Well, that's just the thing. How do we know? What if he isn't? What if they're out there just waiting for us to come out again? Or worse, planning a way to come in and get us?"

"They'd have come in by now, I think, if they were that eager to saddle themselves with a bunch of tourists. No—I think they're busy out there fighting their own war, and I'm pretty sure the men who rounded us up are Janjaweed. So I, for one, am very glad there's a war outside keeping those bad guys busy."

"But, Steve. What if the bad guys win that war?"

His point was taken.

"Are the batteries in your flashlight new?" Steve asked.

That was a good question. Joel considered. He'd bought this flashlight last summer and had taken one camping trip with it; then it had lain dormant until this trip.

"Sort of," he answered.

"Sort of new?" Steve questioned.

"Well, we better not waste what's left," Joel answered, his mind made up. "I'm going in there, and I'm going to see where it goes." He dropped down and started crawling forward, shining the flashlight in front of him against the damp walls and dark shadows.

"Are you coming?" Joel asked, stopping momentarily to hear Steve telling Bill they wouldn't be gone long—hopefully.

"I wonder if spiders taste anything like bacon and eggs?" was the reply he got from the hungry missionary crawling along behind him.

Spiders, indeed, inhabited the tunnel, which stretched farther west, then turned a sharp left, or south, as it began its descent. Joel's flesh crawled, watching them scurrying away from the focus of his flashlight, retreating into darker shadows.

The men picked up speed. The tunnel was mostly downhill, widening out the farther they went until they found they were able to stand up and walk again, their heads hunched slightly to keep clear of the ceiling and webs. Some sections were slippery with little trickles coming from above them, running down in rivulets through the rock. The thought of snakes had passed through Joel's mind once or twice. It was good that they didn't have a bigger flashlight. Ignorance was bliss.

The opening suddenly appeared, tall and narrow, as they came around a bend, the light blinding them. They could hear the *rat-a-tat-tat* of machine guns still being fired outside. The men stepped out of the cavern cautiously and found themselves looking toward the river and the bridge from the west side. They could see the dining hall across the water, and the fighting that still continued, very near to where they stood, at the bridge.

"So who are those guys shooting at the Janja?" Joel asked Steve.

"We are Sudanese Liberation Army, and who are you?" Both men turned in surprise to see a young boy, maybe twelve years old, leveling a Chinese-made assault rifle at them. Glaring fiercely at them, he yelled again, his voice cracking as he did, "Who are you?"

Fighting the urge to pat him on the head, Joel looked at Steve, who answered, introducing himself and adding, "I work at Adramata Camp for *Médicins Sans Frontières*."

The transformation on the kid's face at this information elevated Joel's respect for Steve's profession several levels. The young soldier's mouth split into a white-toothed grin that was infectious; it made Joel suddenly think of a boy with his basketball in an underground parking garage, except this kid wasn't even as tall as Dominic.

"My name is Matthews." He stuck out his hand, slinging his gun smoothly behind his shoulder in a more friendly position and shaking each of their hands vigorously in turn.

"Joel Maartens at your service, Matthews." Joel knew a moment's discomfort, as a strange surge of fatherly concern for this young boy swept over him.

"I knew you for *khawajas*, so that makes you Janja enemy, as all foreigners are, but you"—he nodded up at Steve—"you work for the Doctors. They are our friends. Come with me, I will take you to my commander." He immediately set off through the dense brush.

"Whoa, soldier," Joel called to him. Matthews turned around, a question on his face, waiting.

"We have friends back inside the cave." Joel gestured up the hill.

"We were hiding from the Janja in there, but Joel found a tunnel behind the waterfall. We followed it, and it came out here," Steve added.

"Oh." The boy processed this information, considering for a moment. "I think you should go and bring them here. They are safer with us, perhaps. If the battle does not go well, you could go back into hiding. Right now, we need help. Can you fight?"

If Joel had had any thought of neutrality in his head, at that moment it disappeared. He knew he wanted to fight. He needed to help these kids somehow. Steve raised his eyebrows, nodding in silent agreement, and they made an unspoken decision.

"We'll help you, Matthews," Steve spoke for them both. "We'll stay and help. The people in the cave will be all right for a while."

"I don't think they'd want to be involved in this battle, in any case," Joel added, after considering and quickly discarding the possibilities of Robert, Bill, Anita, or Mark picking up a machine gun to kill a Janja. No. He and Steve would stay and fight.

# Twenty-five

~

The most traumatizing condition in the body occurs
when disloyal cells defy inhibition. They multiply
without any checks on growth, spreading rapidly
throughout the body, choking out normal cells.
White cells, armed against foreign invaders, will not
attack the body's own mutinous cells. Physicians fear
no other malfunction more deeply; it is called cancer.

DR. PAUL BRAND AND PHILIP YANCEY, *FEARFULLY AND WONDERFULLY MADE*

JULIA COVERED HER EARS, TRYING TO block out the vicious cries of the
Janja militia being whipped into battle frenzy outside the cell window.
They had broken the stillness of the morning with the muezzin's call
to prayer, loud and clear, coming through the camp speaker: *"Allah u
akbar, Allah u akbar; ash-hadu al-la llaha Allah."*

The prayers had lasted for half an hour; then the chanting picked up
energy and volume.

On a mat along the opposite wall, Kelly had somehow slept through
all the noise and was just beginning to stretch, locking her knuckles
together above her head. The sun filtered through the iron grating in

the overhead window, slanting beams of light alive with tiny dust particles. She covered her eyes with her arm and sighed heavily. Sleep was sweet with the bliss of forgetting their situation and the reality of the Janja camp. Waking up felt unreal, more like a dream—a bad one. Julia watched Kelly's eyes turn from forgetting to remembering in a moment, and then she gave a little nod, almost as if she were receiving some secret assignment. When she looked up to meet Julia's eyes on her, she was smiling.

"Good morning, cellmate. They're pretty noisy, aren't they?" Kelly said.

She squinted at Julia, shielding the rays of light from her face with her arm, the sunshine picking up the highlights in her caramel-colored hair.

"I'm not sure about the *good*, but it is definitely morning." She was fighting a feeling of powerlessness that threatened to engulf her, a feeling she had known before, but not one she was comfortable with. Yesterday afternoon when the guards had opened the cell door and she had seen Kelly alive and well, she had been euphoric with possibilities of escape. Kelly had listened to her, nodding and smiling, but—Julia could tell—not believing.

"What?" Julia had asked. "What is it that you're thinking? It's easy to see you aren't convinced."

"Julia." Kelly had sighed, reaching over and squeezing her hand. "I was so glad to see you step through that door; you have no idea. But it was actually selfish, I was glad you came because now I've got company. But Julia, this is a terrible place. Terrible things are done by these men, and our lives are totally dispensable to them. The fact that you're here does make it more bearable for me, but I'm scared for you, Julia.

"It would be wonderful to get out of here, and I pray that God will provide a way for us, but a plan to escape? Didn't you see the arsenal outside?" She had waved her hand vaguely toward the window.

"This is a military base, make no mistake. There are Jeeps outside with mounted machine guns, Antonov bombers, Kalashnikovs hot off their Chinese presses, and helicopters dropping off food supplies and more arsenal. This is not a place where we can sneak around unnoticed in our burqas."

Julia knew Kelly was right. But accepting their powerlessness stumped her. Maybe Kelly was content to pray and wait for God to rescue her whenever He was good and ready, but it seemed pretty passive and . . . well . . . lame.

Somewhere outside their room, they heard a door open and close. Then footsteps. Kelly sat upright on her mat, pulling on her burqa and motioning for Julia to do the same.

"It's breakfast," Kelly explained, "but you don't want the guard to see your face."

The door handle rattled as someone inserted a key from the outside, unlocking it. Mustafa, the same Janja as before, entered the cell, placing a basket of thin dark bread on the floor between them. He reminded Julia of a crocodile, complete with a big fake smile and cold, dead eyes. He crouched beside the bread, taking his time, a tic twitching high on his scarred and pocked cheek, his gaze suffocating the women with its weight.

"*Kissra,*" he pointed at the basket, "is very good with these dates I bring you." He pulled a small paper parcel from inside the folds of his robe and placed it carefully beside the basket; his hands and fingernails were black with filth.

"*Moya?*" Kelly asked.

"Water, I will bring some." He left the room, and Julia let out a deep breath. Her relief was short-lived, however, as he returned almost immediately with a jug, which he set down beside their food. Crouching down again, he made no move to leave them, his eyes ranging over them and leaving little pricks of ice along Julia's spine.

Kelly stood up, crossing to where Julia sat huddled with her back pressing against the wall. Taking Julia's hand in hers, Kelly squeezed it and said, "Let's ask the Lord to bless our food, shall we?" Without waiting for an answer, she launched into a very loud prayer. Julia bowed her head and listened.

"Heavenly Father, the only one, true God, we thank You for loving us so much that You provide us with our daily bread. We are grateful to You, Lord, and ask You to bless it to our bodies, even as we ask You to bless this guard for bringing it to us. We thank You for Your protection this day over us from all evil and danger and harm. Thank You, Father, for all Your blessings, and especially for the blessing of Jesus Christ and His shed blood that washes us from our sins. Amen."

Raising her head, Julia looked at Kelly and smiled sympathetically.

"I know it comforts you to pray, Kelly, and I'm glad that you have faith . . ." Kelly wasn't listening. Smiling too smugly, she pointed a finger toward Mustafa. But Mustafa, Julia realized finally, was no longer there. She hadn't even heard him go.

"It's amazing, Julia, but it works every time. They bring the food and stay to watch me eat it. They make my skin crawl. But when I talk to God out loud, I guess it makes them feel more uncomfortable than I do." She shrugged.

"Hey, if it works, it works," Julia said, impressed in spite of herself.

An hour passed by in relative peace. It felt good to talk. They reminisced about "normal" life, sharing stories from their childhoods and laughing together over favorite movies and rock bands. They both loved *Sense and Sensibility* with Hugh Grant, and U2 was, they agreed, still turning out quality music.

A comfortable silence settled between them as they considered the oddities of North American society, so familiar yet so distant from a cell in a Janjaweed training base.

"What was it that Joel Maartens wanted to tell you about your father that night, Julia?" Kelly asked out of the blue.

Julia smiled, shaking her head, a bit embarrassed. "My father wrote a letter to me and made Joel promise to give it to me."

"Really? So your father made sure before he died that this letter would get into your hands? Wow. Must be important," Kelly said, her eyes alive with interest.

"I don't know. I never took it."

"But you read it, right?"

"No. I left it unopened."

"Julia, how could you just leave it? Weren't you curious or anything?"

"I don't know. I just couldn't." Julia looked up, her brow furrowed. Uncertainty suddenly washed over her. She had been so confident that she didn't want to know what her father had to say. For the first time, she wondered if she'd done the right thing.

"It's all right, honey," Kelly said. "There's no point worrying about it now, but if you ever get out of here—and I'm praying that you do—you have to promise me that you will get that letter and read it. You owe it to your father."

Julia smiled. "*When* we get out of here, I will make a beeline for a certain lawyer and read that letter, just to make you happy."

Apparently satisfied with this assurance, Kelly let the subject go. Sort of.

"So I guess that means you have two letters to read, hey, Julia?"

"Two?"

"Yup, two letters from two Dads."

"What are you talking about, Kelly?" Julia stared at her, baffled by the possibility of another letter from her stepfather, James Douglas.

"Granted, it is a bit longer, I'm sure, than the one your dad wrote you, but still . . . I bet you've never opened it, either, have you?"

Her thoughts suddenly clarified, and she responded coolly, "God.

You're talking about God, and I assume the letter you refer to must be the Bible, is that it?"

"Yup. Like I said, two Dads, two letters."

"Well, you're right again, I have never opened the Bible. You're my friend, Kelly—and I would never want to do something that would compromise that—but don't be too disappointed in me if I never become a Christian like you, OK?"

"OK," Kelly answered, unperturbed, "but I'm not going to quit praying for you, Julia, and one day, I hope you'll open both Fathers' letters." Kelly reached over and gently laid her hand on Julia's knee. "There's so much love waiting for you."

Feeling tears threaten, Julia stamped out the emotion and gave a promise she doubted she would ever need to fulfill. "Kelly, if I ever read the Bible, I'll call you from wherever I am and let you know so you can stop praying."

It was still early when Mustafa came back to their cell with Nassir An-Nur. The women were told that if they would confess "There is no God but Allah, and Muhammad is his prophet," they would be spared certain punishment. They had till sunset to consider this decision. Mustafa grinned at them with a sickening smile while Nassir made their choice very clear. Confess to being infidels and turn to the one true faith, Islam, or come under punishment.

When Julia asked Nassir how it made any difference if they confessed, he told her that the Qur'an said, "Muhammed is Allah's apostle. Those who follow him are ruthless to the unbelievers, but merciful to one another."

"'Make war on the unbelievers and hypocrites, and deal harshly with them. Hell shall be their home: an evil fate,'" Mustafa added, his tic twitching as he spoke. Nassir glared but said nothing to his soldier in front of the women.

After they left, the women could hear the men arguing loudly through the cell window.

"Mustafa, I will not have these women killed. I do not want their deaths on my hands. Do you understand?"

Although they strained to hear it, they could not make out Mustafa's reply.

⟡

The day wore on, pushing in on them with its heat in the small room. Kelly and Julia didn't speak much. Julia felt completely powerless. She thought morosely about the short articles that would explain her death as an international incident and wondered how long she would be remembered. A year? A month? Eventually, she fell asleep, drifting into a heavy slumber induced by the emotional drain of the threat lying over her. When she woke up, it was to a familiar sound.

The door had creaked open on its hinge. Julia looked up in dread, expecting to see Mustafa again. But it was a woman.

She wore the colorful, traditional covering over her head, shoulders, and lower garments. Her face was uncovered, and Julia thought she looked familiar but couldn't decide why. Placing what looked like a bowl of stew and a plate of *kissra* beside the door, the woman scrunched down, encircling her legs with her arms, her chin resting on her knees, watching them.

The smell of the food reminded Julia how hungry she was. She dug right in. Kelly bowed her head, and so Julia paused from taking the bite that was on her lips and waited for Kelly to finish praying. She was getting into this routine.

"You are Christian?" the woman asked.

"Yes, I am," Kelly answered; Julia noted that Kelly responded in the singular.

"I am so happy to know you are Christian." The woman's shy smile lit up her face. "Many of the Janja have gone to burn more villages. I was given orders to bring you food," she added.

Kelly and Julia looked at her with compassion, dimly comprehending what it must be to live as a slave to Janja.

"Is it true you come from Hassa Hissa?" she asked.

They nodded.

"I come from a village near there. My home was Qasar." The woman covered her cheeks with her hands, peering at Julia and Kelly through her fingers. "The Janja burned Qasar and killed my family. Now I am Janja slave. My older sister is maybe alive, maybe, in Hassa Hissa. I don't know. Her name is Edith Yusuf. Maybe you know her?"

Kelly and Julia glanced quickly at each other, as Kelly immediately moved toward the woman huddled by the door.

"Are you—could your name be Margaret?"

"Yes." Margaret looked at Kelly in confusion. "How do you know?"

Kelly dropped down on her knees in front of the Sudanese woman.

"I helped to take care of your children, Samuel and Mary. They are alive, Margaret. Your children are not dead; they are alive," Kelly whispered, tears streaming down her cheeks, tears that Margaret reached out and touched, palming Kelly's face.

"Is it true?" she asked, hope suddenly pushing away the darkness of her existence. "My children live," she whispered over and over. Finally, she covered her face with her *taub*, her shoulders and body shaking as she silently wept for joy.

Julia joined the other two women and stated what was no longer an option.

"Kelly and Margaret, we have to escape from this place. We need to think of a plan."

Margaret's face shot up, a tiny spark of light in her eyes that quickly dimmed. "Is hopeless. No way past guards. No places on outside of camp for hiding."

"There must be a way. We need to think," Julia insisted.

"Maybe one way," Margaret said slowly, "at night."

"We're listening."

Margaret slowly explained to them, drawing a crude map of the camp in the dust on the cell floor with her finger. Julia nodded. It might work. They agreed to try it that night. Time, for all of them, was running out.

"I go now." Margaret got up, turning to the door. "Before, I don't care if I die. Now . . . now is different. My children live."

"Margaret, I will pray for you, that God will protect you and guide your steps." Kelly spoke softly, conviction in every word. "And I pray that one day soon you will be with Mary and Samuel again."

Then Margaret was gone. The door opened and closed almost silently behind her. Kelly and Julia strained to hear sounds from the guard for several moments after she left, but all was quiet.

At sunset, Nassir and Mustafa returned. Their eyes were bloodshot—from the burning fires, or the lust of killing, or maybe both.

When Julia and Kelly both refused to turn to Islam after more attempted persuasions, only one man was disappointed. Nassir left their cell in disgust, without so much as a glance over his shoulder. Mustafa lingered at the cell door, leering at them. In the morning, he said, Nassir would be away and would not be able to stop Mustafa from taking what was his by jihad law.

"You will scream," he said, his face contorted with a sadistic insanity, "and no one will care."

# TWENTY-SIX

Probably the number one reason prayer
malfunctions in the hands of believers is that we
try to turn a wartime walkie-talkie into a domestic
intercom. Until you know that life is war, you cannot
know what prayer is for.

JOHN PIPER, *LET THE NATIONS BE GLAD: THE SUPREMACY OF GOD IN MISSIONS*

SHE WAS HANGING CRISP WHITE sheets out on the clothesline. It was
a beautiful summer day, puffy clouds sailing across the blue sky. Julia
and the lawyer man were running back and forth under her clothesline, playing a game. They laughed and giggled, the wind carrying their
voices to her, far, far away at the top of the porch step. Why were they
so far away? She could hardly hear them. She squinted her eyes into
the sun, trying to see them playing. One of the sheets had fallen to the
ground. It was covering the children; that's why she couldn't see them,
couldn't hear them.

Carefully, she stepped down the rickety back stairs; several steps
were in need of repair, and the railing was rough with peeling green
paint as she held onto it for support. At the bottom, she started running

to where the children were struggling under the sheet, her hip aching from the effort, but she couldn't reach them. She could see them still moving. Could barely make out their little voices. But she couldn't get near. No matter how fast she tried to run, no matter how many sheets she walked past hanging on the line, she could not get to them. They weren't giggling anymore. They were calling her name and crying out for help.

Rose sat up in the pitch dark, her heart pounding in her chest. Something was wrong with Julia and Mr.—what was his name? She couldn't remember. He was here the day she had dug up the dahlia bulbs. She remembered he'd been asking about Julia. That must be why he was mixed up in the dream. Too many dreams and lives and crises had come and gone in Aunt Rose's life for her to doubt that the dream was important. Those young people needed her prayers. When the Spirit said pray, she prayed.

Getting out of bed, she knelt on her worn carpet and cried out to her heavenly Father, the Maker and Revealer of every dream.

The morning shone bright with a fine dusting of new snow. Rose had slept deeply after responding to the urgent need for prayer the Father had sent her. She never lacked from Him what she needed when she listened and obeyed. In her younger years, she had often spent long, exhausting hours worrying and anxious about burdens that had not been hers to carry. But as she learned to respond to the ones He gave her, she found His load was never too heavy. Sorrowful, sometimes, yes. Last night, she had wept before the heaviness of the prayer had lifted, replaced with a peace in knowing her petitions were heard. She had slept soundly afterward, waking refreshed, a song in her heart.

Thanksgiving was next week. The record player was scraping out a nostalgic rendering of "Come, Ye Thankful People, Come" while Rose fried an egg and slathered toast with marmalade. She sipped her tea appreciatively as she read the brown leather Bible on the table beside her.

When the phone rang, disturbing the quiet moment, she frowned, wondering who it could be. The call display said Evans. *That's right.*

"'Ello, Ella, I almost forgot," Rose told her friend.

"I'll be waiting for you, honey." Ella called everyone *honey*. She wasn't from the Deep South, but she had raised five children and had twenty-three grandchildren. She had long ago lost her ability to get everyone's names straight, so she just used *honey*.

Rose concentrated on the road; the new snowfall was almost gone, but the temperatures were still too low to assume there wouldn't be hidden ice. She stopped at Anne's house, picking up the third member of their weekly Wednesday morning prayer meetings. They used to go to the church on Wednesday nights to pray, but several years prior, the pastor had told them that he would prefer it if they met in one another's homes, saving him the trip out to open and close the building for such a small group of people. They hadn't minded, although their numbers were further reduced, from only eight or nine at a good turnout to their faithful little trio. When all three of them remembered. They used to rotate their homes for the meeting, but since Charles's stroke, it had become more difficult for Ella to get out. So now the ladies came to her. Rose had had a stroke herself several years back, which had left her incapacitated for a time. Gradually with physical therapy, she had been able to resume almost all her former activities; her friends had prayed her through those difficult, frustrating days.

Anne had on her winter boots. Rose smiled a greeting. Anne didn't take chances with her sidewalks since her fall two winters before. She proudly showed off the new ice grips that clamped to the bottom of her boots, making her almost impervious to icy perils.

They chatted like professionals, recycling old conversations with teeny pieces of new news added sparingly to make conversation stretch through the morning.

Arriving at the Evanses', they made their bundled way up the walkway. Rose wondered who would shovel it for them if snow really did fall and stay.

Ella opened the door, the fragrance of her blueberry muffins pouring out like a blessing on the visitors.

"Come in, come in." Her cheeks were bright like Mrs. Claus. "My, my, my, you ladies brave all weather."

"'Ello, dear." Rose pressed a kiss to her friend's cheek. "Not to worry. The snow's all gone from the roads."

Their coats were put away, and they gathered around Ella's small kitchen table, covered in a green-flowered plastic tablecloth.

The warm muffins were served on a pink-flowered china plate on top of a lace doily, with cold butter on a butter dish and homemade raspberry jam in a little crystal cup. They ate and chatted some more until finally Ella asked Rose to read a passage from the Word.

Rose opened her Bible and read from Psalm 116.

When she got to the part that read, "Precious in the sight of the Lord is the death of his saints," she saw Ella dabbing her eyes with a tissue. Stopping for a moment, Rose laid her hand on Ella's. "Are you all right, dear?"

"Oh, honey, I just can't believe that our day is so close. Charles . . . Charles could go any time. I'm glad our passing is precious to Jesus, but it's sure hard on the ones who have to stay behind." She sniffed, her eyes filling up again.

"I remember my mother explaining that same passage to me in quite a different way. It wasn't so much that the Lord looks forward to seeing us on the other side, although I know He is waiting for us there, but rather that the deaths of the saints themselves are carefully planned and ordained by Him. He isn't just waiting on the other side; He's in the passing."

The ladies stopped and considered this, an unusual silence resting over them.

"Thank you for that, Rose. I think we should pray now," Ella said, smiling though still teary, and giving Rose's hand a little squeeze.

They made a long list. Rose added Julia's name and "the lawyer," telling her friends about the dream she had had in the night.

"Where has that niece of yours gone to this time, Rose?" Anne asked.

"She's in Sudan, writing about the terrible things that are happening to those poor people."

"Let's pray for the Sudanese people, too, then," Ella suggested, "and the church there. We should remember our brothers and sisters across the world who are suffering—more often than we do."

Rose nodded, smiling at her friend and the compassion she was known for, always at the ready, always sincere. The Lord had blessed her indeed with these women whom she trusted as her friends and sisters. Bowing their heads, they began a vigil that lasted for more than an hour, knitting their hearts together in prayer.

# Twenty-seven

The aim of the attacker is to destroy you,
and cut you off from Christ, and bring you to final
ruin without God. You are a conqueror if you defeat
this aim and remain in the love of Christ.

JOHN PIPER, *DON'T WASTE YOUR LIFE*

MATTHEWS GRINNED AT JOEL and Steve as he turned and led them out of the jungle foliage into a small clearing hidden from view of the bridge. The SLA were holed up there during this skirmish. Joel didn't think he'd ever seen anything so miserable. They were just little boys—some couldn't be more than nine or ten years old. Several lay bleeding on the ground. A young kid carrying strips of cloth moved from boy to boy, binding machine-gun lacerations in arms and legs. Two bodies lay to the side of the clearing. The fallen.

Steve groaned.

Joel understood. Sorrow and shame mixed together, creating a physical pain in his chest. How had the world come to this? What grotesqueness had mankind come to?

Matthews left them for a moment, returning with two extra guns retrieved from the corpses at the clearing's edge.

"I know this is not a good time," Steve confessed, looking more than a little uncomfortable, "but I—well, I don't know how to use a gun, and I'm not sure I could ever shoot a man, Janja or no Janja. Let me stay here and help with your wounded."

"All right, you stay here," Matthews agreed. He turned to Joel.

"We fight, now. I will show you," he said, his eyes shining with an unholy gleam.

Joel accepted the gun gingerly. He really hadn't been planning to shoot anyone today, either, but wasn't about to say so.

Following him through the brush, Joel moved carefully and slowly until they crested a slight rise where they were in range of the bridge. Other boys lay armed and waiting. Joel saw the Janja truck in the distance, parked on the bridge. Abandoned, he assumed, when the SLA troop caught them in the surprise attack that morning. Across the river, he could see several headless bodies lying by the roadside where Eddy had greeted them just yesterday morning. Bodies wearing Jebel Marra Camp shirts. Bodies that were black-skinned, just like the SLA soldiers. Eddy? Arnold?

Joel had felt adrenaline kick in at the falls, but now he could feel the blood rush to his head as rage over such senseless murders filled him. Tightening his hands around the smooth steel of the AK-47 that Matthews had entrusted to him, Joel narrowed his eyes. His gun experience was patchy, but on the rare occasions that he had gone hunting with an uncle or college buddy, he'd done himself proud. A machine gun was a different beast from a rifle, but he figured it couldn't be that complicated.

And a minute later when bullets pinged past their ears from the direction of the river, he found that firing back wasn't difficult at all.

When one of the Janja toppled and fell, directly across the river from him, Joel was certain it was his shot.

These SLA corps were experts at diversionary tactics. Every few minutes or so, one of the boys would run out from a new and unexpected spot, having sneaked carefully through long grass to achieve a good position, drawing Janja fire toward himself and exposing the enemy's positions while they attempted to pick off the kid.

Joel's eyes began to stream as the intense focus, the heat of the sun, the smoke, and the din began to distract him and play havoc with his aim.

A volley of bullets came raining down on them, and they flattened themselves, waiting for it to pass.

"When will these Janja give up?" Joel muttered to Matthews, on the other side of him.

"They never will." Matthews grimaced as he doggedly continued firing.

"There's got to be a better way." Joel grunted, wondering how they could possibly continue under this onslaught. They were simply outnumbered and out-munitioned by the Janja. The SLA boys would be picked off one by one, until no one was left.

When the solution occurred to him, he wondered why he hadn't thought of it sooner; it was perfectly simple.

"Matthews!" he yelled over the bedlam. "What if we took some of these guys back up the tunnel?"

Matthews let fly a volley. Joel waited until the ringing in his ears began to subside.

"Down," Matthews called. They dived, keeping themselves to the ground as return fire zipped and zinged over their heads.

"We could work our way over to the other side of the river and surprise them from behind." Joel thought his idea had potential. Matthews lay on his back, breathing hard, and apparently considering. Finally, he turned onto his belly, crawling away from the gunfire.

"Come." He beckoned to Joel with his hand. "You need to talk to Joseph."

Joel followed, slithering like a snake as they made their way through the jungle back to the base camp.

Noticing Steve's red, blistering nose and cheeks, Joel realized that they must have been out here for a long time.

"You forgot the sunblock, you dummy," Joel told him.

"Yeah, and you forgot your shades," Steve retorted.

Joel explained his idea to Steve about using the tunnel to get behind the Janja. He nodded slowly, thinking it through, then whistled between his teeth. "It might just work."

Matthews hurried Joel along a short path, where they approached a young soldier who looked to be about sixteen years old. He had facial hair, but it was new and soft. A black bandanna covered his forehead, and he wore a loose, navy blue shirt, unbuttoned.

"Commander Joseph." Matthews stood at attention and addressed his leader.

"Matthews, how are you doing, little one?" Joseph spoke to Matthews like an older brother might to a younger. Joel shook his head slowly, reminding himself that boys this age were in high school back home, playing basketball, hanging out, watching TV.

Matthews introduced Joel, who immediately launched into an explanation of the plan as Joseph listened intently, raising his eyebrows at the description of the tunnel that led to the waterfall.

"If this is true, we could use this tunnel and take our wounded to a safer place," he said thoughtfully.

The young commander did not have his rank by accident, Joel decided, nodding in quick agreement. "And if we could get the injured out, we definitely might be able to surprise the Janja by coming in from behind."

Drawing in the dirt, they discussed Joel's idea, sketching out a rough map of the tunnel, the layout of the cabanas in the camp, and identifying which buildings might be used for reconnaissance. They nodded in quick agreement, the decision made.

Calling over some of the wounded fighters who were still able to move about without assistance, Joseph quickly organized a transport detail for all the wounded. He also sent Matthews to round up ten of his crack snipers to reconnoiter a trail into the back side of the camp.

The trick was to continue engaging the Janja, at least sporadically, and have fighters drop out of the firing gradually as though they were suffering casualties. These fighters would join Joel and Steve and cross the river via the tunnel, while a contingent remained in place, continuing to volley gunfire at the enemy in an attempt to hide the fact that most of their troops had left. Messages were sent quickly down the line, putting the plan into action.

Making their way back into the tunnel, Joel and Steve retraced their steps with eleven boys, including Matthews, Joseph following more slowly with the wounded.

The group of tourists evidenced varying degrees of relief and strain as the men and boys emerged from the tunnel into the cavern.

"It's about time! Where have you—" Bill stopped when he noticed the SLA soldiers. "Hey, who are all these kids?"

"We thought," Joel said, dusting himself off from the tunnel debris and any possible clinging insects, "that since we were in Africa, we should start an orphanage, you know, like Oprah."

His attempt to defuse the fear and tension with a bit of humor did not go over well.

"Very funny, Joel." Anita spoke quite crossly. "But did you stop to think how we might be feeling, waiting in a damp, dark cave with the sound of gunfire outside, wondering how long it will be before some Janja soldiers come out of the tunnel to shoot us?"

"Sorry everyone," Steve said calmly, "but it's no picnic out there, either." He briefly described what had happened and then carefully explained that they would have to make room for and, if they could, try to help with the wounded boys being brought into the cave. Even as he spoke, they were entering the cave.

The irritation on Anita's face softened into sympathy as she gazed at these boys on their makeshift stretchers.

Steve continued to tell the safari group the rest of the plan to overcome the Janjaweed by surprising them from behind on the resort side.

The SLA boys, following the dialogue as best they could, nodded occasionally, but looked restless and worried as the gunfire outside continued.

Silence fell over the group as they pondered what might happen next, moving instinctively closer to the streams of daylight shimmering through the waterfall several feet beyond them.

Matthews nudged Joel. It was time.

"Let's go, Steve," Joel said.

"I think it would be a good idea if we asked God to help us first."

Joel nodded. It was a good idea. Pulling the boys around them, Steve prayed over the tourists and soldiers, white and black.

"God, we are facing an enemy that would destroy us. We ask for Your hand to guide us on right paths, to protect us from every bullet, and to bring us victory. We ask not for our will, but for Your will to be done, Father. We will give You all the praise. In Jesus' name, amen."

Steve stationed himself at the mouth of the tunnel, waiting there with the safari group, ready to lead the fighters who were still working their way from the main conflict to join the new endeavor.

Joel grimaced, the air all but choked out of him, as Steve grabbed him in a rough bear hug.

"Go with God, my friend."

Joel nodded, unsure of how to respond, and gave Steve a friendly cuff on the side of his shaggy head before slipping into the water with eleven boys moving quietly behind him. Moments later, he stood with them on the eastern side of the riverbank, inside Jebel Marra Camp once again.

They cut north into the jungle, using its cover to work their way toward the cliffs on the eastern boundary of the camp. They planned to slip back inside the camp from the eastern end in order to station themselves well behind the Janja. Once they were back in the camp, they could use the cabanas and outbuildings for cover.

It went more smoothly than Joel had hoped.

Before he realized it, they were at the back of the dining hall, groups of SLA boys behind each building, ready and waiting for the signal.

They held their positions for several moments until Steve and his troop appeared. Tension wiped away Steve's usual carefree smile. He had led the boys to Joel and the other fighters, but Joel knew Steve wasn't a fighter. He wasn't even carrying a gun. Making eye contact with him, Joel was surprised by the look of determination in Steve's gaze even as his mouth moved silently. He was praying. Joel knew it with absolute certainty. The man had come to the battle to pray.

Joel looked down at Matthews standing at shoulder height beside him. Matthews, in turn, looked back at him, winked, and whispered, "You the man."

Shaking his head and grinning in spite of himself, Joel glanced over this motley crew of young boys he was about to lead into combat. He hated who he was in that moment.

A thumbs-up response from Matthews. It was now or never. Turning to the boys standing around him, he nodded three times, the agreed-upon signal. Moving swiftly, they used every possible shadow for cover until they had the Janja in their sights and within range. These kids knew what they were doing and how to do it, Joel suddenly realized with admiration and shock.

At least two dozen Janjaweed—more than Joel had estimated—were still busily engaged, returning fire at the SLA on the other side of the river. He looked at their backs for a moment, panicked for another, and then pulled himself together, remembering the sight of the decapitated Jebel Marra guides.

"Now!" he yelled, giving the order to open fire and letting loose his own AK-47 as he did.

Gunfire burst out around him from both sides, making his ears ring.

Taken so completely by surprise, the Janja were easy targets. Most of them were picked off within the first several minutes. The few who escaped alive ran into the jungle and were chased down. Joel had a fleeting thought of pity for these Janja. The machine guns' *rat-a-tat-a-tat-tat* rang out occasionally from that direction, making him apprehensive, but one by one, the boys returned, their guns hanging by their sides.

It was over.

Walking slowly as if in a dream, or rather a nightmare, Joel counted Janja corpses. They would need to dispose of these somehow, he dimly realized.

The afternoon had waned, and rain began to fall, warm and gentle. Joel found himself kneeling beside the pool of water by the falls, several dead bodies on the ground nearby. This was what he had done. He submerged his hands in the cool water and saw blood. Blood-stained soil was leeching into the cleansing water. *In Sudan*, Joel thought, *even the earth bleeds.*

Staring intently at the ripples of water the rain was creating on the surface of the pool, he didn't see the Janja raise himself up, lift his machine gun, and point it directly at him.

"Joel! Look out!

Joel immediately dropped and rolled to the side. Managing to get a grip on his weapon, he raised himself up slightly and pulled the trigger. The shot went wide, grazing the Janja's shoulder; Joel steadied himself to shoot again. There was no need. Matthews was there before him. Standing with the barrel of his AK-47 against the Janjaweed's head,

Matthews's face wore a look of detached hatred. Joel braced himself against what he was about to see.

"No!"

Matthews paused, cocking his head even as Steve's long strides covered the distance between them. Removing the gun from the Janja, who had fallen back to the ground, Steve handed the weapon to Matthews as his hands gently assessed the Janja's body for wounds.

"It's over," Steve said. "We won. We fought against the enemy who would have probably killed each and every last one of us without mercy. But Matthews"—he raised his voice just a notch above the controlled anger he was speaking through—"does that mean we should sink to the same level? If we behave like our enemy, we become our enemy and will never know any peace. If we overcome our enemy with the goodness of God's mercy and love, we might see an end to this fighting. But even if we don't, it's the only defense we have to keep ourselves from becoming the same monsters they are."

The Janja, uncomprehending, watched Steve tear off his shirt, rip it into strips, and begin to wrap it gently around the gaping wound in his arm, forming a tourniquet to stanch the flow of blood. Joel moved in closer to cover the Janja with his gun while Steve ministered to him. *Just to be on the safe side.*

During the last part of Steve's argument, young Commander Joseph had rejoined them from his station on the other side of the river.

"It is true," he said, his face wearing a pained expression, "but while you care for the enemy, I have nineteen soldiers who lie bleeding in the cave and eight dead who must be buried. I must make decisions of importance every moment: what I must do, not what I can do."

Steve did not argue. He nodded as he finished with the bandaging. "I understand, Joseph, and this was what I had to do," he answered. "You are a good commander. You treat the boys kindly and lead them well. I will come and help you now, and we will take care of them together."

They walked away quickly, Steve's arm over the younger man's shoulder, talking in low tones, which left Joel and Matthews with the Janja and the predicament of what to do with him.

"It is easier to kill him than to take him alive," Matthews pointed out.

"No doubt," Joel agreed, "but I think we can make a nice prison for him in one of the cabanas where he can wait while we decide what to do with him."

After they tied up the surviving Janja and organized a guard over the cabana, they piled all the corpses into the government-issued Jeeps the Janja had arrived in, shoved the gears into neutral, and pushed the vehicles over the mountain's edge in an attempt to hide what had happened from the eyes of any Janja who might come looking.

It wasn't the most luxurious travel arrangements that the safari group had ever had, but it was the best they could figure out in the aftermath of the Janja raid. They would head back down to the valley with the SLA the next morning to be dropped off at an IDP camp, where they would have to make their own arrangements for getting back to Khartoum. Joel wondered if they might even end up at Hassa Hissa camp. He would like to see Julia again. No, he decided, being perfectly honest with himself, he *longed* to see her again. Something about the fighting and killing had left a bad taste in Joel's mouth. Maybe seeing her again would take it away.

The Janja prisoner would be taken to one of the SLA bases where he could be put under guard and where it would be decided what would happen to him. The logistics of the situation left Joel shaking his head. The boys complained to him that it was very difficult for them to take prisoners since they had such little manpower. They explained how the

Sudanese government itself was supporting the Janjaweed, so there was no national security that would deal with the Janja. The SLA and other "rebellions" like them were considered the criminals. No jail or prison in Sudan would incarcerate a Janja.

Later, much later, that night, Joel asked the question that had surfaced repeatedly during this terrible, strange day. He spoke quietly to the boy who lay awake on a mat beside him.

"Matthews, why are you fighting? Why do you keep at this terrible war?"

There was no answer at first. Joel wondered if the boy had already fallen asleep. Then Matthews started speaking, his voice small in the darkness.

"When I was six years old, the government soldiers came to my village and burned it down. They shot my father. They cut off the arms of my two little brothers and laughed, saying they would never have to worry they might shoot a gun at them. John died soon after, but Simon is still living with an auntie. They raped my sister and my mother."

His voice dropped to a whisper. "And they laughed as they shot them. My mother had hidden me in the durra sack, covering me with grain."

After a long pause, the twelve-year-old continued in a steadier voice, "I hope one day I can be like you. Today, I saw you fight good." Joel smiled at this—high praise from a superior soldier. "But you do not hate. Maybe someday I won't have hate. Now, it is all I have."

Joel had no words, and his tears were silent. Reaching out his hand, he rested it on the boy's dark, curly hair until his breathing grew steady and even, sleep bringing a short reprieve from memories.

*Why, God?* The question filled Joel's heart, pounded in his head, and choked him. But the sound of the rain pouring down outside was the only answer he heard.

# Twenty-eight

᷑

In all these things we are more than conquerors
through him who loved us. For I am sure that neither
death nor life, nor angels nor rulers,
nor things present nor things to come, nor powers,
nor height nor depth, nor anything else in all
creation, will be able to separate us from the love of
God in Christ Jesus our Lord.

Romans 8:37–39

Peter looked to the fire he was patiently tending. The pot of *waika* simmered in the embers. The scent of the meat and onions made his taste buds water. The *asida* was already prepared and waiting.

Peter was not the only one who would enjoy his small meal. Every day, he cooked the portions of food he was allotted in the camp, and every day, hungry, orphaned camp children would hover and wait for him to set the bowl and pot down several feet in front of the fire, signaling that he had had enough. Then they would scurry toward it, licking it clean in no time. Usually, between three and ten children waited for and watched Peter with their hollowed eyes and extended stomachs.

Every day, he went a little hungry. But he was satisfied to have these children share his meal. Satisfied to have less.

"Peter, you must eat, my friend," Hassan said, encircling Peter in a warm hug. "All I feel here is bones. You have no fat."

"I am an old man, Hassan. I don't need food the same way I used to. These children"—he gestured to those gathered around his fire—"they have no one to provide for them. We must give what we can."

Hassan nodded. "But you must take proper care of yourself, or the children will miss more than your food."

"You are wise, Hassan, but I believe the Lord sustains us when we care for those who live next to His heart."

Dave approached the two men who were crouched as far away from the heat of the fire as they could be while Peter still tended the pot. Squatting down clumsily, Dave took his place with the other two men. They had met together in this way each day since Kelly's kidnapping.

"How are you, brother?" Peter asked.

"It's the third day." Dave told them what he knew they already knew. "The second day for Julia. So far nothing has happened. We sent messages to Nassir telling him we would do whatever he wants, and nothing. I can't stand this—this waiting. Every inch of me is screaming to grab a gun and a jeep and go and get her back."

Both men nodded, young African and old African.

"We have prayed, and we know that God hears us," Hassan reminded Dave.

"Yes, I believe it with all my heart, but why do I feel no peace? Why is my wife not released?"

"Have you given her to God?" Peter asked, his voice deepened with sorrow.

"Given her to God? She already belongs to Him."

"Yes. But have you given her, your most precious gift on earth, back to the Giver? Are your desires for her that she would be used for Jesus, or used for yourself?"

"But she is my wife, Peter!"

"A wife is the Lord's good gift to a man. But she is not yours to consume. She belongs to her Maker, and one day you or she will pass from this world and leave the other alone. The Lord gives, and the Lord takes away."

Peter's words resonated in Dave's mind, but images of barbecue picnics and Christmas dinners and grandchildren—if God granted them—playing on a rope swing flashed through his mind. Weren't all those things normal dreams? To plan toward and hope for? He and Kelly devoted their lives to others; they were not selfish people. Was it too much to ask to grow old together?

"I think," Hassan said, sympathy etched in the lines on his face, "we must pray."

They prayed for the women, for their release, for God's will to be accomplished in the situation.

"And Father," Dave finished, "I guess I never thought of giving Kelly back to You before, but it makes sense. Thank You so much for the blessing that she's been to me. Thank You for such an incredible gift. And Father—" His voice broke. It took him a few moments to choke down the painful lump in his throat. The rest of his prayer came out at little more than a whisper. "I give Kelly back to You. Do with her what pleases You the most. Our lives are not for ourselves; our lives are for You. Amen."

"Blessed be His name," Peter added.

"Blessed be His name," Hassan and Dave echoed.

# Twenty-nine

All shall be well, and all shall be well,
and all manner of things shall be well.

St. Julian of Norwich, *Revelations of Divine Love*

Julia's cheek pressed against the cool brick wall. The burqa served at night as a kind of a blanket, not because she was cold, but to keep the eyes of Mustafa and the other Janja off her body, and for that she was grateful, but wished it wasn't so hot. Glancing at Kelly, she could see perspiration beading her brow. The lengthening shadow of twilight accented the dark hollows under her friend's eyes. Julia knew the signs of exhaustion and strain were mirrored on her own face, but sleep eluded her. Instead, she worried over the details of the escape plan.

"God, if You are who Kelly thinks You are, then we need Your help." The whispered words seemed very small and weak, as when she tried to scream in a nightmare but it came out as a whisper. The prayer was not strong enough, she thought, to make it through the roof. A tear escaped down her cheek. Dashing it away, she squared her shoulders and set herself to wait, wanting to be ready as soon as Margaret sent the signal.

With a start, she opened her eyes. Had she heard something? She had fallen asleep; for how long, she didn't know. The room was utterly dark. *Just as well, for what they were attempting.*

Had the signal arrived while she slept? Crawling on her hands and knees to the wall directly underneath the barred window, she felt gingerly across the rough cement floor. It was there. Margaret had succeeded. A key wrapped in a soft cloth was lying on the floor.

Confident that she would be able to obtain a key for unlocking the door, Margaret had refused to answer their questions as to how she would accomplish this. The sign would be the thump of the key landing on the cell floor, wrapped in cloth so it wouldn't alert the guards, but if the women could stay alert and wait for it, they would know for certain when it came. Julia thought the key had just arrived, but she wasn't absolutely confident. Had she heard the key and woken straight away, or had there been a lapse of time? If there was, she didn't think it could have been long. Reaching over to where Kelly was sleeping, she gently shook her friend's shoulder. Kelly sat up. Julia could hear her shuffling herself together.

"Is the key here?" Kelly whispered.

Julia slid her arm around Kelly's shoulder and gave her a little squeeze.

"It's here. Let's go." She didn't say it, but she hoped they were ready. Darkness surrounded them in this cell in more ways than one. The risk of escape had been calculated against the risk of staying and hoping for rescue. Escape it was, ready or not.

"Julia, let's pray."

Somehow, even though Kelly's prayer was whispered as quietly as her own had been, Julia thought that it had a better chance of getting past the roof. Kelly prayed as if God wasn't just listening, but was interested.

Julia froze. What was Kelly saying? She hadn't been paying much attention to her friend's petition, assuming that she knew what to ask for, but the words she spoke jarred Julia's sensibilities.

"And open their eyes to see, and their ears to hear. Thank You for protecting us, Father, and please forgive these Janja for the evil that they have done and plan to do to us. Set them free from the bondage of darkness that they are in. Help them to find Jesus, too, and through Your grace, the miracle of love and forgiveness. And Lord, help Julia to know it, too. Give her Your precious gift of faith. In Jesus' name, amen."

"I don't think I like that prayer, Kelly. How can you pray for these men?"

"Oh, Julia, it's not me—"

"Shhh," Julia cut her off. "We need to go."

Kelly made no reply as Julia inserted the key, turning it as quietly as she could. Slowly, the door inched open, as they waited for what seemed like long moments to see if it made so much as a creak.

Once the door was open sufficiently wide, they tiptoed down the short hall, Julia's hands leading the way, sliding along the wall by their side. They moved carefully, trying to hide inside the darkness, aware that the guard would be just around the corner at the end of the hall. It seemed like an eternity, but finally they were there. Julia could see him. It was Mustafa. She knew that odiously familiar head, now sagging in slumber.

Kelly gently tugged the end of her burqa twice. *Go or stay?* Julia answered Kelly's unspoken question by grasping her hand tightly, and together they started toward the door. The women crept along the shadows of the main entry until finally reaching their goal: an iron door with an iron bolt. Impossible to get through without a clang or a squeak. This was the weakest part of a desperate plan. They knew the guard changed during the middle of the night. But when? Had it already happened while they had slept? If Mustafa's breathing and slight snore were any indication, Julia expected they would have company soon. Waiting in the shadows across the room from a sleeping

Mustafa, her heart raced like a sprinter's. Silently, leaning together and clutching each other in fear, the women waited. And waited. While Mustafa snored.

Julia had started to touch her toes every few minutes, stretching her legs to relieve muscle fatigue. Kelly followed suit. It helped. When the doorknob turned, neither of them could see it in the darkness, but they heard it. Julia felt her legs turn to jelly. Everything depended on this moment.

The door swung wide. Oblivious to the women huddled against the wall, the guard came walking in, swinging his flashlight in front of him, narrowly missing the women's forms to the side of the door.

"Mustafa!" The arc of his flashlight surprised the sleeping guard.

The girls didn't wait to see what happened. They glided as smoothly and silently as they could through the doorway into the night. No one yelled. No one fired a gun. They were out, and they were free.

Almost. Hugging the walls of the block buildings that composed the Janjaweed base, Julia and Kelly flitted from one long, dark shadow to the next, expecting at any moment to hear a shout, but the only voices they heard were those of the cicadas. Making their way to the back of the camp where the Zurgha slaves were kept, they avoided the main path, skirting the huts until they reached the northwest corner of the boundary wall.

She was there. Shaking with fear but ready to guide them out, Margaret reached out her arms, embracing both of them.

"God be praised you are here. I began to wonder if you would come," she said, speaking so softly, Julia had to lean close to hear her. "I will take you to the opening. Come. We are in the hands of God now."

They turned up the path, following Margaret southward along the wall for several minutes. Julia realized she could dimly see the ground. The darkest part of the night was over. They needed to cover as much ground as they could before morning gave them away.

Stopping abruptly, Margaret turned and signaled for quiet. Bending down between the wall and a random bush, she worked at something that sounded like digging and scraping. Still in a kneeling position, she beckoned with her arm and disappeared through the wall. Julia crouched down and felt in front of her with her hands, trying to ascertain the size of the opening. What she felt was broken brick and pieces of mortar surrounding a roughly oval space. Crawling on her belly, using her hands and feet to pull and push herself through, she left the Janja camp.

As Kelly made her way through, Margaret explained, "We use it for goats. You call it shortcut, yes?"

Julia smiled at her and nodded. The swallows and swifts had begun their morning song. With a rising sense of panic at how little time they had left, Julia placed her hand on Margaret's shoulder, pushing slightly.

"Hurry, please," she said. "We must move as fast as possible."

Margaret glanced back, nodded, and quickened the pace.

Julia worried. This country was such a barren land. Except for an occasional lonely shrub or bush, and rarely an acacia tree, places to take cover or hide were few and far between. Her ears strained constantly for the sound of a vehicle approaching, the sound that would warn them to run for cover.

And so, sometime later, when she heard camels' hooves, she realized she had made a mistake. All three women turned; all three saw the fear in each others' eyes. These experienced Janja must have seen them a long time before the women could possibly have heard the desert beasts.

As if on cue, the shrill "ay-yi-yi-yi-yi-yi-yi-yi-yi" of the nomadic hunter reached their ears. The women stopped, powerless to move, knowing that they were the prey; they huddled together in fear.

"Father, save us. Oh God in heaven, help us now." It was Kelly. Scared, but praying.

"Ay-yi-yi-yi-yi-yi." A devilish shriek.

"Run toward the road!" Julia ordered.

Grabbing Margaret's hand in hers, Julia pulled the woman with her. But Margaret was exhausted. She was wheezing and gasping uncontrollably, and Julia realized that malnutrition and abuse had left her depleted.

Hope lay in the road alone. Public vehicles might stop. *And might not*, Julia thought. But it was all they had. Glancing back over her shoulder, she saw the ungainly beasts coming on with their odd, loping gait. Five of them traveled in a V formation like geese. They didn't appear hurried. She knew that the Janja wouldn't hurry the camels if they were sure of their prey. Rage such as she had never known built up in her. Half carrying, half dragging Margaret, she saw that Kelly had gained some distance but seemed to be slowing. Exhaustion must be getting the better of her. Exhaustion and fear.

"Run, Kelly! Get to the road!" Willing her words to keep her friend moving, sweat poured off Julia's brow. The sun had not come up yet. The morning was gray. The ground was gray, the camels and Janja were gray. Everything seemed colorless. *It's the end.* For a moment, she imagined herself dead.

Then everything slowed. She felt disconnected, as if she weren't really there at all. Shock. Somewhere in the back of her mind, she knew she was going into shock. All the tension of the night followed by the physical push of these last three or four miles . . .

"Julia, look!" Margaret was pointing at the camels behind them. One of the Janja had separated himself from the group; even as they watched, he picked up speed, and headed toward Kelly. Pure frustration and helplessness overwhelmed Julia.

"Julia," Margaret's eyes searched her own, "if I die, please care for my children."

The words fell on Julia like clear, cold water, and suddenly she felt real again. Real in a horror story that so many others had already lived—or not lived—through. Tears pouring down Margaret's cheeks bore testimony to that. And to something else: a hard, stony look in her eyes. A woman facing the ultimate nightmare.

"I will, Margaret. I promise."

The men on camels suddenly were upon them, the animals' hooves flinging up sand. The camels brushed close against them, jostling them off balance. The strong, pungent odor of the beasts filled Julia's nostrils as she raised her eyes and found a machine-gun barrel pointed straight at her heart. A man's gaze met her own. His eyes showed no sympathy. Mustafa, Julia realized, is experienced in hunting women.

"Where did you think you could go to get away from us?" Mustafa spat the words at her. "You run, but it does no good."

He dismounted with an agility that surprised her and with a single step was beside her, grabbing her arm roughly and making her cringe. "We will have to teach you, now, to never run again."

Julia stared in horror, unwilling to see, but unable to tear her eyes away from the potent evil in Mustafa's eyes. This was no normal hatred that was held in check by society's boundaries, justified or unjustified. This was hatred unleashed, bordering on madness; total evil for evil's sake. This was a person who had lost his very soul. What had taken its place was ugly, glinting, and cruel.

Out of the corner of her eye, Julia saw Margaret suffering at the hands of the other three Janja. But there had been five. She knew there had been five . . . where . . . Kelly! She yanked herself out of Mustafa's grip, turning toward the road where her friend had headed, calling as she did so, "Kelly!"

The sudden blow caught her unexpectedly and with such force to the back of her head that it knocked the wind out of her and made her teeth and ears ring. Doubling over, she fell to her knees, stunned. Tears stung her eyes shut and squeezed out of her lids.

From somewhere far away, she heard Kelly calling her name. Kelly. They had captured her, too. God had not saved her.

"I hate you! I hate you! I hate you!" Her screams shook her, leaving her trembling. "I hate you!" she screamed at Mustafa. With her fists beating the dusty, hard earth, she screamed at her father and at all Janja. She screamed at misery and injustice and pain. She screamed at God.

"Stop!" Mustafa's shout did not make sense in Julia's mind. "Stop!" She could not. She continued shrieking like a mad woman.

When he kicked her, she paused, the pain of it sucking the breath from her body. But when he kept kicking her, the rage spun out of control again, and she did what she would never have thought to do. Grabbing his dirty, scuffed boot with both her hands, she yanked his leg before he could make contact with her bruised body again. Pulling with all her might, Julia watched as Mustafa crashed to the ground like a huge, felled tree.

"Timber," Julia whispered. A giggle escaped her lips before her senses returned. Which they did as soon as she saw the look on Mustafa's face.

Julia stared aghast as his finger flipped the safety on the AK-47, lifted it toward her, and—

"No!"

Julia heard Kelly scream and then, from out of nowhere, her friend threw herself between them.

The gun went off, making her ears ring.

Then silence.

Mustafa and Julia both stared at the stain that spread over Kelly's abdomen, where she had fallen between them.

Julia's comprehension returned more slowly than Mustafa's did. He got up, walked over to Kelly, and pulled off her wedding ring.

"Stop it, stop . . . stop, please, stop . . ." Sobs began to shake Julia. Trembling, she lay over Kelly's bloody body and wept, smoothing the hair from Kelly's face, holding her cheeks and searching her eyes. Kelly looked at Julia, her eyes clouding over even as she whispered something. Julia bent down, trying to hear.

"Read your letters," she whispered. Her mouth went slack, and her eyes stared up at the blue sky—unseeing.

"Kelly. Kelly, don't! No! Please, no . . ."

Whimpering, Julia knelt with her arms wrapped tightly around Kelly's body, the red-stained ground filling all her vision.

Camels' hooves clomped restlessly in the dust. Janja stood a few feet away, shouting and arguing loudly with one another in Arabic. Julia, awash in grief, did not comprehend the cause for all this commotion. Then suddenly she understood. A camel was missing, and so was Margaret.

Please, God, let Margaret get away. Let her go free. You took Kelly. Don't take Margaret, too. Please, God.

Mustafa's voice sounded louder and angrier than she had ever heard him. So loud that, at first, no one noticed the sound of the Jeep coming toward them over the savannah.

Never, in all her worst dreams, had Julia thought she would be so relieved to see Nassir An-Nur. But she was. As the general stepped out of the Jeep, the wind catching at his robes, the steel of his assault rifle glinting in the early morning's dawn, Julia instinctively fell back. Nassir's gray eyes took in the situation at a glance: Kelly's body, Julia, the Janja, who cowered before their general. They had disobeyed the order, "Do not kill the white women."

Yelling sharply, Nassir directed two Janja to help him carry the body into the back of the Jeep. Issuing orders and flinging insults at his men, Nassir directed Julia into the passenger's seat. Woodenly, Julia obeyed and climbed into the vehicle, even as the Janja mounted their camels and turned back toward the base.

"Where are you taking me?" she asked, glancing sharply at Nassir as he turned the Jeep away from the Janja base.

Nassir's mouth worked; his knuckles turned white as he gripped the steering wheel. "I am taking you to your people."

"But why?" Julia persisted. "You are too late. Kelly is dead. Why did you not take us back before?"

"Last night Abdul, my son, had a fever." Nassir did not look at her. "I am a Muslim, a Janjaweed general. Every day, I say that this will happen or that will happen if it is the will of Allah: *Insha Allah*. My son is very sick. He may die from this fever. So I prayed to Allah, like I have never prayed before."

He paused. "I can not believe my son's death is the will of Allah."

His words were hard, angry. Julia could well imagine that this Janjaweed general would have difficulty accepting Allah going against his personal wishes. In a world where his status gave him what he wanted, when he wanted it; where he, himself, was the author of life and death so often that the possibility of not being able to exercise control over his own son's life would be a bitter pill, indeed.

"Finally Abdul woke up. His fever was still high, and he had been dreaming. He looked at me and spoke clearly. He said he had seen the *khawaja* woman. The woman with no head covering. He said that God spoke to him in his dream and that you must go free."

Much later, Julia would remember that Nassir said "God" and not "Allah" had spoken to the boy. And she would say a prayer for Abdul, that he would truly find God's love and break the pattern of hatred and violence in his family and in his country. But for now, she was still confused.

"Once you helped Abdul. Now I have helped you. We are, as you say, even."

Those were the last words the Janja general spoke to the woman reporter from Canada.

The sun had risen blood red over the African veld when Nassir dropped Julia off at the outskirts of the IDP camp. He called to a man who stood a short way off, staring wide-eyed at the Janja general speaking curtly to him. Gathering Kelly's body into his arms, he obeyed the instructions. Ordered by a Janjaweed to carry a corpse, one did not disobey.

Julia walked back through camp, leading the man with his burden as if in a daze. They walked past hundreds of dilapidated shelters and shacks, past the eyes of countless children, men, and women, all accustomed to the same pain Julia now bore, weighting her every step the closer she came to the relief base. She shared a piece of their lives now, but only a small piece. She could leave.

# THIRTY

❧

But God has so composed the body, giving greater
honor to the part that lacked it, that there may be no
division in the body, but that the members may have
the same care for one another. If one member suffers,
all suffer together; if one member is honored, all
rejoice together. Now you are the body of Christ.

1 CORINTHIANS 12:24–27

DAVE RESTED ONE HAND ON THE casket while the other held the Bible.
He read from the book of Isaiah. His voice was steady, but Julia had to
strain to hear each word.

For you have been a stronghold to the poor, a stronghold to the
needy in his distress, a shelter from the storm and a shade from
the heat; for the breath of the ruthless is like a storm against a
wall, like heat in a dry place. You subdue the noise of the foreigners; as heat by the shade of a cloud, so the song of the ruthless is
put down.

White and black faces gazed together at the simple wooden casket. *Kelly is dead.* Julia repeated it every once in a while, to convince herself it was true.

> On this mountain the Lord of hosts will make for all peoples a feast of rich food, a feast of well-aged wine, of rich food full of marrow, of aged wine well refined. And he will swallow up on this mountain the covering that is cast over all peoples, the veil that is spread over all nations. He will swallow up death forever.

Dave stopped. He cleared his throat, heaved a great breath, and opened his mouth. Nothing came out. Inhaling and exhaling deeply, he leaned heavily on the casket. Peter moved out of the crowd and stood beside him, laying his arm across Dave's shoulders. Dave's weight shifted from the casket onto Peter's small, wiry body, braced and able to offer support.

Clearing his throat once more, Dave continued,

> And the Lord God will wipe away tears from all faces, and the reproach of his people he will take away from all the earth, for the Lord has spoken. It will be said in that day, "Behold, this is our God; we have waited for him, that he might save us. This is the Lord; we have waited for him; let us be glad and rejoice in his salvation."

Julia glanced up to see Margaret standing a short distance away, holding baby Samuel in her arms, with Mary huddled against her, holding her mother's hand as if she would never let it go.

Margaret had arrived at Hassa Hissa, still riding the Janjaweed's camel. Margaret's sister had been happy to see her but unhappy to let the children leave, especially young Mary, so useful for gathering firewood and other chores. Julia wouldn't let herself dwell on the idea that the woman was willing to send Mary into danger instead of herself or her own daughter.

"Kelly would have wanted me to read one more thing. It's written by a man named John Piper, and it's something she had written on the first page of her Bible. It helps to show who she was—who she is.

"'Let love flow from your saints, and may it, Lord, be this: that even if it costs our lives, the people will be glad in God. "Let the peoples praise You, O God; let all the peoples praise you! Let the nations be glad and sing for joy." Take Your honored place, O Christ, as the all-satisfying Treasure of the world. With trembling hands before the throne of God, and utterly dependent on Your grace, we lift our voice and make this solemn vow: As God lives, and is all I ever need, I will not waste my life . . . through Jesus Christ, amen.'"

Then someone started singing, and the song kept growing, filled with rich harmony and depth and a wailing that was faith:

> We know God is strong and He will save us
> It is well, It is good.
> His way is truth, His way is life.
> We know God is great and He will keep us
> It is well, It is good.
> His way is safe, His way is sure.
> We know God is love and He will heal us
> He is good, He is good.
> His way is peace, His way is joy.

The music and the words encircled Julia, engulfing her with strength—and hope.

One song led to another and another.

Afterward, there was embracing and kissing, but not much talking.

It wasn't, Julia decided, what she would describe as a sad funeral—although there was sadness. It was more like . . . triumph.

Over the next few days, Julia watched the light flicker in Dave's eyes like a small candle on a stormy night, but then slowly, surely, she saw it begin to grow steady and warm again. She feared looking into his eyes at first. What kind of hatred would she see there for herself? He had every right to lay the responsibility for the pain he felt at her feet. Julia knew it well. The truth that she was to blame for Kelly's death was like a sword in her soul. The ache would not leave, and she knew that if she were to die as well, it would be less hell than it was to stay alive this way.

Julia was sitting at Peter's fire with Hassan, Bekki, Margaret, and the babies one evening when Dave approached them.

"Jonathan told me I have to go home. He says I need to grieve properly, but I'm going to come back to Hassa Hissa as soon as I can."

"When do you leave us?" Peter was nodding, but the catch in his voice betrayed him.

"I fly back to Khartoum in the morning, then on to the States as soon as it can be arranged." Dave reached for sleeping Samuel, and Margaret placed the child in his arms.

"I'm going to miss each one of you so much," he added, cradling Samuel gently. The ache of tenderness on his face as he gazed at the child pierced Julia's heart.

No one spoke; each one sobered by the contemplation of all that had happened to them and the mystery of all that could happen still. The stars were so big above them it was as if they were inside a painting. Julia could not get over the African nights. Every once in a while, the fire crackled and shot a spark into the blackness.

Peter's voice finally penetrated the stillness.

"God, He is good always, children. Deep sorrow comes to all. But God, in His goodness, does not leave us alone. He is here. He is faithful even here."

Three days later, Julia, too, was packed and ready to travel back to Khartoum the next morning. Sitting on the picnic table surrounded by children, with Mary scrunched up beside her, Julia was barraged by questions.

"Why are you leaving us?"

"When will you come back?"

"Please, don't go away."

Her gut wrenched. How to leave these children in a place like Darfur was something she could not get her head around.

In the morning, she would get up and walk away.

But the children were condemned to more suffering and premature death, as surely as if someone had set them on death row and thrown away the key. And the worst of it was they would suffer because the nations of the world had chosen not to flex their political muscle. Rwanda all over again.

"Julia."

It was Jonathan. Julia hadn't seen much of the camp director since the funeral. He was being run off his feet with both the needs and the lack of resources. His face was tired and strained.

"I'd like you to come and help me with a little problem I have, if you don't mind."

"Not at all," she answered, unwinding her arms and hands—but her heart, never—from the grip that several of the children had on her.

Bemused as to what Jonathan might need her to help him with, she followed him to the mess tent while he explained. "It seems that there was a skirmish between some Janja and SLA fighters at a tourist camp in the mountains not far from here."

Julia nodded, not surprised.

"Interestingly enough, it appears that some of the tourists got mixed up in the fighting and even assisted the SLA. Which is where we come in. Once the Janja were dealt with, the SLA did not want to be hampered with a bunch of Americans on safari—stupid Americans to be on safari in Darfur, I might add—so they've dropped them off here for us to take care of. Probably don't think we have anything else more important to do, like keeping this camp together, for instance.

"I know that you're traveling back to Khartoum tomorrow. I've arranged it so they will travel with you and"—Jonathan shot a quick, guilty look at her—"I need you to take care of them until then. Keep them out of trouble. Can you do that?"

He was right to question, Julia thought, after all the trouble she had caused.

"Jonathan, it's the least I can do after all the heartache and pain I've brought to you. I know when we talked after I got back you said that God has a purpose in it, but Jonathan, how do I live with it? I can't stop thinking that if it weren't for me, Kelly would still be alive."

"You don't know that, Julia. Besides, you already are repaying us."

"I am? How?"

"You're telling our story. You're letting the world know. Ultimately, I believe that this is the only way things will ever change for the better here. People need to understand the crisis we're in. Christians need to pray. You can tell them."

He patted her shoulder. "And entertain our guests for me."

"How many of them are there?" she asked, trying to push down the lump that had risen in her throat at Jonathan's words.

"Six."

They stepped into the mess tent, pausing for a moment as their eyes adjusted from the bright sunlight outside.

A group of disheveled strangers looked up at them as they did.

He recognized her first.

"Julia Douglas."

Joel. *Joel with whiskers.* The smile on his face was impossible to resist.

"What have you been up to? Fighting Janja? And Steve? I thought you were the sensible type."

"Oh, believe me, compared to him," he said, jerking his thumb toward Joel, "I am."

They introduced her to the other people with them, their names evaporating in the inordinately happy buzz that was filling her head.

"But how did you get to *this* camp? I mean, it's not the first one you passed coming down from Jebel Marra, and it's definitely not the biggest."

"But when I asked the SLA boys if they were going by Hassa Hissa, they said, 'Sure.' It didn't matter to them which camp we went to. But it mattered to me." Joel's eyes pulled her in, forcing her to struggle to keep focused on the conversation.

"So Mr. Armani-sunglasses made friends with the SLA?" she asked him in mocking disbelief, deliberately changing the direction and tone of the conversation. She knew about the SLA, the skinny-kid peace-keeping corps that was undersupplied, underfed, underpaid, and up against Mr. Bully Janjaweed.

So many things had changed since she'd seen him in Khartoum. That felt like another lifetime ago. But the strength of—whatever it was—between them hadn't changed. Sitting down with the group, she found herself listening to one story after another. It didn't take long to grasp what had happened at Jebel Marra. Unfortunately, the images were only too clear.

Joel's expression grew serious.

"Julia, what's happened with you? You seem . . . different, somehow," he said, concern edging his tone.

She shook her head, appealing to him with her eyes; the words she had to say were too difficult to form. This was not the right moment for a heart to heart. Instead she carefully assessed Joel. He looked different himself. She knew there were things he wasn't telling.

Steve cut in, giving her an excuse to not answer just yet. She could have kissed him. Steve, that is. "Hey, Julia, I'd love to find a place to clean up a bit."

This met with immediate group consensus. Julia took them to find beds for the night in various staff housing, managed to come up with a few towels, and agreed to meet Joel in exactly thirty minutes. He said he'd be waiting for her.

And he was.

In all his fresh-shaven glory and smelling clean, he offered her his arm. She paused for just a minute, feeling self-conscious in the dusty clothes that she'd worn and perspired in all day. But there was no fixing that now.

"Shall we take a stroll through this beautiful oasis?" he encouraged, leaning toward her, arm still extended.

It wasn't a beautiful oasis. Nothing like. They stood looking at the rows upon rows of makeshift shelters; some covered with thin plastic tarps, poor protection from the rains that would come. Smoke from the fires filled the air. It had been very warm earlier that day, but now it was finally starting to cool down. It was a breath of relief after the hot spell they'd been having.

Gallantry was nice, Julia decided. Sarcastic gallantry, she wasn't sure about, but she slipped her hand through the crook of the elbow being proffered. They walked for a while without saying anything. Joel was taking in all the sights and sounds of the camp.

"What happened, Julia? You are going to tell me about it, aren't you?"

"Did someone talk to you?"

"No one talked to me. Your face tells its own story, girl."

"As does yours. Are you going to tell me what really went on at Jebel Marra?"

Joel nodded thoughtfully in assent. "If you want me to, I will."

"I want you to."

"Alright, but ladies go first." He was smiling but his voice was serious. Julia nodded, taking a deep breath. It was hard to tell it: the memories that she worked at blocking out every night so she could sleep and then again in the morning so she could get up again, even after they all came rolling back down on her like some horrible nightmare that wouldn't go away. As she started talking, a dam broke open.

"Kelly was killed five days ago by Janjaweed. They abducted her because of an article I wrote. The bullet that was meant for me, killed her instead and—oh, Joel, it's horrible. I know it wasn't me who pulled the trigger on the gun, but I feel so responsible. There's no way I can ever fix this."

"Whoa! Captured by Janja?" Joel asked, incredulous, his face paling significantly. "It's a miracle that both of you weren't killed. Slow down, Julia. Tell me everything that happened, from the beginning."

In the end, it was a relief. Somehow, telling Joel the whole story made the weight lift off her, at least for a while. He didn't say much. He just listened and kept her hand, still tucked through his arm, close against his chest. So close she could feel his heart beating.

The picnic table—bereft of the children, who were having their story and "craft" hour—was already occupied by the refreshed safari group. Hassan was busy briefing them about life at the IDP camp.

"We try to provide the basics for life: a water jug, a tarp for shelter, a bit of food—" He suddenly noticed Julia and Joel standing together, listening to him, and paused, taking the two of them into consideration, then continued on with a big smile. "It is not much, but it makes a big difference to these people who have had everything in the world taken away from them. To know that someone cares enough to help you—it is so important."

Feeling a bit conspicuous, Julia pulled away from Joel and went and stood instead beside Peter, who was smiling at her just like Hassan.

"I am glad you like old, ugly black men better than young, handsome, white ones, my daughter."

"Peter Kuanen . . ." The tone in Julia's voice warned.

The African looked at her, emanating wisdom and understanding.

"Come and talk with me, daughter. I see all is not well, even though your new friend does not stop staring at you."

Julia's eyes immediately sought out Joel's to see if this was actually the case. It was. Blushing, she looked away, disconcerted.

"He's just a lawyer my father hired," she tried to explain.

"Yes, as the sunrise is just a new day and water is only life. I know, daughter. Dave has told me of your lawyer."

"He did?"

Peter nodded. "Dave and I talked about you and prayed for you many times before he left."

Julia hadn't considered this before. She was thoughtful for a moment before admitting, "I've prayed for Dave every day since Kelly died. I've promised myself to pray for him every day for the rest of my life. It's hard; but there is nothing else I can do. I can't bring Kelly back, and I can't take away the pain Dave feels. Peter, how will I live with this?"

"You cannot live with it."

"I can't?"

"No. It will devour you as surely as the lion eats those who try to pet him."

"Then . . ." Julia was at an impasse. "How? How can I live at all? I've spent my life and my whole career trying to help others. I never wanted to hurt anyone, to cause such pain. I am not evil like the Janjaweed—or my father." It slipped out. She hadn't meant to say it, but she had thought it. It had been there the whole time: waking her up covered in sweat in the middle of the night, weighing her down during the day so that every simple thing became a huge chore. She had been thinking she should get checked for malaria. But she knew it wasn't malaria. It was her fear. She had become her father. She knew she hadn't deliberately caused Kelly's death, but she could not stop thinking, if she had never come to Darfur, Kelly would be alive now. She squeezed her eyes shut hard, trying to push down the pain.

Peter had led her away from the group during this conversation; now they had come to his shelter. The evening fire was already lit, and stew bubbled in the pot over it. He brought her his best chair, an upside-down plastic water bucket, and she sat on it gratefully while he squatted, his arms comfortably draped over his knees and moving easily to stir the stew with a wooden stick now and then.

"Julia, you are not alone. Everyone who has ever lived hurts other people and is hurt by others. Everyone, except One—Jesus Christ. He lived without sin—for it is sin that brings pain in life and the sting to death. He lived, God's own dear Son, a perfect life as a real man, so that He could die instead of us for your sins and for mine."

The sun was setting, inching its way over the horizon, splashing the trail it left behind with a riot of colors and hues no one had ever invented words for: glowing crimsons flecked with golds, ambers and fuschias that melted into pearly pinks and mauves. The evening sky blazed with the glory of it. Julia ached with the beauty of it, listening to Peter. Listening to the sky.

"Julia, Kelly died so that your body might live. Jesus died so that your soul might live. He did not take only the punishment for our sin, He took on Himself the shame sin brings. The Bible says that God made Jesus 'to be sin who knew no sin, so that in Him we might become the righteousness of God.'"

The children had arrived. Their noses brought them. Peter started scooping tablespoon-sized servings into the children's broken cups and saucers. Their faces beamed as they devoured the stew, scooping it up with grubby fingers, too hungry to wait for it to cool.

Julia smiled at them and was immediately rewarded as two little girls climbed onto her lap, their fuzzy heads resting against her arms. This was the Africa Julia knew she would never forget. Would never want to forget.

This was the Africa she would fight to salvage from corruption and genocide. It wasn't over yet. The Janjaweed would not—must not—continue their course of madness and terror.

It made her wonder.

"Did Jesus die for the Janja, too? Did He take their sins?"

"Yes, He died for all our sins. But to be forgiven, we must believe Him. Even you, Julia, can have no peace with God unless you have faith in Jesus. He is the only way."

Julia marveled at the love that shone from Peter's face. She knew he loved her; she couldn't think of Peter not loving someone. But the love that she saw, the yearning and the holy desire filling his eyes with light was the love the man had for his God. It filled her with an aching sense of hollowness. As the sun dipped and then was gone, the darkness that covered her felt dark, indeed.

When she left his fire to go and check on Joel and his friends, Peter told her that he would always pray for her that she would grow in faith toward Jesus. His words felt like a benediction, raining down on her head, soothing the pain and the remorse that she carried.

"Remember the lion, Julia. You cannot bear this guilt alone. You need to let Jesus carry you through this dark water of sadness. It has been my whole comfort to study His face through my darkest hour. It is there, in knowing Him and watching Him, that I find the strength I need to keep living, and the grace and love that heal my soul."

Julia listened, and for the first time, she knew she could not live without God's help. She could not get through this without Him.

Peter prayed with her then, his large, calloused black hands enfolding hers. Afterward, she felt different. Peter's prayer—or Peter's God—had somehow lightened her load.

Sitting beside Joel in a small cargo plane the next morning—she and the safari group were the only passengers—Julia clutched a book to her heart. The drone of the propellers filled her ears as she gazed out the window. They rose up, far above the dry, arid land growing hazy in the distance and the shimmer of heat.

She had not opened the book yet, but it was dearer to her than anything she had ever owned before. Hassan had handed it to her before she stepped into the plane.

"It's Kelly's Bible; Dave told me to give it to you when you left." Hassan had hugged her, told her he and Bekki would be praying for her, then turned, walking away quickly.

Julia waited while Joel said goodbye to Steve. They did what men who really love each other do. They punched each other's shoulders—more than once—called each other names that didn't sound very kind, then semi-embraced. Another punch, and they were good to go. She knew they would miss each other.

She would miss Hassan and Bekki, too. They had become good friends. And Peter. Peter Kuanen, who was, she imagined, just what a father should be: understanding what she could not say, giving her wise advice that would last her for a lifetime, turning eyes full of love toward her with acceptance and . . . delight.

She would never forget him.

The Blue Nile snaked along, far below the aircraft, Khartoum and

Omdurman like some prize at its apex. With a surge of longing, Julia wanted to go home to her own tiny piece of beautiful, green, democratic, Vancouver, British Columbia.

"So, you said you would tell me about your e-mail from this woman you met up with in Khartoum," Joel interrupted her reverie.

"Joel, it was so strange. It said, 'I have good news to share with you. Call me.' That was all. And a phone number."

"Did she know that you were in Darfur?"

"No, she had no idea, I'm sure. She thinks I'm visiting friends in Khartoum."

"Will you call her?"

"I think so. The poor woman—her life is so meaningless and tragic. I would like to see her again."

Adila agreed to meet Julia at the hotel. They sat outside in the shade sipping *kakaday* and making small talk. It was hot, but Adila was in her burqa. She spoke softly, carefully lifting her veil to drink the tea, taking very small sips. This uncharacteristic behavior made Julia begin to wonder about the good news that Adila had mentioned in her e-mail.

"Adila, it's good to see you again. I didn't know if you would e-mail me, but I'm glad you did. Tomorrow, I head back to Canada. So this is the last time I will be able to talk to you like this." Julia hoped this information would make her friend a bit more forthcoming. It did. But the delivery was all wrong.

The woman hung her head.

"I'm pregnant," she whispered.

"Why—well that's wonderful, Adila. Congratulations are in order then."

"Yes. But I've run away from Ahmad."

"Oh . . . I see." And she did. "Well, that must be good, isn't it?"

There was no answer. After a moment, the ramifications began to settle in Julia's head. Khartoum. A Muslim city of men. You did not see women in public very much here. And if you did, they were in burqas or were foreign women like herself. There would be no jobs available that were decent. No family to support her. No place to live. Especially for Adila. Ahmad would be feared too much for anyone to risk helping her. No, it was not good.

"How are you living? Where are you staying?"

"I am staying at the Hilton right now—under a different name, of course. Last night I stayed here, and tomorrow will be somewhere else; the burqa does have advantages. I was able to steal a significant amount of money from my husband. Which is good and bad. Good, because I can live well until I figure out a plan. Bad, because when he finds me—which he will if I don't get out of Sudan—he will kill me."

"What can I do? How can I help you?"

"I don't know, Julia." The eyes that searched hers from behind the veil were definitely Adila's; Julia recognized the fear.

"What about the U.S. Embassy? Couldn't you seek sanctuary?"

"From one of the most powerful men in Khartoum? I don't think they would risk sheltering Ahmad Barak's wife. No, it must be something else. I don't know what, but I will risk everything now for the sake of this child. For the first time, I have hope. Hope for something better. Hope that I can be needed by someone, that I can still know the happiness of being loved for myself."

"What about Rashid?"

Adila was silent for a moment, then took a long shuddering breath.

"My heart is torn. I would take him if I could, but my son is so firmly in the grip of his father's indulgences. Ahmad controls his every waking hour and I rarely am allowed to see him anymore. The truth is, I lost him long ago. I would do anything, Julia, to keep it from happening again."

"Adila, do you believe in God?"

"I am a Muslim. I believe in Allah."

"Well, I don't know God very well, and Allah not at all, but I think we need to pray." Everything that had happened to her in the last two weeks was coming to this, Julia thought wryly to herself.

"Yes. Please. Please pray for me."

So Julia did.

In a hotel courtyard in Khartoum, she beseeched God, whom she didn't know very well, but who knew her in every fiber, cell, and unexpressed hope of her being.

"God, just the real God, please—I don't want to talk to anyone else—Adila needs Your help. It seems too hard to get her out of Sudan, but that's what I'm asking for. She needs a safe place to raise her child. She needs to be free. Amen."

Julia kept her head bowed for a moment. Silently she included a PS: *God, I think only You can do this thing. So will You, please? Thank You for listening. And I think You are real. I don't understand why You didn't rescue Kelly, but help me to trust You and believe the way Peter and Dave do.*

The two women raised their heads.

"Thank you so much, Julia. It makes me feel better already. I can know that somewhere, no matter how far away, I have a friend. A friend who prays for me." Adila's voice was husky.

"And I will never forget to pray for you," Julia promised. She had two people on her prayer list already. This was almost as bad as Facebook. How, she wondered, did God ever keep track of all His people?

Adila insisted on paying the bill for the tea. They hugged goodbye, and Julia left to get a taxi to the museum where she was supposed to meet Joel.

"Wait!" Adila called.

"Please e-mail me sometimes. It will make me feel less lonely."

Julia hugged her quickly, assuring her that she would e-mail often, and climbed into the taxi. When she looked back, she saw a woman dressed in a black burqa, faceless and standing alone.

Joel and Julia had decided to meet again at the museum, filling in time while they waited for their flight out of Khartoum. They had said goodbye to the other tourists at the airport the night before, leaving them to go their separate ways. Joel and Julia had then taken a taxi to the Grand Hotel and said a shy and proper "good night" to one another in the lobby; but only after Julia promised to meet him the next day at the museum after her visit with Adila.

Now Joel found himself standing with Julia—whom, he had discovered, liked to read each plaque on each artifact before moving on to the next one—in front of the "Angel of the Lord" mural once again.

It was seven feet tall. Shadrach, Meshach, and Abednego were rendered as small men, making the angel seem even bigger. There was something significant about this mural, but Joel couldn't quite grasp it. He looked at the flames of fire, large and menacing, and remembered Matthews' story of his village being burned to the ground. Just like so many others had been. Every one of those SLA kids had stories that were almost identical. Joel had listened to more of them on the trip to Hassa Hissa.

"What do you think, Joel; is it Darfur?" Julia asked him softly, tracking his thoughts. She had a way of doing that.

He pulled his eyes away from the distraction of her, focusing back on the mural.

"All that fire."

"Did you know that when the rebellion started in Darfur in 2003, in that first year almost four hundred villages had been destroyed by Janjaweed activity, most of them burned to the ground?" Julia asked.

"The SLA boys call it a 'scorched earth' campaign."

"Yeah, I've seen it firsthand." Julia's eyes sobered at the memory of Qasar, still smoking, filled with the stench of death.

Now she would go home, and in the meantime, Darfur burned one village at a time, leaving hundreds of thousands dead in its wake, while the world tried to pretend it didn't happen. Well, the world that she affected would know. And if they didn't do anything about it, God would judge them—Julia sincerely hoped.

"But Julia, if this mural represents Darfur burning in the furnace of an evil tyrant, then who is being saved by the angel?" Joel asked, looking up at the tall, celestial being.

"It's a good question, Joel," she answered softly, "and I don't know the whole answer . . . probably I never will, but I think one of them . . . might be me."

Joel saw that Julia's eyes had grown misty, a faraway expression in them that he could not fathom. But as he looked at the mural with her, he realized that she was right.

"I think I might be one, too."

They smiled at one another then, understanding and not understanding each other perfectly.

"So we just have enough time for me to buy you an early supper, I think, before we need to pack up and head to the airport. What say you?" Joel asked, a hopeful smile teasing the corners of his mouth.

Julia liked his mouth. She liked how he could show the tiniest bit of expression with a movement of his lips.

"I say yes," she answered, smiling back at him.

They ate at the Grand Hotel, in the air-conditioned dining room, looking over the Nile moving slowly past them. Julia told him more about her concerns for Adila. He raised his eyebrows at her in his funny way when she told him she had prayed out loud for the first time in her adult life. Somehow, that led to her telling him more about the time she had spent with Kelly in the Janja camp. He listened to her as she described Mustafa and their attempt to escape, and how Kelly had prayed for the Janja.

"I'm sorry, Julia." He shook his head. "With all due respect, none of you should have made it out of that kind of situation. It's a miracle that both you and Margaret are still alive."

"I know it, now," Julia said, "but at first, it was just too hard. To be alive because someone you know and love died instead."

They both pondered that for a moment before Joel spoke again.

"Steve talked to me a lot about God. Actually, your dad did, too."

"My dad?"

"Yeah, I have an old diary of his. It should really go to you now." Joel watched her carefully while he spoke. "But . . . you didn't want the letter, so . . ."

Julia looked down at the white linen tablecloth, the gold-edged plate, and the silver cutlery. Taking a breath, she lifted her chin and met Joel's gaze with a steady look.

"I want it now. I want the letter my father wrote to me."

He smiled. "So he's your father now, is he?"

"Yes," she said, "I guess he is—or was. It's weird. First I never wanted to think about him, and for most of my life I managed to pretend to myself that he never existed. I would make up this perfect father image in my head—it was actually quite elaborate."

"I can believe it." Joel's head was tipped to one side. She couldn't fathom the look in his eyes.

"And then you show up, saying he's died and written a letter," she continued. "I didn't feel anything. No sadness. No regret. A lot of anger. I had never known or wanted to know him. How could I miss what I never had?"

"You couldn't."

"Exactly," Julia agreed. "But now it's different. I think it's time I meet him—even if it's only through this letter you have for me."

*And*, she added to herself, *I promised Kelly.*

"Wait here. I'll be right back." Joel excused himself from the table, retrieving the letter and Fred's diary from his travel bag in his hotel-room closet. He smiled. "Thanks for the introduction, Keegan. How could you have known?" Then he made his way quickly back to the dining room and the table where Julia sat waiting for him . . . talking animatedly with some other guy.

Steve? No, it was Dave. Sure as there was apple pie in America, it was Dave.

"Hey! Dave. How come you're still hanging around this place?" Joel clapped him on the back while Dave power-hugged him back, forcing the air out of his lungs.

"You know Khartoum. Sometimes your flight leaves, and sometimes it doesn't. Mine keeps being delayed. I'm supposed to be on the 11:45 tonight. If all goes well. Boy, is it ever nice to meet up with you guys!"

"Dave, that's the same time our plane leaves," Julia told him, her head shaking in disbelief.

"But are they the same airline?" Joel asked, taking his ticket from his money belt to check. Dave did the same with his, but as he did, his passport fell out. Automatically, Julia bent to pick it up. But the face that looked up at her from the photo wasn't Dave's; it was Kelly's. *Dear Kelly.* Julia's heart squeezed as she looked at her friend's picture.

Light blue eyes. Long brown hair. Beautiful face.

"Dave." The idea was preposterous. But it might work. "Dave, we need to talk."

An hour later, Julia sat in her room, impatiently waiting beside her laptop. "I know she's at the Hilton, but she's not using her real name. It all depends on this silly e-mail."

"It actually depends on a bunch of other things, too, Julia," Joel reminded her with a concerned smile.

Dave had straddled the back of a chair, cupping his chin in his laced fingers.

"I think this is the perfect learning opportunity to teach you two kids about the sovereignty of God."

Julia and Joel stared blankly at him.

"Everything that happens in creation has been pre—" He never finished. Julia and Joel both swiveled their heads at the tone indicating that there was a message in Julia's in-box.

"It's her!" Julia wasn't quite jumping up and down, but her eagerness was infectious.

"What does it say?" Dave asked, apparently unflustered.

Joel craned his neck over Julia's shoulder, breathing in the smell of her as he did so and reading the e-mail out loud: "I think we should try. I'll be there at seven."

Dave checked his watch. "It's six now, and we need to be at the airport by eight, preferably. She'll still only get on standby, if at all. It's a gamble."

"So what were you going to tell us about God's sovereignty?" Joel asked.

"Right." Dave's worried expression relaxed. "He is. And we need to pray."

They each prayed, one after the other. They didn't use a lot of words, but the message was clear: "Help!"

"It reminds me of something I read once by Anne Lamott," Julia said.

It was Dave and Joel's turn to look blankly at her. "Her two favorite prayers. The first one is, 'Help me, help me, help me.' And the second, 'Thank you, thank you, thank you.'"

Dave sighed and nodded.

"I hope we get to pray that second one," he said softly.

Julia shot him a look of concern. He had seemed so natural and at ease. It had been easy to slip into the friendly camaraderie she had enjoyed with him and Kelly. But without Kelly it was different. Dave was different.

He got up and walked over to the bed, picking up his wife's Bible from Julia's bedside table.

"May I?" he asked her.

"Oh, Dave. Please. You know you don't need to ask me. And if you reconsider the gift, I understand."

"I don't think that's necessary, Julia. Mine says exactly the same thing."

He lay on the bed, the Bible open above his head, and started reading it. Out loud.

Julia could not follow it all, but it did have a relaxing effect. She was ready to lie down, herself, when the knock came, making her jump.

The woman who entered the room in a flowing burqa was Adila.

Forty-five harried minutes later, the woman who left the room in the company of Dave, Joel, and Julia was, by all appearances, Kelly. Or at least, that's what her passport said. And that's what the name was on the standby ticket she bought at the airport, the ticket that lay crumpled on her lap as she tightened her seat belt.

Circling above Khartoum, the lights twinkling below them, Adila said a silent, tear-streaked goodbye to her son, who might think of her sometimes when he wasn't distracted with all the luxuries and pleasures his father lavished on him.

Julia, sitting a few seats across from her, leaned forward to see how she was doing once they were well on their way.

Fast asleep, Adila's head rested against her window, her hands protectively spread over her womb.

# THIRTY-ONE

Suddenly it hits me what an utter inconsistency it is
to feel indignant as a Christian about the Holocaust
of the Jews and the holocaust of abortion, but not
about the holocaust of sinners perishing in unbelief.

JOHN PIPER, *A GODWARD LIFE*

HIS HANDWRITING WAS HALF printing, half cursive. Almost italic, but not so fancy. Julia was learning about him, this man who had been her father, and he intrigued her. Humorous accounts from his journal of prison life that a month ago would have made her frown with disapproval, now made her smile with amusement. Contrasting that life to a prison cell in a Janja camp, she realized her father had enjoyed an amazing amount of conveniences: running water and plumbing in his own cell, for instance, and a varied meal plan for every day of the week. Julia's mouth twitched in amusement at having such empathy for so many elements of her father's life.

Now that she knew she would read it, Julia wanted to save the letter. If she was going to have only one communication with her father, she wanted to wait for the right moment.

Christmas came and went, then New Year's. A few days later, she visited Aunt Rose. The old lady had been so pleased to see her.

"Darling child, you are such a sweet sight for these tired old eyes! Let me look at you." To do that, she had to first release Julia from a fierce embrace.

"Oh, I am so grateful to the Lord for bringing you out of that desolate place in one piece. Come sit down. You must be freezing after that hot African sun." Julia was tugged and fussed into a little wingback chair beside the natural gas fire, replacing what once had been a proper wood-burning fireplace. Still fussing, Aunt Rose pulled a small ottoman up for her feet and placed a cushion in just the right place behind her head. Julia watched as Aunt Rose bustled about. Steaming tea was poured, cream and sugar offered, then a homemade, chocolate chip cookie, before Aunt Rose began her cross-examination.

"Was it terrible?"

Looking into her tea, Julia considered. Aunt Rose would want to hear the details. Even the hard ones. She thought for a moment before answering.

"It was the hardest thing I've ever seen. People watch their loved ones brutally murdered in front of them at the hands of their own government, their homes and entire villages are burned, and then they escape to an IDP camp where they wait for someone to help. And the help that does trickle in isn't enough. So they die. In a line for food aid. Or from opportunistic diseases they don't have the strength to resist. In a world with enough food and enough medicine but not enough will to enforce basic humanitarian rights."

"But why—" Aunt Rose started.

"Why won't the world's powers stand up to the government of Sudan? I don't know, Aunt Rose." Julia shook her head, her eyes dark and troubled. "Is it because 60 percent of Sudan's oil is being exported to China, the United States' biggest trading partner? Is it because of the close alliance and the support Sudan gives to the most powerful terrorist organizations in the world? Or is it just because the powers that could help are overextended in other places? Maybe it's simply because people are too busy with the next soccer game or New Year's Eve dance. I don't know.

"I saw the haunted eyes of young girls who have been raped more than once and who live in terror of the next time.

"I saw a friend give her life for me." The words felt like sawdust as she said them slowly. "Then I helped her husband bury her." Julia groaned, her hands covering her face as the sobs wrenched from her soul.

"Honey." Aunt Rose's arms wrapped around her, rocking back and forth, holding on as Julia finally let go of all the grief she had carried and tried to contain.

Aunt Rose's face was wet with her own tears when she finally spoke into the hush that settled over them. "She died for you, Julia. She died so that you would live. Accept it. It is a precious gift. A precious, precious gift.

"I think I will talk to God about this now, if you don't mind, Julia." And Aunt Rose did. She prayed for the people of Darfur and their plight, for healing and redemption. She prayed for Dave. She prayed for Julia, that God would make clear to her what He would have her do with this burden He had given her for Darfur. She prayed that God's children all over the world would somehow become more aware of the crisis and that their prayers would rise to His throne, and mercies would flow out, as God's own sorrow and grief for Darfur were shared and lifted up by the body of Christ.

Julia couldn't make sense of everything Aunt Rose prayed. And after Aunt Rose said, "Amen," it didn't feel right to speak out loud right away. For the first time in a long time, Julia didn't feel overwhelmed by evil. Evil was there. But so was God.

"Thank you," Julia finally said, as she rose from her chair.

Wrapping her scarf around her coat's collar and slipping on her red mittens, Julia hugged her father's auntie goodbye, and suddenly she knew. It rushed up inside her with a longing as strong as it was unexpected—a longing for her dad. For Fred Keegan. It was time to read the letter.

Julia drove with her dog Goliath to Stanley Park; the hundred-acre park—she had always thought that this meant it was Christopher Robin's park—in the middle of Vancouver. Climbing onto an outcropping of rocks that lie scattered along the beach and stretched out into the water, she clambered and picked her way to the farthest possible rock. Goliath, exhausted from their game of fetch, lay panting on the beach. She knew that he would stay where she had told him to until she came back.

Crossing her legs under her, she lifted her face to the sun, wrapping her arms around her red and black lumberman's jacket, enjoying the January sunshine full on her face. The seagulls called—oh, how she had missed that sound; the smell of seaweed and briny saltwater filled her lungs and cleared her head. The sculptured "Girl in a Wetsuit" sat daintily on her own rock, a short stone's throw away, but Julia ignored her bronze friend today, having come here with a specific task to carry out. Reaching into her backpack, she pulled out the manila envelope. Inside were three sheets of notebook paper. Clutching her father's letter in her hand, she read:

September 8, 2008
Dear Julia,
    I want to die better than I've lived. So I ask you, please read this letter to the end.

It's the only one I'll send. If you receive this, it will mean I am gone from this world—so you can relax. I won't come and disturb your life.

There are some things, however, that I'd like you to know about me.

One is that I've always loved you.

Julia breathed slowly in and out. She felt as if she'd just run up a flight of stairs.

I guess your mama didn't spend much time talking about the father you probably had no trouble forgetting. I don't blame either of you for having nothing to do with me. I was a real jerk. I was guilty, as charged, for the crimes I committed. That life, I am ashamed of, and I paid a high price. Thirty years in the slammer. And counting. I won't bore you with the sorry-old-me stuff. Mostly, I want to tell you about the last eight years. Something important happened, and you should know not just who I was, but who I got to be and the Treasure I found. This is why I write to you.

I've got a picture of a cute kid taped to my wall. You're missing your front teeth and have two of those pony things. You're a cute gal and no mistake. Pretty, like your mama. The picture came in the last letter with the divorce papers. I guess you were seven in that photo. That means you'd be thirty-three now. I wonder if I'd know you if I saw you today. Can a man walk past his own kin and not feel the bond of blood that connects them? Recognize the spirit in the other who shares his same history, ancestors, and perhaps God? Maybe that's why we get goose bumps. Maybe I'm a crazy old fool who's had too much time to think about the inner workings of this thing we call life.

A smile played on her lips as she read this man's musings. He sounded . . . nice.

> In any case, sweetie, you need to know some things.
> First, by now you will have met a certain Mr. Joel Maartens. He's a good, honest lawyer, Julia, and you might want to keep him.

Keep him? Julia and Joel had seen each other only once in the six weeks that they'd been home. Feeling awkward and a bit strained, they were both having difficulties adjusting back to real life, complete with fast cars, fast food, and fast-track careers. After telling him the latest news she'd had from Adila—about the immigration program in Portland, Oregon, and the church there that Dave had introduced her to— there just hadn't been much left to talk about. Maybe the Canadian cold had chilled them.

"Call me sometime," she'd told him when he dropped her off after a nice dinner at an expensive restaurant. His answer had been cryptic. Something about needing to work out a few things. Or had he said "make a few changes"? Anyway, it didn't matter. He hadn't called, and everything in her very limited dating experience told her that he wouldn't call if he hadn't by now. It hurt. She wasn't going to lie about it to herself. She missed Joel. She missed his eyes, she missed his humor, but most of all, she missed his friendship. It wasn't any good. Thinking about him didn't bring him closer.

> There is a bank account number included in this letter, and as of this moment, it belongs to you. Sorry. This does not make you a millionaire, but it might help with a mortgage or something like.

Secondly, I made you a dining room suite. I know. I took a chance. Maybe you'll hate it, and if you do, do whatever you want with it. But woodworking is something that I've really grown to love. I made this for you, honey. Joel Maartens has it in storage until, and if, you're ready for it. I hope one day that you will have a family. And I hope that they can grow up remembering good times together, eating, laughing, and praying around the table I made.

Any control she'd had, she lost as tears trickled down her cheeks, running off the end of her nose.

Thirdly, and most important, over the last several years in prison, I made a decision that changed my life. I started going to church here on Sundays, then to Bible studies during the week. Then I accepted Christ as my Savior. I believe, Julia. I know it may sound trite, but it's changed everything.

Look at me: I'm a convict, I've lost any family I ever had, I have cancer and will likely only live a few more months, but I can tell you that there is no place so alone that Jesus can't fill it. There is no darkness that He cannot bring light to. There is no life that He touches that isn't changed forever.

Julia, if you don't know Him, find a Bible and start reading for yourself about what our heavenly Father has done for us through Jesus Christ.

Julia laughed, wiping away the tears as she thought of the other item in her backpack. It was Kelly's Bible. Today, she had promised herself that she would fulfill Kelly's last wish. Read both letters. This one was, just as Kelly had said, shorter than the other one, but today was only the beginning.

Julia, I wasted an entire life. I lost so much. I never had the chance to tell you how much I love you. But most of all, I lost the chance to live my life for Jesus. I hope that somehow your life will make up for the loss mine has been. Don't be afraid; loving Him is the best and most fulfilling thing I have ever done. To do less is to not really live at all; to do more is impossible.

The days I have left are filled with my prayers for you. Not only that, but right now while you're reading this, I'm waiting with Him in glory for you, honey. Every day I'll be asking Him when you're coming, and one day when He says, "It's today, Keegan," I'll be waiting for you with all the hugs and kisses I never gave you there.

Till then, sweetie,

With love,

from Dad


Julia sat on the rock by the ocean called *peace* for a long time, her heart speaking volumes to a heavenly Father who cared so much and with such detail in sending her His love. Finally, she picked up Kelly's worn, leather-bound Bible. Keeping her promise, she flipped it open, and it naturally fell to the place where a lovely, pressed daisy lay. Julia read: "In the beginning was the Word . . ."

# AUTHOR'S NOTE

The prayer of a righteous person
has great power as it is working.

JAMES 5:16

AUGUST 2009

Genocide, by the definition ascribed to it by the UN in 1948 at the end of Hitler's Holocaust, is the intention to destroy, in whole or in part, a national, ethnical, racial, or religious group, as such. Genocide is generally understood to be the worst crime a government or ruling party can commit against its people.

On July 14, 2008, the International Criminal Court prosecutor Luis Moreno-Ocampo applied for a warrant of arrest for Omar Hassan al-Bashir, president of Sudan since 1993. The warrant was granted and on March 4, 2009, al-Bashir was formally charged with five counts of crimes against humanity and two counts of war crimes. From threatening the entire world with disaster to denying those charges altogether, President Omar al-Bashir, since that time, has not stopped acting to expel the NGOs who were working in Darfur, leaving a desolate situation in extreme emergency and need.

To learn more about the situation in Darfur and related topics, visit:

- http://www.sudanreeves.org (an excellent source of "from the ground" facts the media may ignore)
- http://www.savedarfur.org (things you can do *right now* to effect change)
- http://www.wagingpeace.info/
- http://www.persecution.org (the Web site of International Christian Concern)
- http://www.eyesondarfur.org (see the proof with your own eyes)

I also recommend the following books:

- Don Cheadle and John Prendergast. *Not on Our Watch: The Mission to End Genocide in Darfur and Beyond.* New York: Hyperion, 2007.
- Os Guinness. *Unspeakable: Facing up to the Challenge of Evil.* New York: HarperOne, 2006.
- Mark Steyn. *America Alone (The End of the World as We Know It).* Washington, D.C.: Regnery Publishing Inc., 2006.

With 50 percent of the NGOs pushed out of the country, the 4.7 million people who have been surviving through receiving aid in Darfur are compromised (see Eric Reeves, "Darfur Enmeshed Within Sudan's Broadening National Crisis" at http://www.sudanreeves.org). Most of the region has only a tenuous and fitful humanitarian presence, and many distressed populations are completely beyond reach (see UN humanitarian access maps at http://www.unsudanig.org/library/mapcatalogue/darfur/index.php?fid=access). Genocide by attrition is what happens next, along with the loss of eyewitnesses. Who will care? Who will tell the story? Who will pray?

What can you do?

- Pray.
- Write a letter to your newspaper.
- Write a letter to your MP or Senator. (Many of the Web sites listed on the previous page walk you through how to do this.)
- Start a prayer meeting for suffering Christian brothers and sisters in Darfur and other areas of the world.
- Send money.

Prayer has never been so obviously our best recourse. God in heaven, who alone can quell evil, listens to people when they pray. Will you pray with me for Darfur? For all the children and widows and impoverished people. For your brothers and sisters in the Lord who suffer there, that their faith would not quit. That they would be bold for the sake of Jesus Christ. For the power of the gospel which speaks of Love conquering hate, of Life conquering death, and of Hope dispelling despair. For the sake of Jesus who laid down His life for every one of us so that sin would no longer have power to hold us in its grip. True freedom is this alone. I pray that if you have not discovered freedom from sin, that you will now.

⌒

"If my people who are called by my name humble
themselves, and pray and seek my face and turn from
their wicked ways, then I will hear from heaven and
will forgive their sin and heal their land."

2 CHRONICLES 7:14